LAST WORD

A KATE REID NOVEL
BOOK 7

ROBIN MAHLE

HARP HOUSE PUBLISHING, LLC.

Published by HARP House Publishing
July, 2017 (1st edition)

1

The melodic echoes of the four-piece orchestra drifted among the guests whose chatter eclipsed the haunting strings. The formal dinner and, more importantly, fundraiser, was being hosted by one of Washington's most influential lobbyists.

This, however, was just another dinner for Congressman Grant Copeland, who knew better than to miss out on the opportunity to grease palms and pick the pockets of donors. With a cocktail in hand, he searched for the woman he had grown fond of in recent months. An ambitious woman looking to advance her own career and who sought out Copeland's mentorship. And he jumped in at the prospect with both feet. A second-term representative of Virginia's fifth district, the independent congressman was still considered a junior member compared to the longer-serving high-ranking congressional members who had averaged 8 terms.

Copeland was elected at a time when the people of his district were seeking change and had grown tired of the political system that seemed ever more corrupt and dysfunctional. His independent status allowed him to pander to both sides and win his seat. A seat he had protected at all costs, which was exactly the reason for his attendance tonight.

"Congressman Copeland, pleasure to see you." A nameless man with a forgettable face approached him.

"Good to see you too. Shrimp is fantastic. You should give it a try." Copeland nodded and took his leave, continuing on the path of his initial intent—to see her. He moved through the clusters of Vaseline smiles, pearl necklaces, and sideways-glances, eventually approaching the woman he'd thought about all day. "You look stunning." He placed his hand on the small of her back and lightly kissed her cheek.

"There you are. I was wondering if I would see you tonight." Janine Atherton returned his greeting with a warm smile and placed her hand on his chest, her red-painted nails and pale skin contrasting with his black suit.

"I escaped the clutches of Chairman Dominguez in time to make it here just so I could see you."

"And chat up your donors, no doubt. You don't fool me, Congressman." She raised her glass to her lips, her eyes fixed on his. "And where is your lovely wife tonight?"

He peered at his watered-down cocktail. "My son is down with a bug, unfortunately. She's looking after him."

"That's too bad." Her gaze implied otherwise.

The moment was interrupted by Copeland's chief of staff. "Grant, glad I found you. Do you have a second?"

"I haven't even finished my first drink and you want to talk shop? Can this wait?"

"I don't think so. I'll keep it brief." He glanced at Janine. "Don't you clean up well? Pleasure to see you, Janine. Please excuse us."

Copeland followed him toward the ballroom's entrance. "What's so important that it couldn't wait until tomorrow?"

"I apologize, but I think you should know that the new poll numbers are out."

"And?"

"And, your numbers are slipping. I think it's time to reach out; conduct a few town halls during recess."

"Fine. Might I rejoin the party now?"

"Of course. I just thought you would want to be the first to know." He began to walk away. "I see Janine is keeping you company this evening. Where's Mrs. Copeland?"

His expression hardened. "Home."

"You should know Janine's been doing a great job for us running interference. She's to be commended for her tireless efforts on your behalf."

"I'll be sure to let her know. Thank you." Copeland turned and surveyed the room in search of Janine once again. Upon spotting her, he thrust his hand in his pants pocket and smiled.

She had been a loyal member of his staff for some time, having started as a volunteer during his re-election campaign this past fall. He'd been so impressed by her work, he took her on as his media relations advisor.

Copeland continued to make the rounds alone until sufficient time had lapsed that would allow him to slip away with few questions. As he exited the ballroom and passed through the lobby doors of the museum, the music and voices faded, replaced by the sound of cars and horns and a bustling city street on a steamy summer's night. He reached for his valet ticket. "I'm ready to go now."

"Of course, sir. We'll bring your car around." The man in the white jacket took hold of Copeland's keys and directed another to fetch the car.

The silver Lexus sedan approached with a smooth purr from its engine and the valet driver stepped out. "Here you are, sir."

Copeland slipped inside, cradled by the supple leather seat while the valet closed his door. Examining the grand entrance of the museum a final time, he pulled away and pressed the call button on his steering wheel. "Call home."

The line rang and an undemanding voice answered. "Hi, honey. Is everything okay? Are you on your way home?"

"I'm afraid I was called into a late night session. I'm leaving the dinner now, but I have to head back to the office. I'll probably pull out the sofa bed and sleep there tonight."

"Of course. You thought that might happen. I'm glad I didn't bother attending or I'd be stuck for a ride home. Kids are upstairs and I'll be heading off to bed soon anyway. Don't work too late."

"I won't. See you tomorrow. Goodnight." He ended the call and pulled onto the highway, opposite the direction of his office on the Hill. A hotel was nearby. One he'd frequented on several occasions in the past.

A KNOCK SOUNDED on his hotel room door, and as Copeland approached, he paused to check his reflection in a mirror that hung near the entrance. The first two buttons of his white Oxford shirt were undone and his full head of black hair was no longer slicked back and had begun to sprout wavy strands. He pushed it into place and opened the door. "I thought you'd never arrive."

Janine stepped inside without awaiting the invitation that would undoubtedly come next. "It was harder for me to slip out than I expected, but here I am."

"Here you are." He closed the door, which brought him within inches of her lips. "You want a drink?" Rather than take advantage of his proximity, he instead took her hand and led her into the suite. "Anyone see you leave?"

"Sure they did. If you're asking did anyone follow me, then no, of course not. You're not that important—yet." With a soft titter, Janine lowered herself onto the sofa. "I'm certain we'll be able to fix that soon enough."

He stepped toward her, offering the drink. "With your help, I have no doubt."

JANINE AWOKE to the door across the hall closing shut with a resounding thud. She reached for her phone and squinted when the screen illuminated, displaying the time. "Shit." She pulled herself from the bed.

"Hey, where are you going?"

"I'd better leave before daylight. It's already three. Go back to sleep." She leaned in to kiss him before heading into the bathroom to pull on the cocktail dress in which she had arrived.

Returning to the sitting area, she pulled on her strappy heels before slinging her evening bag over her shoulder. A brief peek inside the bedroom of the suite and she found Grant had returned to his slumber.

Upon making her way into the parking lot, Janine pressed the remote entry and stepped into her car. Staying so late had been unintentional, but both had fallen asleep after what turned out to be a raucous romp in the sack. In fact, she couldn't remember the last time he was quite so amorous. He was almost 15 years her senior and she'd become accustomed to his stamina. Perhaps talk of his impending success was a bigger turn on for him than she'd expected. His time was coming and she would be the one to propel him. But it had to be sooner rather than later in order to avoid any hint of their scandalous relationship. He'd promised to take care of it, but she was still standing on the sidelines.

With the turn of the key, Janine pulled out of the lot and onto the main road, heading home, which was a good half-hour away. The roads were quiet, at least for D.C. and she turned up the radio to help keep her awake. But what seemed more effective were the headlights shining in her rearview. She turned away from the glare and tried to refocus on the road ahead. "Turn off your damn hi-beams, asshole."

She changed lanes so whoever was behind her could pass. Instead, they pulled back into her rearview. "Jesus! What the hell is wrong with you? There's no one on the road. Go around." She pressed down on the gas pedal to gain distance, but the car caught up and began riding her tail.

The hairs on the back of her neck raised and her pulse quickened as her eyes shifted between the road ahead and the rearview. Gaining in speed again, the headlights remained closer still. Janine studied her navigation screen to find the nearest gas station or other public places that might offer refuge, but there were none close enough to solve her immediate need. Another option was to divert onto the road that was still about a quarter-mile ahead and see if the car continued to follow.

She veered off the exit and stared into the mirror. The momentary relief diminished when the car appeared once again. "That's it. I don't know who the hell you think you are, but I'm calling the police." She pressed the call button when the lights behind her grew brighter and the revving engine grew louder.

"Shit." The voice activated system finally kicked in. "Call..."

The car plowed into her, thrusting her head forward and then back again. The bumper dragged on the ground, throwing sparks, as the back-end of her Audi coupe had crumpled and she began losing control of the wheel. Stunned, Janine swerved toward the side of the road and the car slowed to a stop. She unbuckled her seatbelt with trembling hands, still peering in the rearview at the car that stopped moving, but was still behind her. The driver's side door was jammed as she tried to push it open. "Damn it!" Tears streamed down her cheeks and her shoulder throbbed as she slammed the door in an attempt to force it open. It wouldn't budge.

When she again tried to call 911, a figure appeared at her window, shadowed by the bright lights still shining from the rear. She strained to see who had run her off the road. An object—a crowbar or something similar—appeared out of nowhere and smashed her window. Janine turned away from the glass that flew inside, shielding her face as she screamed. Half-dazed and in shock, she began, "What are you doing? What the fuck is wrong with you?" It was then she spotted the unmistakable shape of a gun and the arm that raised it nearer to her head. "No. Please, don't. Please...

A moment later, Janine's world turned black.

ASAC Campbell waited for a response. "Nothing? No one's got anything else?"

"I don't believe so, sir." SSA Dwight Jameson turned to his team. "Reid? Vasquez? Is there anything else?"

"That's it for me." Agent Kate Reid grabbed her tablet and began to rise along with the others. "Thank you, sir." She stepped into the hall and headed back to her office.

"Hey, hold up." Dwight caught up with her. "You didn't mention to him that you'd be training at Quantico next week. Why not?"

"It's only for two days. I'm sure he has bigger fish to fry."

He pressed his hand against her shoulder. "Kate. Come—talk with me."

She considered his request as Agent Alicia Vasquez reached them.

"Everything okay?" She seemed to notice Kate's hesitation.

"Yeah. Go on ahead. I just need to have a quick word with Jameson."

"Okay." Vasquez eyed them both for a moment before making her departure. "Whatever you say."

"See? Even she knows you're hiding something." Dwight walked into his office, holding the door for Kate.

"I'm not hiding anything. There's nothing to hide." She dropped into the guest chair. "I'm going to train, just like we discussed. That's all it is."

Dwight took his seat and leaned back in his chair, regarding Kate with dubious eyes.

"Stop trying to read me. This will be no different from the last time I took hours at Quantico. It's part of the deal, right?"

"It is, but this time, you'll be meeting with the profiler, right?"

"Yes. Doesn't mean anything, though. He still doesn't know me from Adam and I don't know him, so there's no story here."

"Okay, fine. Have it your way. I'd just hate for Campbell to be caught off guard when the time comes for you to leave."

"I won't do that to him. Nick's departure was expected and if I am lucky enough to get a job at BAU Headquarters, then I'll give him plenty of advanced warning."

"It was expected but not appreciated," Dwight continued. "Especially after they'd finally seemed to put the past behind them."

"Campbell understood what it meant for Nick to get that position. It was an opportunity of a lifetime and he can't hold that against him. It's not fair."

"Still, he's been different since Nick left."

"I think he's been better, if you ask me, and that's because you've picked up and taken the reins without hesitation, Dwight. So don't sell yourself short."

"Oh, I'm not. I've got big shoes to fill, but I have no doubt I'll be able to do it."

"Good. Then if there's nothing else?"

"On a personal note, how's things going with you two?"

"Great. Nick's really happy there. We don't see each other that much, but maybe that's a good thing. I feel like I'm getting a chance to spread my wings a little. And if I hope to move forward, it has to be that way. Like I told Nick."

"You have to do this on your own." Dwight smiled. "I wouldn't expect you'd want it any other way, Kate. Go on. Get out of here. I'll let you know when we get the next round of consults."

"Thanks." Kate turned toward the door but stopped short. "Oh, how's Abby? She get moved in yet?"

"As a matter of fact, she did. This past weekend. Been pretty crazy with all of us in there, but I figure eventually we'll have to get a bigger place."

"I'm really happy for you, Dwight. You deserve it." She turned the corner and disappeared. As she returned to her desk, her cell phone showed a missed call from Nick.

With a press of a button, she returned his call. "Hey. Sorry I missed you. We were meeting with Campbell."

"Right. It's the weekly meeting. How could I forget?"

"Exactly. You haven't been gone long enough to forget that. They were never your favorite thing. So, what's going on?"

"Plenty, actually, but that's not why I called. I thought we could grab dinner tonight, if you're free."

"Sure. Free as a bird. I'd love to. I should be able to wrap everything up by 7 or 7:30. You want to shoot for 8?"

"Sounds good. I'll text you later with a place. Any preferences?"

"Nope. You should pick tonight. I'll see you later, babe. Bye."

"Bye." Senior Unit Agent Nick Scarborough slipped his phone back into his pocket and stood from his desk. He was still getting used to life at BAU Headquarters in Quantico. It had been eight weeks and yet everything still felt so foreign. The case load was different, his team was different. He hadn't once been in the field yet. They had people for that, apparently. Oh, he could go if he wanted to, but the bulk of his days were filled with bureaucracy; obtaining expenditure approvals, processing requests. Not exactly what he had envisioned. The few consults he'd taken part in had been fulfilling, and once he was fully integrated into the system, he expected there would be more involvement on that end.

What he missed most was the interaction he had with Kate. Her enthusiasm, her insight. Watching her wheels spin when they were working on a case was nothing short of watching genius at work, in his humble opinion. And the fact that she wasn't here was a testament to her confidence and how much it had grown, especially over the past six months or so. She had come into her own and he was witness to the transformation. Her wish had been that he not offer any special treatment when it came to training or applying for work at BAU Headquarters. And he'd kept to his end of the bargain. Kate had been in a few times for various courses but had only recently applied to work under the direction of Unit 4's profiler, Noah Quinn. She hadn't even met him yet. But Nick hoped that was all about to change.

He left his office, which was a far cry from the one he had back at the Washington Field Office. Larger, better views, and with superior technology at his fingertips. The time had come for him to meet with Quinn to discuss his options for hiring another to work beneath him. Resumes had been submitted, including Kate's. Her letters of recommendation from Quantico instructors, colleagues, and other law enforcement officials included. And it was all her own doing. She had worked tirelessly to obtain the required information and had sent everything to Quinn via email last week. She, along with several other candidates, was in the running.

"Quinn?" Nick appeared in his doorway. "You got a minute?"

"Scarborough. How's it going? Sure, come on in."

"I wanted to follow up with you on your quest for a trainee."

Quinn leaned back in his seat. "I'm still in the process of reviewing the applications. So far, I've seen a few strong candidates, but I haven't made any calls to meet yet. Why?"

"Just interested. I'm sure we'd like to get fully staffed as soon as possible."

"I understand, but this is an important decision. We need to bring in the right person. Someone who has proven him or herself and you know as well as I do the type of person it takes to do this job."

"I do know."

"That being said, I should be finished whittling down the list by the end of the week and will be looking to set up meetings for next week."

"Great. Well, I'll let you to it, then." Nick began to leave.

"Scarborough?"

"Yeah?"

"I know there's a history between you and candidate Agent Reid and I hope you understand that I can't let that affect my decision-making process."

"I wouldn't expect it to, Quinn."

"Good. I'll see you later."

2

The officer spotted the car ahead, noticing the extensive rear end damage. His shift had only just begun as had his patrol around the 57-acre grounds of the Washington National Cathedral. The Cathedral's auxiliary police force worked in conjunction with Metro PD and operated with full legal authority when on the grounds of the Cathedral.

He pulled up behind the two-door Audi and cut the engine. "Well, that's a shame. Damn nice car." Stepping out into the morning air that had warmed considerably so early in the day, he began his approach to what appeared to be an abandoned vehicle.

The officer's black rubber-soled shoes struck the pavement with a heavy thud as he made his way toward the car. His eyes shifted in search of anyone nearby who might be the owner, but the Cathedral was still closed at this early hour and no one was in sight.

Given the proximity to the heavily-traveled Massachusetts Avenue, it would not have been unusual for a driver to pull off down this road if he was in need of assistance, as it certainly appeared this driver had been.

The officer was steps away from the rear window on the driver's side and palmed his weapon. The cloudy skies reflected off the window and he struggled to see in until he moved closer to the driver's door, noticing shards of glass clinging to the door frame. He slowed his approach and leaned in. "Holy shit." He stumbled back and pressed the button on the radio receiver strapped to his shoulder. "Requesting backup. Unit 4-2 in need of immediate assistance."

"Unit 4-2, what's your location?" the dispatcher replied.

"Pilgrim Road, opposite Bishop's Gardens. I think I've got a dead body here."

"Units are responding."

With his elbow, he cleared the shards and reached inside. "Oh my God." He pressed two fingers against the woman's neck and knew she was gone. The hole in her head was also a pretty good indicator.

Within minutes, two patrol cars raced behind him, screeching to a halt. The officers jumped from their vehicles and rushed to his side.

"She's dead." An unusual sight for sure, the officer blurted out the words before the others could draw near, as though he was preparing them.

"You break the window?" one of the officers asked.

"Already broken. Door's jammed. I had to see if she was still alive." He peered inside again. "And then there's this. Take a look."

The officer angled his head inside to get a view of her face, which was slumped to her right. "Jesus!" He pulled away. "What the...?" He turned to the other men. "She's got something shoved in her mouth."

"Like a sock or something?"

"Hell, I don't know. It's soaked in blood. Son of a bitch. We got to call Metro. Get them down here now before we open the grounds."

It didn't take long before Metro PD arrived en masse and with plenty of force. The reason was simple. This place was an American institution that held presidential funerals as well as prayer services after the inaugurations of the past several presidents. Right now, no one knew what this was and so nothing could be ruled out, not even the possibility of terrorism.

Detective Anthony Phelps approached the officer still standing next to the driver's side door. "You the one who called this in?"

"Officer Brooks." He offered his hand.

"And you broke the window too?"

"No. It was already smashed. The door is jammed shut. I confirmed the status of the victim."

"Okay. You mind if I take a look?"

The officer stepped back and allowed Detective Phelps a closer look. "She's got something in her mouth."

Phelps placed latex gloves on his hands and leaned over the door. "We need to get this door opened." He continued to peer at the body. "Let's see what we've got here. Anyone run the plates yet or look for an ID?"

"No, sir. As soon as I saw she was dead, I just been waiting for you guys."

"Hey, Guzman, you mind running the plates?" he shouted to one of his men. "Let's see if we can find out who you are, Miss." Phelps tilted the woman's head and reached for the scrap of fabric lodged in her mouth. "Christ, it's wedged in there good." He continued to pull as gently as he could. "Got it."

"What the hell is it?" Brooks appeared squeamish at the sight of the fabric that dripped with blood and saliva.

Phelps began to unravel the bunched-up material, though the type of fabric was too difficult to ascertain. What he did know was that it had writing on it. Holding it with both hands, he pulled it taut. "'Whore.' Written in what could be lipstick, possibly red, the word 'whore.'" He turned to the growing crowd of officers around him. "Okay. Let's see what else we can find. How about a name, to start? Guzman?"

"The car is registered to a Janine Atherton, twenty-seven years old, Bethesda, Maryland."

"Get me a bag, would you?" Phelps asked.

"Sure thing." Brooks walked toward the ambulance that had arrived.

"Any police reports of a recent accident in her name?"

"No," Guzman continued.

"Which means we have to assume that someone hit her either before or after she stopped here."

Brooks returned with the bag. "I didn't see any broken glass around the back of the vehicle or any signs a collision occurred at this location."

"Thanks." Phelps placed the evidence in the bag and began walking around to the back of the car. "Let's get CSI down here now. And get that ambo over here so we can get this poor girl loaded up."

THE HOUSE WAS EMPTY. Not a scrap of furniture left inside. Just exactly as Kate had seen it when she arrived after the days-long journey from San Diego. Starting a new life. And now she was ready for the next chapter. Years had passed since she lost Sam and then Marshall. She was a different woman now. No longer afraid of her past, no longer fearful that it might still catch up to her. And that was the only saving grace in all of the pain she had endured.

Happiness now awaited her. Something she never thought would again be possible, but it was waiting for her outside, right at this very moment.

Leaving this house had been a difficult decision she had spent many sleepless nights pondering. And while moving into Nick's condo wasn't ideal, it would do, for now. The little old woman and her son who owned this place decided now that she was moving out, the time had come for them to sell it. The market was better. Everything was better.

A final check of the rooms. Nothing had been left behind, except maybe the woman Kate used to be. She made her way outside, locking the deadbolt a final time.

Nick stood in front of the moving truck, hands in his pockets, sun shining on his face, and waiting for her to say her final good-byes to a home that had been truly hers, even if she hadn't owned it. The first and only time she'd ever lived alone.

Kate turned away from the door and stepped off the porch, slinging her bag over her shoulder. Hair pulled back into her trade-mark ponytail, wearing shorts and a t-shirt that had been dirtied by the final cleaning of the house, she smiled at Nick. "I'm ready when you are."

He placed his hands on her shoulders and they both peered at the quaint cottage-style house that had been Kate's home for nearly three years. "I'll drive the truck to the storage unit if you want to take your car to the condo and start unloading it."

"Sounds good." Kate kissed his cheek. "Dwight leave already?"

"I told him he could take off. They'll unload the truck when I get to the facility, so no need for extra hands. I'll meet you at home soon."

"Home. Okay. See you later." She smiled and walked to her new car, the one she finally broke down and purchased last month. Her old Nissan had seen better days and the time had come to move on from that too. With her probation over, it was an easy decision to make, one she had put off for far too long. Still, she refused to use the money Marshall had left her. That would be for when she and Nick decided to buy a house together. He would have wanted it that way. He would have always wanted nothing but happiness for her.

The engine of her new Ford Explorer droned softly as she pulled out of the driveway. Nothing extravagant. Not like Nick's car. Then again, he made quite a bit more money than she did. Especially now that he was the senior unit agent. Never mind. It didn't bother her. She was happy with her purchase and headed out onto the road toward Nick's place. "I guess it's my place now."

She pulled into the parking garage with her very own parking pass. Nick had set everything up for her. But it didn't change the fact that this was still his home. Not hers. A part of her had felt the same after moving in with Marshall. His place, his rules. That wasn't what he intended, of course; it was just the way she felt. And the familiar feeling crept inside her here too.

Kate grabbed a box from the back and headed into the elevator. Upon reaching his unit, she used her brand new key and opened the door, shutting off the alarm in the process. She was home. Only once again, a home that was not hers. Setting the box on the floor, she walked inside. Certain her presence here had reached a minimum of a thousand times before, Kate knew every nook and cranny, even where Nick hid his stash of cigarettes. It was a vice he picked up only recently, though he wasn't a regular smoker. But every now and again, he would stand on the balcony, peer at the bay, and smoke to calm his nerves. She never gave him grief about it. It was enough that she served as a constant reminder for him to keep his drinking under control, which he had—mostly. But to deny him a few drags from a cigarette after the type of work they dealt with would be denying him the chance to release stress how he saw fit. And she wasn't his mother.

But looking at this place now, it was all different. They'd already come to the conclusion that the goal was to buy a house in the near future. Whatever that meant. This was simply a temporary arrangement in order to keep from renewing her lease, thereby liberating her in the event she was offered a position inside of Quantico. A probability that still existed, though she hadn't yet heard anything back after submitting her application—ensuring Nick did nothing to further it ahead of anyone else. As she'd stated that fateful day in November, she would not ride on his coattails. Ever again.

The upside to her living here was that they would see each other more often. Since his transfer, if they got together more than twice a week, they'd count themselves lucky. It would be a nice change to see him on a daily basis again. And perhaps even better that it was privately and they were no longer working together. She had felt freed by that, without expressing it directly to him.

Kate stepped outside on the balcony and looked out toward the bay where Nick's boat gently swayed in its slip. "Maybe we'll actually get to take it out this summer."

"I certainly hope so."

A flinch at the oncoming unexpected voice. "You're back? That didn't take too long."

"Nope. You're all set."

"Thank you for taking care of that for me."

"That's what a good boyfriend would do, right?"

"I guess so." She snuggled against his chest. "It'll be strange waking up to you every day."

"Strange? In a good way, I hope." Nick wrapped his arms around her waist.

"In a good way."

"Hey, I was talking with Quinn and he said he'd be contacting the applicants next week."

"Hopefully, I'll hear from him. Assuming you made no suggestion that he should reach out to me."

"We had an agreement and I'm sticking to it. I promise you. I will not interfere with the process."

"Good. Now that we've got that settled, we should celebrate."

"What kind of celebrating?" A seductive smile crept upon his lips.

"Take out. Maybe a glass of wine on the balcony. The warm breeze on our skin."

"Sounds perfect."

GRANT COPELAND's chief of staff, Philip Vega, stood at his door. "Excuse me, Grant. May I come in?"

"Sure, Phil. Come on in. How was your weekend?" Copeland set his phone down and turned his attention to Vega.

"Fine, thank you. Listen, I—um, I got a call; a message, actually, and I haven't returned it yet. I wanted to talk to you first."

"Who was it?"

"Metro Police."

"Oh? What, did I forget to pay a parking ticket or someone on the staff forget?"

"They said it was important I call them back as soon as possible."

"I see. Then what are you waiting for? Call them back. Do I need to do it?"

"I don't think so. They called the mainline and Theresa forwarded it to my voicemail. I think they'd have asked for you directly, if that were the case."

"Okay, maybe you'd better make the call and let me know what this is about because that look on your face is making me a little nervous. Is there anything you need to tell me first?"

"I'm not sure if the two events are related, but I also got a call first thing this morning from Janine Atherton's roommate. Said she hadn't seen her since Saturday morning and wasn't answering her phone. Wanted to know if she'd shown up for work today."

Copeland's mouth gaped and his eyes blinked as though in slow motion. "She's not in?"

Vega shook his head. "I haven't heard from her since the fundraiser on Saturday night. That's why I came to see you. Now that Metro PD has called, I'm starting to get a very bad feeling about this."

"Okay, okay, before we jump to conclusions, why don't you just return their call and find out what the hell is going on? Let me know as soon as you know anything, you hear me?"

Vega nodded and left the office.

Copeland began to search his memory for her final words before she left the hotel. Nothing came to mind that would speak to her absence now. He hadn't tried to contact her on Sunday because he was with his family. Now his concern grew and his focus on anything else had vanished. "Calm down. She's okay." He reached for his cell and was ready to press the button and make the call to her himself, but something stopped him. Self-preservation. Both for his political career and his marriage. If something had happened, his call would show up on her phone and phone records if her voicemail picked up. "Just wait for Phil."

Several minutes passed and his patience was running thin. He had to know if Janine was okay. Just as he was about to rise, Phil returned and Copeland knew right then and there, bad news awaited him.

"I spoke with a Detective Phelps." He lowered himself onto a chair. "Grant, Janine was found dead yesterday morning near the Cathedral."

"What? The Cathedral? What the hell?"

"Apparently, her car had been rear-ended, pretty badly, and they found her already dead."

Copeland cupped his mouth and devastation masked his face. He was speechless for several moments until finally lowering his hand. "She died in a car accident?"

"No. She was murdered, Grant. Shot in the head. They think she was rammed off the road and then shot. I guess the cops went to her apartment, but there was no answer. I don't know where her roommate was at the time, but they didn't have her name and the detective said they didn't want to just start calling random people listed as contacts on her cell. They found my name with the words "boss man" next to it. Figured that would be their best bet."

"Janine's parents are dead and I don't even know if she has siblings. Oh my God. I can't believe this. I was just with her."

"I know. I can't imagine who would want to kill her. I don't know if it was a road rage thing or what. Phelps wants me to go down there to talk—and identify her body."

"I want to go with you."

"I don't think that's a good idea, Grant. Right now, the best thing for you is to steer clear of this until I know more. Let me go down and talk to the detective. I'll find out what they know and we'll figure this out." Phil stood. "I'm so sorry. I'm so sorry for Janine."

Copeland watched him leave and continued to stare into the

corridor. His mind's eye took him to a better place. The last few moments when he gazed into her eyes, knowing how much she cared for him, maybe even loved him. And while the feeling wasn't reciprocated, he cared for her deeply. Now she was gone—murdered. It seemed unfathomable. Who could have done this to her? Why?

3

Inside the D.C. Metro Police Department's second district office, Philip Vega approached the counter. "Excuse me? I'm here to see Detective Phelps."

The officer eyed him.

"I'm Philip Vega. He's expecting me."

The grizzled man behind the desk, an officer who appeared to have been on the job for too long, picked up the phone and made the call. "Yeah, I got a Philip Vega here to see you. Got it, thanks." He placed the phone back in its cradle. "He'll be right up. Just hang tight over there."

Phil turned in the direction the officer had pointed and made his way toward a seat. His pulse was racing as he'd never had a reason to be inside a police station before and certainly not to identify a body.

"Mr. Vega? I'm Detective Phelps. Would you mind coming back with me?" He was already walking away before Phil caught up to him. "We did manage to get hold of the roommate. I had one of my guys go back to the apartment and she was there. She's coming too, but not until later this afternoon. Apparently, she's pretty broken up about it, as you'd expect, and needed time to gather her strength."

"I'm sure. Do you still need me, then?"

"Yes, sir. The sooner we can confirm her identity, the sooner we can start the paperwork to release her to the coroner for the autopsy."

"Autopsy?"

"It's important that we find out exactly what happened to Ms. Atherton, Mr. Vega."

"Of course."

"You work for Congressman Copeland, is that right?"

"I'm his chief of staff."

"I see. You must work closely with him?"

"Yes, sir, I do."

Phelps pushed open the door to the room. "She's just inside here. Please follow me."

Phil hesitated but found the courage to continue.

As they reached the draped body on the table in a room the size of a jail cell, with no windows and a concrete floor, he stopped and waited for the detective.

"You ready?"

He nodded.

Phelps pulled away the cover from her face. "Is this Janine Atherton?"

He could only look for a moment before he had to turn away. "Jesus. What the hell happened to her?"

"She was shot in the head, Mr. Vega. Point blank. Is this her?"

He nodded. "Yes, it's Janine."

Phelps returned the cover. "Thank you. Come with me."

They left the room and walked back into the hall where Phelps led the way to an office.

"Would you mind making a statement for me, Mr. Vega? If you can't do it now, I'd understand, but since you're already here."

"A statement? Why?"

"I need to know when you last saw Ms. Atherton and what you know about her that might shed some light on my investigation. There are some things here, Mr. Vega, that I can't convey to you at the moment, but it's vital I piece together the last days of her life. Do you understand?"

"I—I guess so. Yes, of course."

"Good. Please take a seat and we'll get started. Then you can be on your way."

"What will happen to her?"

"I'll wait for the roommate, for additional confirmation, then I'll release her to the Chief Medical Examiner's Office for the autopsy. With your help, though, I can at least get started on the paperwork. So your visit is not in vain. I'm hoping the roommate will be able to confirm whether Ms. Atherton had any family I can contact as well. If not, then she'll receive the autopsy results that will confirm the cause of death."

"You said she was shot in the head. Isn't that how she died?"

"As I said, Mr. Vega. I'm right in the middle of this and there are things I can't comment on at the moment for fear it might jeopardize the investigation. I'm sure you can understand my position."

"Yeah, I get it."

Noah Quinn stared through the window of his office and on to the grounds. Quantico was a beautiful facility with stunning gardens inside the compound's 385 acres. Home to the FBI's training facility as well as BAU headquarters, Quantico was also home to many buildings that housed a variety of laboratories, additional training grounds, and even dormitories for the Academy trainees.

He'd begun to make the calls and schedule interviews for the junior position where he would get an opportunity to groom another profiler. It was unfortunate that another was needed, but his workload was overwhelming at times. It was a testament to what he saw as the decline of civil society, a phenomenon that he believed had only occurred in the past few decades, but was deteriorating at an ever more rapid pace. At some point, he wondered if all the hype about violent video games and the depravity that could be found at one's fingertips on the internet had infiltrated pop culture, creating a cesspool of desensitized individuals whose ideas of right and wrong were so intertwined, the differences became indiscernible to them.

This, of course, was but one reason out of so many that could have contributed to the violence he studied on a daily basis. Quinn was an agent and psychologist. And while the work was fascinating, it was also terrifying, so he searched for help. A profiler who could offer additional insight, although that wasn't an official title, but more of a job description.

There was one candidate, however, who stood out. Not just for her qualifications, which he had to admit, were impeccable, and not because he was well aware of the relationship she had with his boss, Senior Unit Agent Scarborough. It was because he remembered well their first meeting. And doubted she would.

With his phone at his ear, he waited for the line to pick up.

"Agent Reid."

"Yes, this is Agent Quinn, BAU 4."

"Hello, sir. Thank you for the call."

"I assume, then, you know why I'm calling?"

"Well, I hope so, yes. The trainee position?"

"Yes, ma'am. I'd like to know if you might be available to come in to have a chat with me this week? Say Wednesday, 10am?"

"Absolutely. Yes. I will be there. Thank you so much. I look forward to meeting you."

Quinn smiled. "Same here, Agent Reid. I'll see you then. Good-bye." A shake of his head and a half-cocked smile and he turned back to his desk to finish making the calls. There were still three other candidates he wanted to consider. And knew completely the implications of bringing on his boss' girlfriend. Quinn had a reputation to protect and doing favors wasn't in his repertoire. He didn't know Scarborough well enough yet to know what might happen were he to choose another candidate. As he saw it, it was a risk either way and the only way to approach the sensitive matter was to simply hire the best. And if it happened to be Agent Reid, then so be it, but if not, well, maybe his career would suffer for it, or maybe not.

DETECTIVE PHELPS OFFERED HIS HAND. "I appreciate you coming down, Mr. Vega. I'm sure this wasn't easy and I am sorry for your loss."

"Thank you. What's going to happen now?"

"As far as you're concerned, I'll be in touch if I have any other questions, which I imagine I will the deeper I get into this case."

"Do you believe it was more than a simple case of road rage or something like that?"

Phelps eyed the man. "Hard to say right now. Again, I thank you for your time."

"There's one other thing, detective. You understand I work for Congressman Copeland and so did Janine."

"I'm well aware of that and before you say anything more, I

have no intentions of bringing the media into this. There's no reason to and it'll only hinder my investigation. So if you're worried about your boss' name, and I suspect you are, unless I have a reason to make mention of the congressman in any way, I will speak with him myself first and we'll just take it from there."

After escorting him to the lobby and upon Vega's departure, Phelps considered the bloodied note, the one piece of information he hadn't relinquished. It was too early to show his hand, but he already knew this was no accident, no road rage incident. Janine Atherton was murdered and the killer was sending a message. Now it was up to him to figure out the intended recipient.

While waiting for the roommate's arrival, Phelps returned to his desk and began searching ViCAP for any similar cases inside the repository and to enter this case. It had become available to local law enforcement on a much broader basis and more easily accessible in 2008. Accessed through a secure internet link, it was the best way to compare markers. And in this case, the note, for lack of a better description, was a very distinctive marker.

In his doorway appeared a young woman who seemed fragile and shaken. She was accompanied by another officer.

"Detective Phelps? This is Anna Soto, the roommate."

"Yes, hello. Please come in." He eyed the officer. "Thank you. I'll take it from here." Phelps took her by the arm and led her to a chair. "Please, have a seat, Ms. Soto."

"Thank you." Her pallor and swollen eyes suggested the news of her friend's death had already taken its toll.

"I appreciate you coming down, Ms. Soto. Before we go back, can I ask you a few questions about Janine?"

"Yes."

"I know how hard this is, so please forgive my frankness. I would like to get to the bottom of what happened to your friend."

"I understand."

"Okay. Was Janine dating anyone?"

"Not that I was aware of. She worked so much, there was never any time for her to go out."

"And she worked on the Hill, for Representative Copeland?"

"Yes."

"From what I understand, she'd been attending a fundraiser of some sort on Saturday night? I already spoke with her supervisor."

"Yes. She's always—was always going to things like that. It was part of her job."

"A media advisor?"

"Something like that."

"What kind of car do you drive, Ms. Soto?"

Her brow knitted for a moment. "A 2012 Honda Accord. Why?"

"What color is it?"

"White."

"Thank you. Why don't we go back now and then I'll take an official statement? Would that be okay with you?"

She nodded and wiped a tear from her cheek.

The congressman waited in his office for Phil's return, unable to work, unable to think about anything else. All he wanted to know was what had happened to Janine. And when Phil finally appeared in his doorway, Copeland gleaned more than enough by the man's downtrodden expression.

"What happened? Was it her? Did you see her?"

He was zombie-like in his approach and finally sat down. "It was her. Jesus. I saw the hole in her head." He began to tremble. "Who would do that to her?"

"What did the detective say? Do they have any suspects?"

"No. Well, none that he told me about. He was waiting to talk to her roommate, Anna." Phil paused for a moment and turned his sights toward Copeland. "We'll have to draft a statement for the press. It won't take long for this to get out."

"Christ, I can't think about the goddam press right now. Janine is dead."

"I know, but we have to think about the optics here. We have to protect you."

"Optics? What optics? A member of my staff was killed, presumably in some kind of horrific road rage incident. How could this possibly reflect poorly on me? It'll reflect poorly if I try to distance myself."

"Grant, look, I know what was going on between you two. It wasn't hard to figure out. And if I could figure it out, the media will too."

"What are you talking about? There was..." Copeland shook his head. "Damn it."

"We need to just let the detective proceed with his investigation. I doubt Janine told anyone about you. The best way we can handle this is one day at a time. Wait to see what Detective Phelps comes up with."

"And if my name happens to show up somewhere? What then? Don't you think he'll wonder why I didn't come forward sooner? It'll make me look guilty as hell and you know it."

"For God's sake, Grant, why the hell couldn't you just keep it in your goddamn pants? You've just put your entire political career in jeopardy and we lost a friend and colleague."

"Excuse me? Who the fuck do you think you're talking to? You think I wanted Janine gone? You think I don't give a shit about her? You're wrong. I cared about her more than you could ever know. So excuse the hell out of me for that, you son of a bitch. Get out of here. Just get out. I need to think, and right now, I don't want to look at you."

Phil's face heated in anger before he finally pushed up from the chair. "Janine won't be the only one getting buried if this gets out."

~

THE COURSES REQUIRED to get to the point of being assigned work with an agent-profiler are extensive and Kate had taken several over the past few months in preparation. She was already at a disadvantage, since most of the other agents in those courses had far more investigative experience than she had. In fact, most had nearly ten years under their belts, while Kate had only finished her two-year probationary period earlier in the year. However, there was the one distinct advantage she had over her counterparts. Not one of them had been kidnapped—twice, by a serial killer, eventually bringing about the killer's death. The tragic incident as a child shaped who she had become as a young adult, then several years later, the monster came after her again, partly due to the discovery of her past and partly because the monster had always been watching her. Waiting for her to remember—and when she did, Kate's entire world turned on end.

The experience, however, was the reason why she was an agent to begin with and had been ushered down a speedier path to find herself here, today, ready to continue her training as a profiler and hopefully get the job so many others sought out for the majority of their careers.

"Agent Quinn?" Kate peeked into his doorway. "I'm Agent Reid here for our appointment."

Quinn took to his feet and approached Kate, offering his hand. "Yes, Agent Reid. Hello. Noah Quinn."

"Pleasure, sir, and thank you for seeing me." Kate wondered why he looked at her in an odd fashion and the silence between them had become awkward.

"You don't remember me, do you?"

"Um, sorry, sir. We've met before?"

"Take a seat, Agent Reid."

Kate flipped through the book of memories in her mind and in not one could she recall ever meeting this man. "Did we attend a class together? You'll have to forgive me; I don't recall meeting you in person."

Quinn took his seat and wore a deliberate smile. "I wouldn't expect that you'd remember. It was quite a while ago. I'd say at least six, maybe seven months ago. It was at the Crush Bar and you were with another woman. Oh, her name is on the tip of my tongue." He looked upward as though thinking hard on the matter. "Anyway, I think your friend was trying to set us up."

The wheels were turning and at last it came to her. "Oh, that's right." She began to chuckle. "Noah Quinn. Okay, wow, that was a long time ago. And as I recall, Alicia—Agent Vasquez—was persistent in her attempt to get us to exchange numbers." Her cheeks flushed the lightest shade of pink. "Now I'm embarrassed. If I'd have known, sir. I..."

"Don't be. I only recalled myself after reviewing your file when you submitted your application. It's hard to forget a face like yours, Agent Reid." Quinn seemed a little flustered himself. "Anyway, you're here now, so let's talk."

While he attempted to move past the discomfiture, Kate began to recall clearly now their first meeting. It had been the night she spoke with Marc Aguilar about the so-called Pretty Face killer. And after the conversation on that wet and cold November night, she went back inside and Alicia had, in a valiant effort, brought Quinn to their table. The ensuing conversation lasted scarcely five minutes before he seemed to catch on that she wanted nothing to do with him. Even before Nick, she wasn't interested in a man like Quinn just based on his seemingly arrogant demeanor at the time, a rash judgment she now reconsidered, especially in light of the fact that if all went to plan, he would be her new boss.

"You mentioned you had reviewed my files. So, what would you like to know about me?"

4

The bartender stepped closer, leaned over the bar, and cupped his ear. "What's that?"

"I said, can I get a vodka martini, dirty."

"Sure. Give me just a minute. I'm short staffed and the place is packed."

"I see that. Thanks." Tasha Brenner scanned the bar in search of her friend, who was late, as usual. She peered at her cell phone. No texts or missed calls. "Great."

It seemed the missing friend had just arrived when she felt a tap on her shoulder. Looking over, alas, she was mistaken. This was not her friend, but a man. A former acquaintance whom she hadn't seen in some time. "Todd Kemper? What are you doing here? Wow, it's great to see you."

"Just having a drink, same as you. I came in a little while ago, actually, and only just spotted you. You here alone?"

"I'm supposed to be meeting a friend, but she's late."

"Ah."

The bartender arrived with her drink. "Nineteen even."

Tasha set her credit card on the bar top. "You mind starting a tab?"

"Sure thing."

The man in the shirt and tie took in the scene. "I haven't been here in a while. This place is packed."

"I know. It's crazy. Took me ten minutes to get my drink. So, anyway, how you been? Where are you at now?"

"Communications Director for Senator Vaughn."

"No. Vaughn, really?"

"Yep. What about you? Last I heard, you were working on a re-election campaign."

"Good memory. I'm actually over at Strattman and Pew now. Better hours and much better pay."

"Lobbying? That's a step up. Good for you."

"Thanks. It's good work if you can get it." Her attention was diverted when her friend finally arrived. "There you are. I thought you were going to ditch me."

"I'm so sorry, Tash. I got held up at the office." She looked at the suit. "Who's this?"

"Todd Kemper. We knew each other back at school. Todd, this is my friend, Layla."

"Layla? Beautiful name." He offered his hand. "Pleasure to meet you. Can I get you a drink?"

She looked at Tasha as though asking for permission. Tasha shrugged her reply.

"Sure. I'll have a gin and tonic."

TASHA BEGAN to get the impression that her friends had every intention of leaving together and that time could well be at any moment. She didn't mind. Todd wasn't her type and she wasn't in the market right now anyway. So, after feeling like a third wheel for the better part of an hour, she made the call. "Hey, guys, I'm going to head home. I've got an early meeting in the morning."

"You want me to walk with you?" Layla asked.

"No, no. It's fine. I'm only a few blocks away. You two stay and enjoy yourselves."

Layla stood and embraced Tasha. "Okay, hon, I'll talk to you tomorrow?"

"Sure. Have fun."

"Oh, I intend to." Layla returned to her seat and to Todd Kemper.

It didn't seem possible, but the tiny metro bar was even more crowded and it was almost midnight. It was no wonder nothing ever got done in Washington. Everyone was too busy staying out all night, drinking and partying. But not Tasha. She stayed on the straight and narrow because she had plans. Big plans that meant there wasn't much time for socializing. She'd made the exception tonight for the simple fact that Layla had begged her to go out.

Tasha let her mind drift into thoughts of tomorrow's meeting and how she would have to present and it was kind of a big deal. In fact, she hardly noticed when she nearly walked into a man only minutes from her home. "Excuse me. Oh, my gosh. I'm so sorry. Are you okay?"

"Yeah. I'm fine." The man had dropped his phone and reached down to pick it up. "I shouldn't have been texting and walking. Dangerous habit." He smiled and tendered his hand. "Jonah, Jonah Jenkins."

"Pleasure to meet you, Jonah Jenkins. I'm Tasha, Tasha Brenner."

"Well, Tasha, Tasha Brenner, you feel like a drink?"

"I was actually on my way home. I live just there." She pointed behind him.

"Oh. It's entirely too early for bed, isn't it?"

She couldn't stop staring at his mouth. His full lips and sparkling smile. Now this was a man she could do with right now. "Yeah, I guess it is. You live nearby?"

"Just up the road."

"Listen, um, my house is literally fifty feet behind you. I've got wine, might have some beer."

"I could use a beer."

The night was shaping out better than she had expected. And while this wasn't how things usually turned out for her, Tasha wasn't going to let this one go and she didn't care what people would call her. He took her breath away. "It's this one here." She ascended the steps with her keys in hand and unlocked the door. And as she entered, she turned to him. "I just realized you must've been heading back home. What brought you out tonight?"

"Just going for a walk. I was on my way home, but nothing is waiting for me there except an empty room."

"Oh." She smiled and closed the door behind him. "Let me get you that beer."

"Thanks." Jonah examined the home while she walked into the kitchen. "Great place you got here. Lived here long?"

On her return with two bottles of beer in her hands, she began. "Not too long. Less than a year. I work in D.C. and the commute's not bad. Here you go."

"Thanks."

When he swallowed it down in a single gulp, he set the bottle on the table and reached around her waist. "How lucky am I to have found you tonight." He tucked her hair behind her ear.

"Oh, I'd say I was the lucky one." She took his hand and led him to the bedroom.

37

THE PATROL CAR rolled to a stop in front of the townhouse in the up and coming suburb of Baltimore, Waltham Heights. Its proximity to D.C. and moderately affordable housing made it attractive to commuters, Tasha Brenner being one of them.

The officers stepped out of their car and approached the home where a frightened woman waited.

"Did you make the call, ma'am?"

"Yes. She's inside. She's dead." The woman broke down.

"Can you show us where she is, ma'am?"

"Yes. Follow me."

"How do you know the victim?"

"I come and clean her house once a week. I wasn't supposed to be here until tomorrow, but I tried to call her and ask if I could reschedule." The woman continued inside toward Tasha's bedroom. "She didn't answer and so I was just going to leave her a note. Her door was unlocked and that's when I knew something was wrong."

"Okay, ma'am. Just stay here, please." The officer entered the bedroom with his partner close behind. "Oh, geez."

Tasha lay on the blood-soaked bed, arms and legs spread wide.

"For God's sake." He moved closer, careful not to touch anything, and leaned over her. "GSW to the head. And, there's something in her mouth."

"What is it?" His partner moved in. "Looks like a cloth or piece of fabric. Don't touch it. We'd better call it into Homicide."

AS THE ELEVATOR DOORS PARTED, Agent Vasquez stepped out into the 5th floor common area of the WFO offices. Carrier bag in hand and on a call, she approached her desk while Kate looked on, anxious to get her up to speed on yesterday's meeting with the

BAU profiler. And even more anxious to tell her it was Noah Quinn.

"I'll get back with you soon." Vasquez ended the call and looked at Kate. "Morning."

"Morning. Everything all right?"

"Not sure yet. Jameson in?"

"Yeah. What's going on?"

"That was the Baltimore Field Office. PD found a body and the detective on the case ran markers through ViCAP and got a match to another victim found in D.C. only a few days ago. Anyway, I'm pretty tight with one of the agents in Baltimore and got a call about it."

"They want us to take a look?"

"Two victims, similar signatures, one here and one in Baltimore. They think there could be more coming. That's why I wanted to talk to Jameson. You have time? We should go see him together."

"Let's go." Kate followed her toward Dwight's office. Whatever she'd wanted to say about the Quantico meeting didn't matter right now. Something else was going on, and she wanted to know what it was.

"Jameson, you got a second?" Alicia Vasquez was a no-nonsense woman and rarely minced words.

"Come in." Dwight's brow knitted as it seemed he sensed the importance of the request. "What have you got?"

She proceeded to update him on her conversation with the agent in Baltimore. Kate listened and waited to see how Dwight would reply. Metro PD hadn't come to them yet, which was a point of concern. Were they aware of Baltimore's findings? If so, why the hesitation?

"Why don't you put in a call to Metro Police and talk to the detective running the investigation? See if he knows what's going on in Baltimore and if he wants to request a consult. There's no denying a link between the two victims and the unique nature of the marker suggests the unsub is fulfilling some sort of vendetta. And based on what you just told me, I doubt the unsub is finished," Dwight added.

"Agreed. If I can get an okay from Metro, Reid and I should head over there as soon as possible and get the download on the status of the investigation."

"Sounds good. Keep me posted and let me know what they want our role to be. I'll run it by Campbell."

The agents began to leave, but it seemed Dwight wasn't finished with one of them. "Reid, can you hang back a minute?"

"I'll make the call." Vasquez continued, leaving the two of them alone.

"I suppose you want to know how yesterday went?"

Dwight peered at the time. "I've waited over an hour and you haven't said a word. Don't know if that's good or bad."

Kate sat back down. "I can't really say. I mean, it went well enough. Quinn's in the early stages of interviewing, so it's going to be a lengthy process, I believe."

"What's your take? You get any feeling at all how he's going to lean?"

"No. None whatsoever. I do know he's considering candidates with a lot more investigative experience than me."

"I'm not surprised. Still, don't count yourself out. You have certain things working in your favor."

"You mean like Scarborough being his boss?"

"No."

"Come on, Dwight. You know that's got to play on his mind a little. I think regardless of my qualifications, he has little choice but to reject my application. People would talk. And I've already been down that road." She inhaled a slow, deep breath. "I'd hoped to be past that now. I wanted to train based on my own merits, not Nick's."

"It will be, Kate."

"I just wish I'd approached him before Nick got the position. Then I'd know for sure. Now, even if I get it, I'll always wonder if he played a part, and I swear to you, that was the last thing I wanted to happen."

"Give this Quinn guy some credit, okay? Whether you get the position or not will be based on your qualifications and recommendations. He has no choice but to display complete transparency or risk the legitimacy of his own career coming into question. Besides, you think you and Nick are the first agents who've ever dated? Please. Happens all the time. In fact, I'd venture to say the Bureau encourages it. Leaves less room for outside influences in an agent's life. Both parties understanding one another's careers. So, anyway, don't discount it yet. This is just the first phase, and by all accounts, it sounds like it went well."

"I hope so." She pushed up from the chair. "I'll check in with Vasquez and let you know if we're heading out to Metro PD."

DETECTIVE PHELPS HAD BEEN SUMMONED to the front desk and arrived to find the two FBI agents who'd contacted him earlier this morning. "Agent Vasquez?"

"Yes. And you must be Detective Phelps. Pleasure." She gestured to Kate. "This is Agent Reid. We appreciate you clearing your schedule."

"No problem. Why don't you two come back and we'll talk?" He led the way to his office. "Please, have a seat." Upon closing his door, Phelps returned to his desk. "After you and I spoke this morning, Agent Vasquez, I did reach out to the detective in Baltimore. Apparently, he wasn't aware the FBI was watching."

"Watching?" Kate asked.

"Well, Agent Vasquez mentioned she received a call from the Baltimore office of the Bureau, and apparently, the detective hadn't made any calls to the Feds."

"Which is exactly the reason why I made contact," Vasquez began. "I got the call from the Baltimore field office after they received a report indicating a hit on two separate investigations with similar markers. He reached out to us because the other investigation was here in D.C."

"So, you come down to see me and those guys over at the other office, they talk to the Baltimore PD? And then what? You all come in and take over my investigation?"

"Not at all, detective." Kate eyed Vasquez noting the man's sensitivity to the issue at hand. "We're here to discuss the markers you input into ViCAP, discuss the similarities with the Baltimore investigation, and then work to come up with a conclusive profile of your unsub so you all can continue to work to find the culprit. This is what we do, detective."

"While your people sit on the sidelines?"

"Something like that. We're here to help. Not to take over." Vasquez offered reassurances and it seemed Phelps might be falling into line now. "That's the great thing about the database. We aren't wearing blinders. We see what's happening elsewhere and that opens up a lot of resources to spread out and catch the person responsible."

"Okay. I can understand that perspective." Phelps appeared to shed the chip on his shoulder. "I had entered the markers into ViCAP and when nothing turned up, I continued on my own path. Now that something else has, then I am more than willing to share information with you and Baltimore to find the killer.

Because I'll tell you one thing, this person is dangerous. And whoever it is, is hunting people he or she already knows or knows through an acquaintance. These are not random killings."

"We couldn't agree more. Not with that message," Vasquez said. "So, why don't you fill us in on the specifics and we'll do what we can to help complete the picture."

Phelps leaned back and puffed his chest a little. "Well, I'll tell you, I've been doing my best to keep this out of the line of sight of the press."

"That's the way we prefer it," Kate added. "Only causes more problems."

"Yes, it does. However, this is due to the nature of the investigation and the fact that the victim was acquainted with a congressman."

"How so?"

"Most people in this city are acquainted in one way or another with a politician. I know she was a member of a congressman's staff, but not the entirety of her role or how close she was to the head honcho. So, tell me, any idea if the Baltimore victim is connected to politics?"

Grant Copeland stared through his car's windshield while he sat on the driveway of his home. The stone exterior was lit by pathway lights leading to the front door. A door he hesitated to pass through. The questions would come, and soon. He would have to tell them how he knew Janine and his wife would learn of his intimate connection to a woman who had been murdered. The fact that this was still a matter of when was largely due to his trusted chief of staff, Phil Vega. He'd been the one to field the questions as Janine was under his charge and Copeland, as far as the police were concerned, had maintained several degrees of separation from her.

He exited his car and walked along the path toward the front door, opening it to reveal his teen son and daughter slouched on the sofa, headphones on and eyes glued to their phones. His wife was nowhere to be seen, but he suspected she was in the kitchen, given the delicious aroma of food wafting through the home. He hadn't told her of Janine's death, and perhaps the best thing to do was to lay the groundwork. Prepare her for the time that was hurtling toward them like a runaway freight train.

The kitchen was just ahead on his right and he continued through, past the staircase, and pushed open the swing door that led into their recently remodeled kitchen. Sue was exactly where he expected her to be, standing in front of the cooktop over boiling pots and sizzling skillets.

"What's for dinner?"

She turned. "I didn't hear you come in." Sue approached him and offered a tender kiss on the cheek. "Glad you could make it home for dinner. What's the occasion?"

"I didn't feel up to staying late tonight. I wanted to be home with you and the kids."

"What's wrong? Are you okay?"

"Not really. Ah, Suzy Q." With hesitation, he continued. "Over this last weekend, a member of my staff, a woman who worked in media relations—Phil knew her well—she was killed on the side of the road."

"Oh my God. Oh, honey, I'm so sorry." She embraced him. "My God. And you just found out?"

"Yeah. Just found out today."

5

The key slid into the lock and turned with ease as Kate entered the place she couldn't really call home but was currently the closest thing to it. Inside, she noticed Nick wearing a broad smile and standing in front of the dining table, arms open wide.

"What's this? I didn't expect you to be home."

"I am and I brought dinner."

She continued toward him and offered a warm embrace and gentle kiss. "Thank you, but what's the occasion?"

"Do I have to have a reason to bring you dinner?"

"Well, no, it's just that you don't often..."

"I know. But before you moved in, I didn't have much reason to. Now you're here and while I didn't cook the meal, the sentiment is the same. Come on; sit down and eat before it gets cold."

"Okay." Kate sat down and was somewhat confused by this new side of Nick. The man who never cleaned his house, always had a housekeeper, ate from take-out cartons or went to a restaurant. This was not the man she'd known for the better part of five years and had been dating for the past six months. "I've never seen you so domesticated before."

He sat down and joined her. "Is that a problem?"

"No. I appreciate the effort. I do. But I also want you to be yourself, Nick. Grand gestures are nice, but we've known each other long enough to understand one another. You don't need to change anything for me."

"I get it. I'm sorry I went the extra mile. I just thought, you didn't say anything yesterday about your meeting with Quinn and I was hesitant to bring it up, so I thought maybe you'd want to talk if we had some downtime. Which is rare, in and of itself."

He was right that she hadn't mentioned anything about yesterday's meeting. In part because there wasn't much to say. It was only the first phase of the process, but mostly because she was hesitant to mention that she had met him previously—and that he had hit on her. It shouldn't matter. It was a long time ago—before she and Nick were officially an item. But it was awkward and maybe it wasn't his business to know. So she avoided the topic entirely.

"It is rare. And I do appreciate it. I just don't want you to feel obligated. But anyway, let's just enjoy the meal. I'm starving."

"Good. I talked to Dwight earlier today. He said you and Vasquez met with Metro PD."

"We did. There's a strong possibility we'll be helping them out on an investigation, along with the Baltimore Field Office. Two victims, same signatures."

"Sounds interesting. How are you moving forward on it?"

"The detective is going to send us the forensics report and we'll cross-reference it with the one from Baltimore. See what other similarities we can find. In the meantime, he's continuing to follow up on the victim's history. Apparently, both had ties to the political world."

"Considering the location, that's not surprising." Nick sipped on his wine. "Sounds like something you guys can sink your teeth into."

"I think so." She noted a change in his tone. "You're not jealous, are you?"

"What? Not at all. I like being a desk jockey. That's what I wanted, remember?"

Kate laughed. "Sure. We'll see how long that lasts."

"So are you going to tell me anything about your interview with Quinn, or am I going to have to continue making small talk?"

She set her fork down and held his gaze. "It's just the first stage, Nick. There isn't much to say right now. He's still whittling down the field."

"I know. But I thought you could gauge his reaction. Get a feel for what he was thinking."

"He didn't go easy on me. I'll tell you that much. It's going to be a tough road ahead and I'll do my best. But that's all I can do."

"Okay."

Kate began to recall the times she'd withheld information from Marshall and how it generally came back to bite her in the ass. Had she learned nothing from her past relationships? Even going back to Spencer, although that was a lifetime ago. Still, if she didn't tell him now and he found out later on his own, he would be pissed about it. Not that she had met Quinn previously, but that she hadn't told him first. "There is something I should tell you about the meeting."

"Yeah?"

She continued to show reluctance.

"Kate? What is it?"

"Turns out, I met Noah Quinn some time ago. I want to say seven months, maybe eight. I can't recall exactly." She could, but it seemed like she would be throwing fuel on the fire.

"What? How did you meet him? Why didn't you tell me before?"

"Honestly, the name never registered. I mean, Alicia and I were at happy hour one night after work, before I went out to L.A. and this guy came up to us. Well, Alicia made sure he came up to us. Offered him some encouragement without my knowledge. Anyway, he introduced himself. Didn't say what he did for a living and I never asked. I think our conversation amounted to a few minutes of idle chit chat and when I implied I wasn't interested, he nodded graciously and left. And that was it."

A half-cocked smile appeared on his lips. "And that's it? You didn't want to tell me that? It hardly counts as a meeting."

"You're right. In fact, it was Quinn who mentioned to me that we'd met before. Even seeing him face to face, I still didn't recall."

"He remembered?"

"Yeah. The guy must have a memory like an elephant."

"I'm sure he must." Nick returned his attention to the food on his plate.

At this, Kate had to smile. "Now that sounded laced with jealousy. What can I say? I have a memorable face."

"I'm not jealous. But you do have a memorable face." He held her gaze with impassioned eyes. "How about we finish this up later?"

"I'm sure it'll reheat just fine."

～

DUE TO ITS 24-hour news cycle, the District of Columbia was a city that never seemed to sleep.

And Detective Phelps, one of Metro PD's finest, wasn't sleeping either. He rubbed the back of his neck, which had stiffened from studying files for far too long. In a cross-jurisdictional coordinated effort, there wasn't enough time in the day to scrutinize all the information about the two victims of the presumably same suspect. He began to consider the possibility that the Feds could offer greater help, as they'd suggested. The files had been sent, but no one yet assigned, as he'd asked to have more time to review what he had.

It was going to be a logistical nightmare, but risking the life of anyone else wasn't an option and so Phelps would have to make clear his need for help. This was something he was never good at doing. Here was a woman who was entrenched in D.C. politics and now another who lobbied for her firm's pet causes. And both were dead. Both with the same note shoved in their mouths. "Whore." A vulgar word written with such obvious hatred. The writing itself was violent in its appearance. What was the more intimate connection between the two?

He retrieved his cell phone. "This is Detective Phelps, Metro PD. Can you patch me through to Detective Ramos, please?"

The line played soft jazz while he waited and finally the man he needed to speak with answered.

"Ramos here."

"This is Phelps, Metro PD. I'm sorry to call so late, but I wanted to talk to you about the Brenner investigation."

"Yeah. I got your files on Atherton. You find something interesting?"

"I'm just sitting here in my office going over what I know about Atherton and her work for a congressman. You get an employment background on Brenner yet?" He heard the shuffling of papers.

"I'm sitting at my desk too. Looks like neither of us is getting any sleep. But, yeah. I got it back today as a matter of fact and haven't had a chance to get it to you or the Feds." He continued to sift through the papers. "Here it is. I printed all this shit off to take it home and still I sit here staring at my computer instead. Wife's going to be thrilled with me."

"See, there's your first mistake. Being married."

The two laughed almost in unison.

"Okay, we know she worked for the law firm. Lobbying. Looks like prior to that, hang on, I've got it here. Right, so prior to that, she worked on an election campaign."

"Oh yeah? For who?"

"She was a paid consultant. Had her own gig, apparently. Don't know what for exactly. Let me see here. Okay, got it. She consulted for Representative Copeland."

Phelps sat bolt upright in his chair. "Grant Copeland of Virginia?"

"One and the same. Let me guess, that's who Atherton worked for? Guess we just found a connection."

"Could you send me that background you have on Brenner?"

"Will do."

AGENT DARYL PEARSON of the Baltimore Field Office arrived at WFO to meet with the team.

"Agent Pearson." Kate offered her hand. "I'm Agent Reid. Come on up." She led the way to the elevators. "We appreciate you driving over. I think if we can get on the same page, we'll be better suited to help Metro and Baltimore PD on their investigations."

"Couldn't agree more." He followed her onto the elevator. "I spoke with Detective Ramos in Baltimore early this morning. They have a new possible connection between the two victims."

"That's good news." The doors parted. "Right this way and we'll get started." She continued through the corridor to

Dwight's office where Vasquez also waited. "This is Agent Pearson."

"Good to see you again, Pearson," Vasquez replied.

"Same here. It's been a while." He turned to Dwight. "And you must be SSA Jameson."

"You are not wrong. Thanks for coming down. Have a seat and let's talk."

Pearson retrieved his files. "As I was saying to Agent Reid, I received new information on the Baltimore victim, Tasha Brenner. The detective discovered she worked for the same congressman as your D.C. victim, Janine Atherton."

"That is definitely worth taking a look at," Dwight replied. "Have you received any analysis on the note yet?"

"Still too early. This is the strongest lead we've got right now. However, the congressman in question has several employees, both past and current."

"Which suggests the connection may not be as strong as we might hope," Kate said.

"That's right. Now, I would like to suggest we meet with both detectives and review what they've discovered to date. I know they've sent over some files, but I'd like to visit the scenes, both of them, in order to gain a better assessment. If that works for you all, I can coordinate it."

"I think that would be a good idea." Dwight turned to Vasquez. "You brought this to us. I'll let you pick sides, so to speak."

"Since Pearson and I have worked together in the past, I would suggest he and I assist the Baltimore PD, and Reid and Detective Phelps work here in D.C., and we can coordinate our efforts."

"I can agree to that," Kate replied.

"Good. As you all know, this isn't going to be easy and we need to be careful not to step on the local authority's toes. Last thing I want them to think of us is as a hindrance, rather than a help. So, while this is certainly within our periphery, let's just keep that in mind. Reid, be sure to get what you need from Pearson here to start compiling a profile of our unsub." He turned to the agent. "Reid is currently training for a position at BAU headquarters."

"Perfect. Sounds like you're the right person for the job." Pearson turned to Vasquez. "You free to run out to the scene this afternoon?"

"Absolutely."

"I'll speak to Detective Phelps and meet with him if he's got time this afternoon as well," Kate replied.

"Great. Then we'll go from there. Thank you and to you, Agent Pearson, for meeting us here. I'll leave you all to do your jobs."

Kate followed the others and returned to her desk. She'd noticed a marked difference in Dwight's demeanor since taking over for Nick. He was poised and logical, yet still let those in his charge do what they did best. He gave her and Vasquez a lot of rope. It made her feel more confident in return, instead of dependent upon his approval of her ideas or plans for an investigation. It was freeing in a way she'd only known briefly in the past. And that was when Nick was on administrative leave. A few short months and she'd seen that very same side in Dwight. He was made for this role and she was glad he was given the opportunity to take it, although the question of her future still hung low in the air; a cloud of uncertainty surrounding her every move. But now she had something to focus on once again. Her classroom training was complete and it was now up to Noah Quinn to give her the opportunity to further her career.

"I'm heading up to Baltimore. Won't be back here tonight, but I'll see you in the morning," Vasquez said.

"Give me a call if you find something interesting. Phelps is taking me out to the scene in about an hour. I'll let you know what we find."

"Perfect. See you later, Reid."

As SENIOR UNIT AGENT, Nick was still in the process of getting to know the rest of his team and his own boss, Unit Chief Cole, the man who previously held his title. He was often there to oversee the issuing of assignments, so Nick felt as though his wings were still clipped and he hadn't yet the freedom to fully grasp the process of how these people worked together or with him.

All extremely qualified agents with years of service between them, they rarely came to him for advice or help or anything in between. Autonomy was king here and it was a new concept for Nick—to a certain extent. He'd been in charge of his team at WFO. The small band of agents who worked and played together relied on him to make decisions. So far, that didn't seem to be the case here. This was a whole new level and one he would need to adjust to if he wanted to gain their trust and loyalty.

"Scarborough, can I talk to you a minute?"

Nick was surprised to see Quinn at his door and felt the slightest twinge of angst. "Sure, come in. What's going on?"

"I wanted to talk to you about Agent Reid." He sat down.

"Okay. What do you want to know?"

"You recruited her, is that right?"

"I did."

"She was working as an evidence tech for San Diego PD and then went through some pretty horrific events, winding up at Quantico a couple of years ago."

"That's right."

"I've read her file. I know what happened and how she came to be here."

"So what's your question?"

"What I want to know is, is she an agent because of you, or in spite?"

"I'm not sure I get your meaning. Agent Reid loves the job. It's who she is. Has been for some time."

"Look, I know she's been under your tutelage for a while."

"I was her designated mentor during her probationary period, if that's what you mean."

"Yes, but in addition to that, during her time at the Academy, you were instrumental in her success, is that right?"

"No. I don't think it is. Her test scores were all of her own doing. She's an extremely bright and incredibly insightful agent. I don't think you'd find another like her."

"I don't doubt that. Not after reading what she's been through. But that leads me to the reason why I'm here. You two recently began a relationship, is that right?"

Nick was growing defensive. "Yes, but I'm not sure what it has to do with her application."

"I'm not sure it has anything to do with it. It was just a point of clarification I needed. My concern is having her here, regardless of the obvious accolades she's received and the recommendations of those whom she's worked with in the past. I've spoken with your former ASAC, Campbell. He said your team was above reproach."

"And?"

"I guess there's no purpose in beating around the bush, here, so I'll get to the point. Agent Reid is uniquely qualified for this position and could allow us to venture into unchartered areas in profiling. Her perspective into the minds of killers is extraordinary."

Nick was waiting for the "but."

"But, I am concerned that your personal relationship might get in the way of her performance, and yours, for that matter."

"I'm sorry? Are you telling me I don't have the ability to do my job if my girlfriend is several offices down the hall? Who do you think you're talking to here? I've put in my time. I've worked more cases and been through more shit with my former team than I suspect any of you have here."

"That's not fair. We were all field agents before coming here. You know that. And, I'm not trying to ruffle your feathers, Scarborough. I'm really not. Before I bring someone on, I have to understand the mindset of that individual, and frankly, there's the possibility of favoritism that I will have to work extremely hard at avoiding, should Agent Reid be chosen." He inhaled a breath. "That being said, I would like to consider her for the second phase, which will be unduly harsh on her. More so than any of the other candidates."

"So you're assuming I'll treat her differently if she works here, but you're about to do the same thing just to prove you're not playing favorites."

"I'm afraid that's correct. And I imagine if Reid was here, she'd agree that it has to be this way to avoid any conflicts and ensure transparency. I already made mention of this in our interview the other day. I don't think she'll object."

"I won't tell you how to do your job, if you don't tell me how to do mine," Nick began. "If you feel it necessary to make Reid jump through hoops others will not, then that's up to you—and her, if she chooses to accept it. I'm not here to obstruct your process in any way and I, most of all, have no desire to bring any opacity to the team. I'm an open book and the same goes for my relationship with Agent Reid. So do what you need to do."

Quinn began to rise. "Thank you. My intent wasn't to upset

you and I hope you understand that this is what's best for Reid, for her career—and mine." He began to leave.

"I understand you met her several months ago."

Quinn turned back. "Sorry?"

"She mentioned you tried to pick her up at a bar a while back."

"Is that what she said?"

"Not in so many words. But sure sounded like it to me. Said she forgot all about it until you said something."

Quinn smiled. "I did recall our meeting."

Nick continued to hold his stare. "She does have an unforgettable face, doesn't she?"

6

The crime scene photos lay before her on the table as Kate studied the images of Janine Atherton slumped back in the seat of her car. Blood caked on her face and lips with eyes casting a haunting glance that seemed to capture the horror she must've felt moments before her death. "You said it was several hours before she was discovered?"

Detective Phelps hovered over her. "At least five, based on what we know from the autopsy. It appeared she'd been dead for at least that long."

"Any forensics come back yet on the scrap of fabric?" She moved the pictures around in a puzzle-piece-like arrangement, attempting to make sense of the images.

"No." Phelps stood upright again and paced his office. "What concerns me most is that we now know the two victims worked for the same congressman."

"Some time apart, though, is that right?"

"Yes. Roughly five months or so apart. Atherton was brought on just before Copeland won re-election. What remains unclear was whether Brenner terminated her consulting agreement or had it simply come to an end when the election was over and she went on her own to pursue a career as a lobbyist."

"That's what we should be looking into, wouldn't you agree?" Kate continued.

"Look, Agent Reid, the last thing I want to do is start dragging Representative Copeland into two murder investigations. I don't want the media circus and I'm betting you don't either. I say we leave Brenner to Baltimore PD and the rest of your team. The best thing for us to do right now is to keep the investigations separate until we can absolutely and without a doubt connect them to Copeland in a way that would confirm illicit involvement in no uncertain terms."

"I've had my share of run-ins with the media, detective. We know how to handle them."

"I'm sure you do, but not when it comes to politics and not in this town. Trust me when I say you don't want that kind of attention."

"Then what do you propose we do? How do we find Janine's killer?"

"I need your help to get a handle on the nature of the suspect we're looking for. Isn't that why you're here?"

"Yes."

Phelps joined her at the table. "Good. The roommate gave a statement indicating Atherton had been at a fundraiser Copeland also attended. I reached out again to his chief of staff, a man by the name of Phillip Vega, and he confirmed his attendance as well. He also confirmed he left before she did."

"And have you spoken to Copeland at all regarding any of this?"

"I've asked Vega to verify with the congressman what time he left and whether Atherton was still there. I'm waiting to hear back."

"What about a boyfriend? Was she alone at this event?"

"She was alone. Roommate says she didn't have a boyfriend, which for an attractive young woman, I find hard to believe."

"I'm sure her job must've kept her too busy to enjoy a flourishing personal life. It happens." Kate had begun to sour on this detective. Wanting to protect, at perhaps the cost of the investigation, a congressman, then throwing out antiquated ideas that a woman should of course have a boyfriend or husband, regardless of her career status.

Phelps glossed over her comment and continued, "Anyway, I was about to follow up with Vega."

"And if you don't get an answer?"

"Then I'll talk to others who attended the event. Find out who talked to Atherton and when and if anyone saw her leave. But what I'd like from you, Agent Reid, as your primary reason for being here is to help formulate a profile on the killer, is to get a history on the men in Atherton's life. I think the more we know about who she dated, her personal record with men, we'll learn if any of them had a proclivity for violence."

"And where would that leave us with Tasha Brenner?"

"I'm not running that investigation, but I would suggest getting word to your cohort and have her run on the same thing. We might find an overlap. D.C. is a small town. You'll find that out real quick."

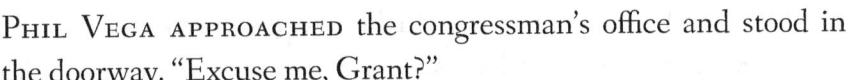

PHIL VEGA APPROACHED the congressman's office and stood in the doorway. "Excuse me, Grant?"

Copeland peered over his glasses and pulled them from his face. "Phil, come in."

"I wanted to discuss some developments in Janine's investigation."

"Close the door, then, would you?"

He shut the door behind him and headed toward a chair, sitting down as though weighed by a tremendous burden.

"Before you begin, I'd like to apologize for my behavior the other day. You didn't deserve the harsh words. It's just, well, it still doesn't seem real to me that she's gone. And looking at you now, I feel as though more troubling news is on the horizon."

"I'm afraid it is."

"Spit it out."

"There's been another murder. A woman who worked on your last campaign."

"What? Who was she and when did this happen?"

"Tasha Brenner. Her body was found the day before yesterday in her home."

"For God's sake. What the hell is going on here?" Masked in bewilderment, he continued, "How do they know this is related to Janine or to me, for that matter?"

"There's something I haven't told you. With both of them gone, I have to say that the reason they believe the murders are linked is because, well, they both worked for you."

Copeland's mouth hung open. "I didn't kill them."

"Since Tasha Brenner was found in her home in Baltimore, the local authorities are working the investigation there, but from what I understand, after receiving an update from Detective Phelps, the FBI has now been brought in."

"Why is that? How is this an FBI matter?"

"The manner of their deaths. The connection between the two women could well mean it's the same killer and the murders crossed state lines, meaning the Feds are coordinating with Metro Police and Baltimore Police. Grant, I don't think I can hold them off. They're going to start asking questions."

"Because they both worked for me."

"Yes. Is there anything you want to tell me? Anything at all that would help me get out in front of whatever concerns they throw our way."

He considered the question but couldn't bring himself to reveal the truth. "No. Nothing I can think of off-hand."

Phil looked at him, appearing uncertain of how to gauge this ambiguous response. "I'll do my best to continue to field their calls, but I don't know how long I'll be able to hold them off. As soon as they sign the registration books for an appointment to meet with you, the press will find out. They're public record. And the last thing we want is for them to start asking questions too." He stood.

"Thank you, Phil. Your loyalty means everything to me."

"I don't know if loyalty will be enough this time."

Copeland watched as he left without another word. This latest news dealt a devastating blow. And this was much more than a mere coincidence. Phil knew it. It was written all over his face. Someone was coming after him. And now the FBI was involved? This was turning into a nightmare and he didn't know how to wake up.

How long would it be before the authorities discovered he'd had affairs with both of those women? The affair with Tasha had been fleeting and meant little to him, but it appeared to have cost her her life—the same for Janine, a woman he might have left his wife for—maybe. Now he would never know because she was gone too.

But the real question remained: who else knew about these affairs? And if this person knew about both of them, what about the others?

In the quiet space of Nick's apartment, Kate curled her legs beneath her and continued to study the files on her laptop. It was the one thing she missed living alone; being alone. The solitude and the quiet gave her a chance to think and she was taking full advantage of the fact that Nick hadn't arrived home yet. Apparently, something had come up on an investigation his team had been working on and so he stayed with them.

She continued to peruse the Atherton file in search of who might have taken the woman's life. It seemed unlikely to her that it was a former boyfriend, though the detective appeared to be leaning that way. Kate had been involved in enough BAU investigations to understand when they were dealing with a vengeful boyfriend or a cold, calculating serial killer. To her, this one fell in the latter category. But she was there to help and if the detective wanted the boyfriends vetted, then she would do so. What she really wanted to know was who was watching Janine that night at the fundraiser, because without a doubt, someone had been. And letting the congressman off the hook at this stage of the game wasn't the right thing to do, and this perhaps weighed the most on her mind.

According to Vasquez, Tasha Brenner had had sexual relations with someone prior to her death who had yet to be identified, though they were uncertain this person was the killer. It appeared no DNA had been left behind, suggesting protection had been used. The forensics team was still pulling prints from her house and searching for fibers. No signs of assault were evident on the body, with the major exception of the bullet to the head. So Vasquez was working to discover who was last seen with Brenner while Kate ran on who Atherton had been with in the past. She didn't expect to find a connection. Neither woman suffered more than the gunshot, which would've killed them almost instantly. This suggested to Kate that the killer wasn't motivated by hatred. Disgust, perhaps, considering the note, but hatred would have been evident in the form of physical abuse. She'd seen it plenty times before. So that lead her to another question. If the killer wasn't motivated by hate, could it have been money and the note was simply meant as a distraction—a red herring? That seemed more likely.

She'd begun drafting her notes, creating a profile of the killer that would help point them in the right direction. The courses she'd taken at Quantico over the past few months taught her how to organize her thoughts. Make a list of personal attributes gathered from the unsub's behavior at the scenes.

Not only that, but draw conclusions based upon social demographics they knew thus far. Locations of the crime scenes—both in the vicinity of Metro D.C. While there were a high number of homicides in D.C., the targeting of these individuals suggested the killer could also be involved in the political world, as the victims had been. Most likely, a male, twenties to thirties, given the age of the victims, although it was still a bit of a leap to assume the man Tasha had sex with before she died was the killer. CSI should determine if there was DNA left from other previous visitors. But for now, the assumption had to be that the unsub was a male.

They were still in the process of constructing the sequence of events for each homicide, meaning a full assessment was still unattainable. However, that information would become the cornerstone on which Kate could build and complete her profile. And she would continue to pursue the angle of personal contacts, boyfriends, friends. At the very least, this could establish Janine's own pattern of behavior, and if that could be done, it was entirely possible the killer saw that pattern and used it against her.

Keys rattling in the door lock diverted her attention. She turned to see Nick enter. "You're home."

"Hey." Nick appeared relieved, as though he'd just seen water after trudging through the desert. "Sorry it's so late." He made his way to the sofa and kissed her on the cheek. "I see you're still up and working away."

"I met with the Metro PD detective in charge of the Atherton investigation. I'm trying to develop a profile."

"Oh yeah? Anything new?"

"Not really. Alicia is working with Baltimore and she's come up with a few things to help round out the profile, but nothing of great significance. Not yet. Hey, did you eat?"

"Had some pizza at the office. Late night working on a serial rapist investigation."

"I remember you were talking about that one."

"It's picking up steam and we're trying our damnedest to find the person responsible. I'd venture to say Quinn's the best in his field. Developed a comprehensive profile the likes I've never seen. You'd do well under him."

Nick was her biggest advocate and never failed to slip in a word or two about her future internship, as it were. "I'm glad you're getting along well with your new team."

"It'd be better if you were there, but we'll have to wait and see."

"Yes, we will." She stood from the couch. "I could use a break. You want to grab a drink and sit outside for a while? It's a clear night and the moon's shining on the water. It's beautiful."

"You're beautiful." He headed toward the kitchen. "I'll grab the wine and glasses. You go on out."

Kate pulled open the sliding glass door and felt the breeze on her skin. She'd finally acclimated to the weather and a sixty-degree summer night no longer felt cold. Which was about what it was tonight. She stretched out on the lounge chair and closed her eyes.

Moments later, Nick's fingertips slid along her arms and her eyes flicked open again. It had been an adjustment, not seeing him at work every day, but it made moments like these all the more precious and meaningful. His eyes conveyed his love for her and she loved him in the same way, never truly believing that was possible. But there was no denying it.

Nick was far from perfect. He still drank too much, was pigheaded as hell, and put more pressure on himself than anyone she knew, except maybe for her.

"Here." He handed her the glass and made a spot for himself on her lounger. "I missed you today. I miss you every day, but especially today. The way we could read one another and play off each other's instincts. The way you can find the minutia in a case. As talented as my team is—and they are without a doubt—it wasn't the same as having you there. It's like a rush of adrenaline when we get a break, you know? I guess I was more addicted to that feeling than I thought I was."

"We do make a good team. That was never in question."

"Then what was?"

"My capacity for doing it without you. I needed to know for myself—for my own sanity—that I didn't need you at my side every day. And that I didn't need you to pull the strings."

"You know I had an interesting conversation with Quinn earlier today."

"Oh yeah?" She sipped on her wine.

"I can see he's hesitant to bring you onboard, no matter how much he might want to."

Kate cast her gaze toward the bay. "Because we're seeing each other."

"He doesn't want to be perceived as favoring you over another due to our relationship."

"So I'm being punished because we're together."

"Maybe." Nick tossed back half his glass in one fell swoop. "And I don't think there's anything I can do about it. It's entirely his call."

"I'm going to be held to a different standard than all the other candidates because you're his boss and I'm your girlfriend. Goddam it." She swung her legs over the edge of the lounger and pulled herself up. "I think I'll go to bed."

As she began to walk away, Nick followed. "Wait a second—please." He reached for her arm to stop her. "I wanted to be honest with you and how I see that this could play out. Doesn't mean it will. I'd like to give Quinn enough credit to see past our relationship and see that you are the most qualified to do the job."

"But I'm not, Nick. And you know it. The other candidates likely have far more field experience than me. In fact, I'd undoubtedly be one of the youngest members they've ever recruited."

"Quinn's not much older than you and I'll bet he faced a similar scenario. Age has nothing to do with it. And it doesn't mean you're any less qualified. You can't tell me any of those in the running have been through the shit you have. Come on. That's just not possible. And you know as well as I do that gives you an edge. It was horrific and terrible and I wouldn't wish what happened to you to happen to my worst enemy, but it has made you different than the rest. Better. Whether you want to admit it or not, it has."

"I can't keep using that card."

"It's not a card. It's your past, it's your future. It's who you are, Kate. And Quinn will see that. Look, I'm not saying he's already decided. He hasn't. But he did talk to me and made his point quite clear. Now you'll just have to make your point clearer. Get him to see what you can do. He'll soon discover that you don't need me and, in fact, it's probably the other way around." Nick held her gaze. "You know I'm right."

At this, she cracked the smallest of grins. "You might be."

He slipped his hand around her waist and pulled her close. "See?"

Their lips touched and the heat between them rose as they pressed against one another. Kate wrapped her arms around his neck and pushed her fingers through the back of his hair. Their grip tightened and Nick lowered her back onto the lounger, raising the tank top that formed to her figure above her breasts, and unhooked her bra.

All was forgotten in the heat of their passion, but how long would that last?

7

An assistant to Representative Copeland stood in Phil Vega's doorway, purse hung over her shoulder and laptop bag in hand. "I'm taking off for the night. You sticking around?"

"For a while longer. Have a good night and I'll see you in the morning." He watched the woman leave and noted the silence in the halls. The time had passed 7pm and it appeared he was alone.

A cursory glance into the corridor confirmed his solitude. Lights in offices were off, and in the distance, he heard the low hum of a vacuum. The cleaners had arrived. He returned to his desk and could now get to work on his reason for staying late tonight.

Phil headed into the hall and toward Copeland's office. It was locked, but he had a key and was the only person Copeland trusted with one. In fact, he was the only person his boss trusted at all.

The flip of a switch lit up the congressman's office and he closed the door behind him, securing it again as a matter of precaution. The office revealed telling personality traits that underscored Copeland's agenda. An innovative man, his tastes reflected a forward progression, similar to his political ideology. He also had the advantage of being a younger man, the youngest Virginia's Fifth District had ever elected to congress. The people wanted fresh ideas and a fresh face. Now that he'd won a second term, he could push his agenda through more easily.

Phil had worked for the man a considerable length of time, going back to his run for state office. Now there was a clear trajectory to his political career that Phil had single-handedly molded from scratch. However, in light of recent events, it was only a matter of time before the authorities would circle back to Copeland and risk all he had accomplished.

He began searching through the personnel files, which the congressman had insisted remain in his office. There were currently fifty people on his payroll, but plenty more who were consultants and had received payments as such. No records of those individuals were readily available here. But it would give him a place to start. Phil had known about Janine Atherton simply by watching the two together. And now there was Tasha Brenner, a woman whom he recalled, but only vaguely. He knew about Copeland's penchant for young interns early on, but his appetite appeared to have refined in recent years, moving up to members of his staff, by all accounts. What he needed to know now was could there be anyone else?

The file drawer was also locked, but Copeland kept the keys in his safe, to which his chief of staff also had access. Upon opening the drawer, he pulled Janine's file. He was fond of her. She was a kind woman, smart and talented. His eyes stung a little at the thought that she was gone and in a most brutal fashion.

There was nothing inside her file that would indicate any trouble had brewed between her and Copeland. She'd not been written up for anything. Her reviews were above par. Nothing at all that would denote a growing animosity from her that might suggest she was about to blackmail him. That was Phil's first inclination: blackmail. One he thought Phelps might question in the very near future.

Continuing his search, he failed to come across Tasha Brenner's records. Her consultancy ended after the election, and in all likelihood, it was with the other files off site. Phil moved on to other files that might reveal another potential thorn in Copeland's side.

He was at a crossroads and the clock was ticking on Copeland's indiscretions. They would catch up to him. This was a career-ending scandal waiting to blow.

THE ROW HOUSE was shadowed by the tree-lined street and a setting sun. Copeland sat in his car, staring at the house, wondering if she was home. He'd considered the possibility that whoever had killed his former lovers might come after her too. Another in a string of women he'd used his power and influence to seduce. But could he tell her that her life might well be in danger? Was it too much of a leap to assume such a thing? Copeland had his share of political enemies, but none he could imagine would commit such heinous acts for revenge or to oust him from his seat.

He feared any suggestion that this woman might be in danger would backfire, and rightly so. Questions would be raised—and answers demanded. But how could he ignore the trend? The odds that the others were murdered due to any other cause was simply too narrow. He wasn't an ignorant man, not when it came to politics. It was a treacherous business and while he'd tried to walk the line and stay in the good graces of both sides, perhaps he had offended someone in the process. An egregious offense it must have been to amount to multiple murders.

Copeland had to dig deep in his soul to determine if he was capable of withholding such information from this woman or any of the others, of which there were plenty in his tenure. But to come forward would mean his death knell.

"I can't. Not yet. Not until I know more." He started the engine and pulled away in hopes that the police would find answers and that he would remain clear of any suspicion. The risk of any other course of action was far too great and it seemed he wasn't as honorable a man as he once believed himself to be.

Copeland continued toward his home and decided to make a call that might change the course of this investigation, a course that would stray away from him.

"Metro Police Department."

"May I speak with Detective Phelps, please?"

"May I tell him who's calling?"

He was reluctant to make anyone other than the detective aware it was a congressman making the call. "I would like to speak to him about the murder of the woman at the National Cathedral last week."

The woman on the line paused. "I'll put you through, sir."

The line rang and he noted the hour had reached 8pm and questioned if the detective was still in, though his deliberation was short-lived.

"Detective Phelps here. And you are?"

"Detective, this is Grant Copeland."

"Congressman Copeland?"

"Yes. I'd like to discuss your investigation into the death of a member of my staff—Janine Atherton."

"I think that would be wise, all things considered, Mr. Copeland. However, I wouldn't recommend having that discussion here. Why don't we meet somewhere? Are you available this evening?"

"I am."

"Good. There's a coffee shop near Congress Heights station. When can you be there?"

"Thirty minutes."

"I'll see you then."

The drive from his current location in Reston to the station would take the full half-hour even in the light traffic, but Copeland needed the time to think and to plan how he would present his situation to the detective. So far, Metro Police had only dealt with Phil Vega and while he trusted Phil with his life, this was something he was going to have to address on his own.

The coffee shop was within view as he pulled along the opposite side of the street and grabbed quarters from the center console of his Lexus. Plunking them into the meter, Copeland crossed the street shielded by the darkened skies and walked into the coffee shop. He hadn't yet met the detective in person and had no idea who to look for, but it appeared that he must've stuck out like a sore thumb because a man quickly approached.

"Representative Copeland, I'm Detective Anthony Phelps." Without waiting for a reply, he started toward the back of the coffee shop. "You need a coffee or something?"

"No, thank you. I'm fine."

Phelps pulled out a chair at the farthest table from the door. "I was surprised to get your call. Sit down." A coffee cup rested on the table and when he sat down, he began to drink. "I've been here for a few minutes. You sure I can't get you something?"

Copeland sat down, peering over his shoulder in search of any interested parties. He was hardly a recognizable figure, but he was wary nonetheless. "I'm sure. I came here to discuss your investigation into the murder of one of my staff members, Janine Atherton."

"Sure. I've been dealing with Phil Vega, your chief of staff, as he'd indicated it was best not to involve you at this time. So forgive me if I'm a little more than surprised to hear from you directly."

"Yes, well, there are things that, frankly, I should be made aware of and I've known Phil a long time. He'll want to shield me from the worst of it. I, however, feel as though that might not be in my best interest."

"What would you like to know? I'm still waiting on DNA evidence to come back on the car. These things take time. And I'm not sure if you're aware, but we've had a similar murder—or maybe you are aware—and there are a lot of similarities between the two cases. So much so, and the fact that these murders occurred in two different states, that the Feds have decided to step in. A few calls were made and now their Behavioral Analysis Unit is involved due to the nature of these unfortunate crimes against the two women."

"The nature?"

Phelps appeared to recall he hadn't made mention of the notes to Vega. "There are things I'm afraid I can't reveal just yet, but when the time is right, I will let you know."

Copeland dismissed the comment and continued, "I am aware that a former consultant was also murdered in the same fashion, which is why I'm here, detective. I need to know how you intend on proceeding and what I can do to mitigate the inevitable damage that will come due to my association with these poor women."

"I'll tell you, I'm not going to have much pull as long as the FBI is involved. That said, I've done my best already to steer them clear of your path, understanding that this is Washington and all that comes with that knowledge."

"That's good to hear and I appreciate it. But how can I ensure that will continue?"

Phelps' skeptical nature had taken hold as he eyed the

congressman. "I can only assume your motives are pure and simply for protection against your political foes. And if that is the case, I can help to the point that I can't. If you understand my meaning."

"Not entirely—no."

"I want to find out who killed these women, particularly Ms. Atherton. She is my primary concern right now. Given that, I feel confident that it was not you who killed her and I'm assuming you have an alibi. If you don't, then you should. So, you, Mr. Copeland, are not in my crosshairs—right now. And I will continue to pursue the angles that I believe will lead me to Ms. Atherton's killer. That is my sole purpose on this investigation. However, others may not feel as I do. And in that case, I will be forced to call upon you to help allay your association."

"And how will I do that?"

"There are ways of pointing evidence in directions that will take me to my end goal and away from you, but it does not come without a cost."

Copeland smiled. "I see. And what value might you assign to that?"

"We'll have to see how things play out with the FBI and the agent I'm currently saddled with. She's a smart woman; eager to find the truth. However, as I said, it's unlikely you are the culprit as I doubt you would be here if you were. So, to me, no harm in finding the person or persons responsible without destroying your burgeoning career in the process. And I'm sure you will remember it when the time comes. That is the only value I can ascribe at this time, until I receive further developments."

"Of course." Copeland began to rise. "I have to go." He dropped cash on the table. "You be sure and let me know what I can do and when. I'll make it happen. Goodnight, detective."

KATE PUSHED her chair away from her desk and peered around the cubicle wall. "You find anything in Tasha Brenner's file that implies she knew Janine Atherton?"

"It appears they did know each other, at least in general terms. Nothing that indicates they were well-acquainted," Vasquez replied. "Pearson received a copy of a statement Phelps shared with his counterpart in Baltimore. It detailed the two women's roles in Copeland's bid for re-election. Said that while they didn't appear to be anything more than colleagues, they did come into contact with one another at the campaign headquarters."

"Who offered this statement?"

"Copeland's chief of staff, a Philip Vega. From what I gather, he's been extremely cooperative."

"That's my understanding as well. What about Brenner's phone records? Anything come through on that end yet?"

"No. Baltimore PD was supposed to send them to Pearson. He doesn't have them yet."

"Right."

"Why? What are you thinking? I've seen that look in your eyes before."

"I just think we need to talk to the congressman and I understand the implications of that. Detective Phelps made that very clear to me."

"What are you hoping to learn?"

"I'd like to know if he has any enemies. And who he thinks those enemies might be. I'd like to get a better understanding of Janine Atherton, her role at Copeland's office. How often they worked together. How often she worked with this Philip Vega guy. There's too much we don't know yet and we need to fill in some holes if we hope to make progress."

"I understand where you're coming from, but you have to remember that the local police are working on their end, likely on those very things. We're here to consult. To help them develop a profile. Look, Kate, I know how you can get. But on this one, you're going to have to take a step back. Just a little anyway. Let those guys do what they need to do. In the meantime, our job is to continue developing a profile of the unsub. Give them something they can work with. Then let them run with it."

"You're right. I just need more. We need to understand the type of people those women hung around with both at work and socially."

"I get what you're saying. Let me put a call into Pearson. See if he's gotten any farther with the locals than we have. He was the one who came to us, so I'll remind him that we need more if he wants us to do the job."

"Okay. Thanks."

"Oh yeah, so, when were you going to tell me that Scarborough's profiler was Noah Quinn?"

"How'd you find out?"

"Talked to Jameson. We're tight, you know. He might have mentioned it in passing. Actually, he was laughing his ass off. Thought it was hilarious that he tried to hit on you way back when."

"Yeah, hilarious. Not so much when you're trying to get a job. And Scarborough thinks he might be hesitant because of our relationship."

"You and me? I told you, Kate, you're not my type."

"You know what I mean. I feel like I'm about to get screwed out of this deal."

"And then you'd have to stay here?"

"Yeah."

"That wouldn't be such a bad thing, would it? Hell, you're

junior to SSA Jameson now. Not a bad place to be. Not like you've hit the ceiling here yet."

"No, I know. I guess I just didn't think this would be a problem, not a big one, anyway. There are plenty of agents who are dating and married. Why is my relationship under scrutiny?"

"Because Scarborough is Quinn's boss. I understand what he must be feeling. Not right and not fair, but what the hell is in this world? You're just going to have to prove to him you're better than the rest. That he needs you, not the other way around." She paused for a moment. "I'll tell you what, you want to impress him, get this profile right. They catch this guy based on what you put together, what leg does Quinn have to stand on then? In fact, I might even go so far as to get his input on what you've got now. Let him see how far you've already come, assuming you make it to the second round."

"Not a bad idea. I need to play up my strengths. He said he'd whittle down the field by the end of this week. I should know then if I made the cut. Maybe you're right, though. Show him what I got, maybe ask for advice. Make it look like I'm a team player."

"Which you're so obviously not."

"Thanks for that." She smiled. "No, I appreciate the advice. I'll make it work. I do deserve the job."

"I know you do, Kate." Vasquez began to turn back toward her desk. "Let me make that call to Pearson and see what he's got."

8

It was Agent Pearson who decided a conference call was in order based upon his recent findings on the Tasha Brenner investigation in Baltimore and the possibility that the press would soon run on the story. He needed to gather a consensus on how best to continue with the investigation.

With arms pressed against his desk, he leaned over the speakerphone. "I received the phone records of Ms. Brenner and forwarded a copy to Detective Ramos this morning."

"That's correct. I have them, though I haven't yet had the opportunity to sit down and review the information," Ramos replied.

"The reason I've asked you all to be in on this call is that I think we need to decide our next course of action."

"I can tell you, detective," Kate began, "I'm struggling to complete a profile without an accurate and complete picture of our victims. So I'll get straight to the point. Did you find anything significant on those phone records? Who was she talking to?"

There were several parties involved in this investigation, but all were after one thing and that was to find out who might have been after Brenner, then figure out if Atherton faced the same situation.

"As a matter of fact," Pearson began, "the primary reason for this conference call was to discuss the records, though I'd hoped Detective Ramos would've had the chance to take a look at them first. But I can tell you that there were several calls made to her personal cell over the period of seven days prior to her death. What makes this particularly difficult is that these calls were from various numbers and not one left a voicemail nor does it appear as though she actually answered the calls."

"So, we don't know who they were from? I don't see the big reveal here, Agent Pearson," Ramos said. "They could've been telemarketers for all we know. We're all plagued by those."

"Yes, however, I don't believe that was the case here. These calls were placed at a single specific time. All at 1am eastern daylight."

"Have you been able to trace the origins of these calls? You said they were from various numbers. Are they all from the same location?" Kate asked.

"Each one was a Virginia area code. And pending review from Detective Ramos, I'd like to begin searching for the callers."

"Of course. I'll review it as soon as we're finished here. I still don't see that this is a major break in the investigation."

"It is if Janine Atherton had calls from these same numbers," Kate added.

"That's something I'll work on asap, Agent Reid." It was the first time Detective Phelps added to the conversation. "There was something else you wanted to discuss, isn't that right, Agent Pearson?"

"Yes. I've been getting calls from a reporter at the *Baltimore Sun*. Says he's got contacts in Washington who've made mention of the Atherton case in connection with Brenner. He's looking for comment. I'm not sure how much longer we'll be able to hold him off."

"Word gets out that these two women worked for the congressman, all hell's going to break loose."

"I couldn't agree more, Detective Phelps. What do you propose?"

"Tell him to hold off. That if he gives you more time, you'll offer up a better story."

"And that would be?"

"Same one, but he doesn't need to know that. Right now, it sounds as though he has no idea this involves the congressman. If he did, it would already be splashed on the front page. And that'll work to our advantage. I think you can handle a member of the press."

There was a prolonged silence on the line from all the parties. It seemed the detective might have overstepped with his comment.

"I'll tell you what, Phelps, do your job and I won't have to hold off the press. As far as the rest of you go, I'll keep you informed of any new developments and I suspect we'll have more once Atherton's phone records are received. I'm sure Detective Phelps will be more than happy to share that information with us all. I'll let you all get back to it. Thank you for coming together on this. We'll continue to make progress."

The call ended on an abrupt note. The fact that there were multiple agencies working this case meant that toes were being stepped on and no one was happy about that. Kate had been here before and it was difficult to keep from ruffling feathers. Still, the conversation left her with the continuing feeling that Detective Phelps had an agenda, that he was being less than a team player. The reason for this behavior was baffling, but raised her hackles nonetheless. The first thing for her to do now was to review

Janine Atherton's phone records, for which she'd already put in a request, circumventing the detective. The investigation was being stalled and that was unacceptable. Upon receipt of those records, she would have to decide if sharing them with the detective was in the best interest of the investigation. Right now, that did not seem like the case. So she would let him retrieve the records on his own and keep quiet the fact that she was already working on them.

Kate headed into the corridor in search of advice and the best person for the job was Dwight. "Can I talk to you for a minute?"

"Sure, come in. What's going on?" Dwight pulled his attention from the trance-inducing glow of his monitor and rubbed his eyes.

"I just got off a conference call initiated by Agent Pearson in the Baltimore Field Office. Both detectives were on the line as well."

"Any new developments on the investigation?"

"I think it was more of a coming-up-to-speed conversation than anything else. Pearson got Brenner's phone records and noted some unusual activity, but what really drew my attention was the reaction of Detective Phelps with Metro Police."

"Is he not cooperating?"

"He is, but not in a manner I would expect. I'm starting to feel like he's either not invested or maybe wants to shove this under the rug."

"I'm sure his case load is heavy. Not that that's an excuse," Dwight continued.

"No. It's not that. He's busy, but so are we all. It's more like he's casting a blind eye to the obvious."

"And what do you want to do about it?"

"Honestly? I'd like to go around him, over him, or whatever it takes to get what I need to work on identifying the unsub." She held off mentioning the records request in anticipation he might make that suggestion himself, thereby letting her off the hook, so to speak.

"You can't do that, Kate. That's not how this works. You know that."

"I do." This wasn't the answer she wanted, so she would keep her mouth shut on that particular issue. "What can I do then?"

"Play to his ego. That's what I think this is. He wants control and between us, the Baltimore Field Office, and Baltimore Police, he doesn't have it. Go visit him. Ask what you can do to offer assistance. You might be surprised. He might just pull you into his inner circle, let you run on things."

"Someone's out there murdering young women and we don't know if that person is done yet and I have to play to some local cop's ego? That's bullshit."

"That's the game."

There was no arguing with him because he was right. While she hadn't come across Phelps' type before, she'd heard stories from her colleagues. "Okay. I'll play the game. I'll kiss his ass and do whatever he wants. But when I get a solid profile, I'm done with him."

"Fair enough. Though I doubt that's a statement you'll follow through with. It's not who you are."

She finally stood. "Yeah, well, cops like that? They tend to change your perspective."

"Hey, before you leave, what's going on with the second round? You hear anything yet?"

"No. Should be in the next day or two. I'll let you know."

WITH HIS PHONE tucked between his ear and his shoulder, Noah Quinn keyed the command and waited for his email to open. "Here it is. I see it. Thank you, Agent Jameson. I appreciate your help." He ended the call and placed his phone on his desk, never taking his eyes off the monitor, which now displayed the much-anticipated email. He'd requested additional information regarding one of his most promising candidates, and her boss had just delivered. With only days left in which he'd agreed to further narrow the field, he wanted to know what she was working on at the moment and it seemed a fairly interesting, if not slightly convoluted, case. His goal was to gain greater insight into her approach to field work. With a stunning letter of recommendation from her current supervisor, SSA Jameson, he needed more, so he began to dig into the Janine Atherton investigation based on Reid's latest report handed off to Jameson yesterday.

According to the report, Reid had been compiling data to develop a profile on a killer who'd shot two women in two different states in the head, then proceeded to shove a piece of fabric into their mouths with the word "Whore" written on it. This was interesting to Quinn because the markers clearly indicated it was the same unsub, however, the means by which this individual took the lives of these women were markedly different. One in her home and one on the side of a road. The former suggested intimate knowledge of the victim, whereas the latter suggested a random act, were it not for the note.

Of particular interest to him were the notes from Reid herself, indicating because the victims both worked for the same person, albeit several months apart, that this person could either be a target of revenge or an active participant in the murders. This was interesting because these assumptions were so polar opposite to one another that it showed him her willingness to consider every possible scenario. Not to mention that the person with whom those women worked was a congressman. And to suggest his involvement opened up a whole new can of worms that it appeared she cared little about.

He leaned back in his chair. "It appears there may be more to you than I originally believed, Agent Reid."

REPRESENTATIVE COPELAND SAT behind his desk, studying the phone records he'd just received from Detective Phelps. It seemed Phelps might turn out to be an ally after all. One who wanted a reward, but it would be well worth the price.

Janine Atherton's phone history for the past sixty days made it to his inbox about an hour ago, after what Phelps described as a confrontational call between the law enforcement participants. While there was little Copeland could do to alter the records, he could at least be prepared to answer questions regarding them. His number appeared multiple times, too many times, and at hours well outside of business. How would he address this when the time came, because it would come—and soon. He considered that it was time to bring Phil in to discuss his options without revealing more than he should, although Vega had known about the affair— at least, this one—and he was a loyal man who had kept his mouth shut.

With the press of a button, he rang the line. "Phil, can you come in here, please?"

"I'll be right there."

The profound sigh that followed suggested he knew this would not be an easy conversation, but Copeland was in deep this time and couldn't afford to take this on alone.

Within minutes, Phil knocked on his door.

"It's open." He waited for him to enter. "I'm not taking you away from anything, am I?"

"No, sir. It's fine. What can I do for you?"

"We're going to need to consider damage control on this Janine situation, as you previously stated." While he was still shaken by the event and had cared for her a great deal, he couldn't allow Phil to pick up on that fact, even if it made him appear heartless.

"I'd say it's a good idea to pull our story together. Both with regard to Janine and to the latest victim, Tasha Brenner."

"Of course. And Tasha as well."

"If we're going to do this, then I need to know the whole story, Grant. No half-truths, no falsehoods. I have to be prepared for any question that may arise. Having said that, why don't you go ahead and tell me what your relationship was with each of these women?"

Copeland was prepared and began to relay what he believed Phil should know. However, he left out a few minor details that, were they ever revealed, would certainly label him a deviant, and he realized with both women gone, there was no chance of that ever getting out. A small measure of comfort in this appalling scenario.

And as he continued to uncover the depths of his relationships, he watched as Phil's expression changed from a man who had once admired him to a man who appeared repulsed by him. Perhaps he had made the wrong call. "So? How do you think we should approach this?"

"And it's just been those two? Grant, I need to be sure there aren't any more out there. First of all, because there's a killer on the loose and we have no idea if this is just coincidence or if someone is looking to get revenge on you. If it's the latter, we need to let the police know there could be another potential victim."

"We can't go to the police, Phil. You know that as well as I do. There aren't any others, okay? It was just them. I made mistakes, I'll admit that. But I never wanted any harm to come to those poor girls. They deserved better. But they're gone and I can't help them. All we can do is protect the seat. I have to keep my seat."

"Of course. You say you called Janine on the night she was killed?"

"Yes."

"We can spin that. She was at the event. She helped organize it and got you there. It shouldn't come as a surprise the two of you spoke during the day."

"And later that night?"

"Right. But that only takes care of the one time. You're telling me there were several instances you called and/or texted her over the past few months, is that right?"

"Yes."

"I think the first thing we need to do is establish your alibi. I've spoken with the detective and he didn't seem interested in talking to you—just yet. But you need to give me a clear picture of what you were doing that night. And I know you weren't in Baltimore when Tasha was murdered. So we can easily establish that."

Copeland knew the detective wasn't going to request an interview for as long as he could possibly hold it off, but that didn't mean he didn't need to come clean to Phil. "I appreciate you keeping the detective at bay and handling this. I suspect there will come a time when that won't be the case, but for now, I'll tell you that I was with Janine after the charity event. We met at a hotel and she stayed with me until about 3am. I didn't hear from her after that."

"Is there anyone at the hotel I need to talk to, then? I'll have to nip this in the bud and make sure we can get the story straight."

"I checked in under another name." Copeland noted his exasperation. "What else could I do? I paid cash too. There's no way I'd use my real name."

"Then we have no official alibi. Unless of course whoever checked you in happened to remember your face."

"You know where I was and when. Isn't that good enough for now? Aren't we just trying to establish a timeline here? No one else is asking and we'll have to take that for what it's worth right now."

"Look, I'll be honest with you, Grant. I've been with you for a long time. I consider you a friend. But I'll tell you, I didn't expect this."

"I know I let you down."

"Not just me. Your wife and your kids. You know what'll happen if this gets out and, frankly, I'd be shocked if it didn't."

"I do know. I'll lose everything. In a split second, everything will be gone. So what can you do to help me prevent that?"

"I'll do the best I can to placate the detective, but the FBI is involved too. They won't be as easily persuaded."

9

_____

Diversionary tactics only worked for so long before suspicions were raised. And Kate was a woman in whom a certain level of cynicism existed in permanence. So when she'd begun to feel that Detective Phelps was operating under a different agenda than the rest of them, her skepticism kicked into overdrive. This was especially true today, when he'd promised to send her Janine Atherton's phone records and had again come up with an excuse as to why he hadn't. She'd put in the same request under the FBI's authority but wanted to understand if Phelps would cooperate, and she'd just received her answer.

Rather than accept this, Kate, as usual, took matters into her own hands. If this detective thought he could out maneuver her, he was sorely mistaken. She had more resources and greater means by which to obtain the required information. Having made more than a few friends at the Bureau, she called upon one of them who willingly gathered the records that she was now reviewing. After all, her team was officially part of the investigation whether Phelps agreed with it or not.

"Those calls that Pearson was talking about on Brenner's phone; you have those numbers?" Kate leaned back in her chair to get Vasquez's attention.

"I thought you had these already. Hang on. Let me forward this to you."

"Thanks."

'You finally get Atherton's records?" she continued.

"I did. With no help from the detective. I'm telling you, something's up with that guy. Like he's working really hard to keep this case close to his chest."

"Sometimes these local cops are that way. I just sent you the file."

"Thanks. I understand that, to a point, but come on. This is on the verge of obstruction, if you ask me."

"Recommend he be taken off the investigation."

"No. Not yet. The last thing I need right now is for the whole of Metro PD to boycott me because I crossed one of their own."

"You're probably right about that. Like this job isn't hard enough. Then you get some prick who refuses to share information. We're all after the same thing here."

"That's what I thought, but I seem to be wrong. I just got the file. Thanks." Kate opened Brenner's records and began to cross-reference the numbers with Atherton's. According to Pearson and the conversation they had yesterday, several unknown numbers appeared over a course of about seven days and at the same time. These were the numbers she had hoped to find on Atherton's records. However, the only ones she'd been able to identify were Copeland's calls. While Atherton had worked for him, it seemed out of the ordinary for him to have called her so frequently and at such odd hours. For the type of job she had, it appeared unusual and fueled Kate's already growing suspicion of the direction this case was headed, which was straight into the abyss.

She continued to study the calls and created a list of numbers on which she would follow up. Uncertain of who Janine Atherton was seeing at the time, any boyfriends, past or present, still needed to be vetted and ruled out as possible suspects. Something she doubted Phelps had completed as of yet, regardless of his insistence he was working on the matter.

Another number had appeared almost as frequently as Copeland's. "Hey, Alicia, have you identified this number on Brenner's records?" Kate wrote it down on a sticky note and handed it to her. "This shows up on Atherton's phone fairly frequently. It's possible it belongs to a family member, which would explain it, but I want to rule out Brenner's records first."

"Sure. Let me take a quick look here." She began typing her search parameters. "Okay, let's see what she's got." The search was running and within seconds, they had their answer. "Yep. This number does appear, and these records only go back six months, but it's on here about ten times. I'd say that's a fair amount."

"When was the last time it showed up?" Kate asked.

"Looks like last month." She turned to Kate. "You want me to run a check on the number?"

"Yeah. I think we need to know who this person is. We might have something here."

"I'll let you know what I find out."

"Thanks. Listen, I need to run downstairs to CID. I won't be long."

"What have you got going on with those guys?"

"Just need to talk to Agent Fraser." Kate was already walking away. "Let me know when you've got information on that number."

The third floor of the WFO housed the Criminal Investigation

Division, or CID, and a colleague who had recently been involved in the exposure of a massive cover up of a domestic terror attack some seven months ago. He was the one who she could ask to complete this very sensitive task with little in the way of prying eyes. Not that he'd been given carte blanche, but he was given a whole lot of extra rope as of late, thanks to his work on that investigation.

It also brought back to mind the surprising reunion with Will Caison, a man she had not seen since her training at the Academy. He'd been there for a meeting with SSA Fraser, and the two had run into one another in the lobby. The surreal moment was still fresh in her mind, though several months had passed.

In hindsight, she wished things hadn't gone down the way they had with him. He deserved better, but she wasn't in the right place then. It had been too much, too soon and he paid the price for it. Still, she was happy to have seen him that day and knew he was back in Washington, working at FBI Headquarters. It was unlikely their paths would cross again, at least as far as their work was concerned. However, the intelligence community was tight and hung out in a lot of the same places. So maybe someday she would take him up on his offer to meet again.

The elevator doors parted and Kate entered the CID. This division was by far the largest in the Bureau with the most field agents and far exceeded the number of BAU agents. She supposed that made sense, though, considering it encompassed far more crimes than her division did. And that was something for which she was glad because if there were more people out there like the killers she had tracked down during her short tenure at the Bureau, it was unlikely she'd still be here. There was a high potential for burnout at the BAU. The human eyes can only witness so much pain, devastation, and horror.

Kate knew where to find Fraser and hoped he could spare a

few minutes of his time. She continued through the much larger space and through the maze of cubicles and offices. Upon arrival at his office, she noted his door was open. "Excuse me, Agent Fraser?"

He turned his attention to her. "Agent Reid? What brings you down here? Decided to slum it for a while? Come on in; take a seat."

"Thanks. I don't want to take up your time. I know you're busy."

"Not at all. It's not often I get to see someone from BAU. What can I help you with?"

"I'm working on a case involving multiple murders with similar markers. State lines were crossed and due to the nature of the deaths, we were asked to consult. The Baltimore Division is also investigating."

"Sounds intriguing."

"I wouldn't know, frankly, because I'm working with a detective at Metro Police and he's been less than forthcoming with information."

"I see. One of those who doesn't like it when we roll in and start taking over."

"Normally, I'd say yes, that's exactly what's happening, but I think there's more to it than that and that's why I'm here."

Fraser leaned over his desk. "What do you need from me?"

"I'm trying to work within the frame of legal and ethical morality..."

"But..."

"But I've got two dead victims and there could be more coming and I think this detective is working hard to keep whatever it is he knows quiet." She tried to assess his reaction. While she'd crossed paths with him on the odd occasion, she would be hard pressed to call him anything more than an acquaintance. So, to help sway him, she had another card to play. "Also, I know you've worked with Agent Will Caison in the recent past. He and I went to the Academy together, and he mentioned you last time we met." She needed to include a slight exaggeration to make her point, without it being an outright lie. "He said you were a hell of a good agent and a good man. That's why I came to you."

"Do you have anything solid that would intimate this detective isn't playing by the rules?"

"No. He's just dragging his feet and making things hard for me. But no, I don't have anything concrete. It's just a hunch." He was silent for an uncomfortable period of time. She needed something more to convince him, a final ploy that often worked on her male counterparts. "Look, I know what you've done for this country. I know you were pivotal in the investigation into the death of the former member of State. I'm asking for your help in what I believe could be another potential cover up, albeit not nearly of the same degree, but a cover up nonetheless."

"Okay. I understand what you need and I'll give it some serious consideration. As you know, it's generally frowned upon to do what I believe you're asking me to do. However, if you truly believe he is obstructing this investigation, I'll consider it. I give you my word."

"I appreciate that, Agent Fraser. If you can get me what I need, I'll take it from there. I won't ask another favor."

"I'll get back to you."

Kate began to rise. "Thank you for your consideration. I can't tell you how much I appreciate it."

"I'm sure there will come a time when I'll need something from you too. I don't know what, but it's possible." At this, he smiled. "It was a pleasure to see you again, Agent Reid."

THE OFFICE of 4th District Representative Pamela Carter was busy with ensuring the latest bill put forth by the ranking house member would have the votes to pass. It was an arduous process that required a fair bit of quid pro quo, the staple of American politics. Heading up that effort was Carter's legislative director, Meredith Bowen, a woman who had put in her time and was recently rewarded with the lucrative position that would finally allow her to pay off her student debt. However, her first priority was to keep making the calls and the latest one would be a check mark for the yeses.

"Got another one." Meredith replaced the cap on the whiteboard marker and raised her hands in triumph. A round of applause from her colleagues soon followed.

She returned to her desk, but before getting the opportunity to make another call, a man she hadn't seen in some time appeared. "Hello. What on earth are you doing here?"

"Just slumming it."

"You picked a hell of a time. It's crazy busy in here right now."

"I see that. I'm sorry, but do you think you could spare just a moment of your time? I won't keep you long."

Meredith looked around at the people on the phones. "Um, sure. I can give you a few minutes. We can go in my office." Only a few feet down the hall, she opened the door and stepped inside, closing it behind her and her unexpected visitor. "I have to be honest with you, I didn't think we'd cross paths anytime soon. What brings you down?"

"It's sort of a delicate situation that I hate to even discuss at all."

"Okay. Maybe you should step off those egg shells you're walking on and just tell me what it is that brought you here?"

"Meredith, I have to ask—have you been in contact with Grant recently?"

"No." The tone of her voice and the way her eyes darkened suggested this was an unwelcome question. "I can only imagine why you're asking me. As his chief of staff, I assume you're trying to avert a potential situation?"

Phil held her gaze. "I know the two of you had history."

"That's right. A not so pleasant history, which I'd just as soon forget as I'm sure Grant would as well."

"Please, I'm not here to upset you. I know you and he haven't worked together for a long time."

"For a very good reason."

"I know. I just—I just have to know that there haven't been any recent efforts to make contact with him."

"Like I said, I haven't talked to him, emailed him, or in any way made contact with him in over a year—not since I started here." She began to rise. "Now, if you'll excuse me, I really am very busy."

He stood. "I do know what happened and I know it wasn't your fault."

Meredith marched firmly to within inches of him. "You're damn right it wasn't. That son of a bitch nearly ruined my career. And do you know how easy it would've been for me to turn on him? Pretty fucking easy. I'll tell you that. But I didn't. Because I know how things work around here. So, I sucked it up and dealt with it. So don't you come here and start telling me to back off of him because I never backed on, you hear me?"

He raised his hands in surrender. "Okay. I hear you. I just had to know. I can't tell you why, but I asked because I always believed you got a raw deal as far as that whole thing went down. But others, they might not see it as it really was."

"Yeah well, you'd better believe that I've protected myself." She pulled open the door. "Now if you don't mind, I really do have to get back to work."

"Of course." Phil walked past her. "I'm sorry, Meredith—for everything."

She watched him leave and shook her head in anger. A final glance to ensure he'd gone from her sight and Meredith returned to the phone banks to finish what she'd set out to do.

"You're back." A young assistant returned the phone to its cradle. "We did it. We got all the votes."

"Are you serious? We're done?"

"That's right. Guess we won't have to pull the all-nighter like we thought." She looked at the time on her phone. "I might even make it home for a late dinner. You should go too, Mer. You did good today."

"We all did. The congresswoman will be thrilled. Has anyone told her yet?"

"No. We thought we'd let you take the honors."

"Great. I'll swing by her office on my way out. Goodnight and I'll see you in the morning, on the floor." This turn of events set her mind at ease once again and after a quick word with Representative Carter, she was ready to head home for what would be the first decent night's sleep in weeks.

"Goodnight, Meredith. Thanks for all your hard work."

"Goodnight, Pamela." With a nod and a smile, she was out the door and heading toward the nearest station to hop on the Metro. An event that had soured her evening was soon overshadowed by her success.

Only a few stops from her apartment, the much less crowded train was just a short jaunt and she was already exiting onto the platform. The cross-breeze lifted her blonde hair, scattering it across her face as she made her way to the stairs and toward the exit.

Upon reaching the top, the dark skies were clear even if no stars were visible. The city lights made sure of that. Two more blocks to her apartment and she could kick off her heels and change into her comfy clothes because all she wanted to do right now was sit in front of the television with a glass of wine and just veg out for a while. She'd earned it.

With the keys in her hand, Meredith unlocked her door and stepped inside. The lights turned on as they sensed her arrival and her modern apartment illuminated with soft light that highlighted the cream-colored interior. She loved her home and she loved her job, even in the stressful times, though working for Pamela Carter was much less stressful than her time around Grant Copeland. It had almost been enough to send her packing, headed back home to Iowa and becoming a teacher.

The earlier conversation with her former acquaintance, Phil Vega, returned to the forefront of her thoughts. And it was most certainly an uninvited arrival. She emerged from her bedroom in full comfort gear and headed into the kitchen for a glass of Chardonnay she so desperately wanted. Meredith wasn't a big drinker, but there were those days when it was all she could think about and today had been one of those days.

With a glass in hand, she curled up on her sofa and switched on the television, but not before reaching for her laptop and reviewing the agenda. She'd lost track of time with her work once again when a knock on her door brought a tidal wave of deliberation that crashed against her skull.

She reached for her phone to check the time. It was 11pm and she hadn't been expecting anyone.

Her legs slowly uncurled as she pulled herself up from the couch and shuffled in bare feet to the door. She peeked through the security lens and pulled back quickly. "What the hell?"

Upon opening the door, her brow knitted tightly. "What are you doing here?"

10

Dispatch relayed the call of shots fired in an apartment building and the responding officer had arrived on the scene. With the growing crowd of onlookers as the patrol cars and ambulance arrived, the officer needed to establish a boundary.

Inside, the paramedics attended to the woman, whom they had identified as Meredith Bowen. Her wallet had been found in her purse, which hung on a kitchen chair.

"I'm not getting a pulse." The EMT looked to his partner.

"Proximate cause of death, likely the GSW to the chest. Immediate cause of death, loss of blood. Take a look here." His index finger lined the second injury. "Bullet graze on the side of the scalp."

"Like she was trying to dodge the shots. Body temp is at seventy degrees. She's been gone close to an hour. Has anyone else seen this?" The EMT pointed to her mouth.

"I don't know. I'll talk to the responding officer. He's outside."

The paramedic headed outside to the cops pulling tape across the building's entrance. "Where can I find the responding officer?"

"Over there." The man nodded in the direction of a group of officers huddled together.

"Thanks." On approach, he continued, "We need to remove the body, but I'll need a signoff first. Who's running the show here?"

"I am. Detective Phelps. Officer Cook answered the call and notified me on arrival. What have you got inside?"

Cook turned to the other officers. "You guys keep the lookyloos away and I'll take Phelps in."

The men entered the building and headed back into the woman's apartment. Officer Cook led the way toward the body. "Dispatch radioed the 911 call from a neighbor who heard the gunshots."

"Gunshots? Plural?" Phelps asked.

"Yeah. She said she heard two but couldn't be sure if there were more. She was awakened by the gunfire. Anyway, I was nearby and as soon as I arrived, I called you guys out. I had already ascertained the victim was DOA and I made no attempt at resuscitation upon determining there was no pulse. In addition, I noted the beginning signs of lividity in the lower extremities."

"No need to impress me with your use of medical jargon." Annoyed, Phelps peered at the body. "But you did see this?" Detective Phelps pointed to her mouth.

"I wanted to wait for CSI. I haven't touched anything except to check for a pulse. This looks to be related to your active investigation of the woman found at the National Cathedral. That's why I called you out."

"Don't do anything until CSI gets here."

"Should be any time now."

"Good. Can we make sure the ambo stays until she's released?"

"Will do," the EMT replied. "I've got plenty of paperwork to keep me occupied in the meantime." He continued toward his partner as the two huddled for what appeared to be an update on the situation.

Phelps pulled Officer Cook aside. "Listen, there's no need for you to wait it out. I'll stay until CSI arrives."

"That's not really... I mean, I guess. If you're okay with it. My shift ended an hour ago."

"You should head back to the station, write your report, and go home and get some sleep. I got this covered."

"Yeah. Okay, thanks. I'll make sure those guys have secured the scene, then I'll head out." Cook walked toward the door.

Detective Phelps began to examine the apartment and came across the victim's cell phone. With a gloved hand, he picked up the phone and pressed the home button. Password protected, of course, but no notifications appeared on the home screen.

Another officer approached him. "I've got the neighbor who called it in."

"Get a statement from her."

"Ten-four."

Phelps continued to make his way through the apartment. He knew what the note in the victim's mouth meant and what it would mean to Copeland, assuming that this woman was tied to him in some way, which seemed an almost certainty at this point. His job now was to keep it from the Feds and that was going to be a challenge, considering Agent Reid had been up his ass since they came on board to help. "Help." Irritation sounded in the huff that escaped him. "Damn Feds are just gumming up the works." If it'd been up to him, this would have remained a local investigation.

But that Brenner woman had been killed in another state. And that made things complicated.

His problems were also about to grow exponentially when word got out that there was another victim with the note in her mouth. While he hadn't removed the note to see what it said, he already knew. But was there a way to keep the Feds from discovering it? He could work this investigation his own way and keep Copeland's name out of the press, at least for a while longer.

Phelps returned to the body and knelt down. Other officers stood near but seemed preoccupied in conversation. If he was going to do this, the time was now. He would have to deal with Cook, but that wasn't likely going to be a problem. And the EMTs. Again, a little green went a long way and he would know pretty quickly how it would play out with each of them. He was no novice.

He placed a glove on his other hand and stepped closer to her head. Leaning over the victim, he lowered his hands toward her mouth.

"Detective Phelps?"

"Shit." Startled, Phelps nearly fell over. "Christ, don't sneak up on people like that."

"What the hell are you doing?" Two officers identified as CSI entered the apartment. The man who spoke was the lead investigator.

"Taking out whatever it is that's shoved in this woman's mouth."

"We'll take it from here. Thanks." The officer continued his approach. "You're welcome to hang out with us, but I'm sure you've got better things to do. I'll let you know when the body's been transferred."

"Yeah. Okay. Thanks." Phelps removed his glove and stood up again. "Bout time you guys got here anyway."

The investigator eyed Phelps with indifference. "Sorry. She's our fourth one tonight. Been a little busy trying to help you guys out."

~

THE CALL CAME in during the pre-dawn hours while Kate still lay next to Nick in their bed. Her phone lit up with the caller ID and she sat up while squinting at the bright light. A quick glance to confirm she hadn't disturbed Nick and Kate rolled out of bed and padded into the hall. "Agent Reid."

"You need to come down here."

"Detective Phelps? What's going on?"

"Another body's been found. Looks like the same M.O."

"The note?" She continued into the kitchen for a bottle of water.

"Yes. CSI is still on scene and they're gathering evidence as we speak. They'll let me know when the body is transferred to the ME."

"Where do you want to meet?"

"I'll text you the address. I'm still here. How long will you be?"

"Um, I can leave in ten minutes."

"Good."

The line went dead and Kate pulled her phone back to check they hadn't been disconnected. It seemed Phelps hung up. "Okay then." She returned to the bedroom and quietly dressed.

"Hey? Where you off to?" Nick turned toward his nightstand. "What time is it?"

"Early. Go back to sleep. I have to meet with Phelps. There's another victim."

"He called you? I thought he was doing his best to keep you away?"

"He is. I'm sure he's got an angle. I just don't know what it is yet."

"Anything I can do?"

"No. I'm heading out to the scene now. I'll call you later." She leaned in for a kiss. "Go back to sleep."

ON HER WAY DOWNTOWN, she wanted to call Agent Fraser, see if he'd given any further consideration of her request. But it was 4am. Still, she didn't want to see Phelps without any ammunition. She was certain he was hiding something and his call was a surprise. Things were about to get interesting and her guard was up.

Within minutes, she'd pulled up behind the detective's car and noted a few other patrol cars remained. No ambulance, meaning they must've taken the body already. "Damn." She'd wanted to see for herself what had happened rather than get it second-hand from Phelps. Now she'd have to make a trip to the ME's office for a full briefing.

Upon stepping out of her SUV, she spotted Phelps leaning against the railing of the steps in front of the apartment building. Smoke billowed out of the cigarette that dangled between his lips and he seemed preoccupied with his cell phone.

"Detective Phelps. Good morning."

"Not so good, Agent Reid." He slipped his phone into his pocket and tossed the cigarette to the ground, smashing it with the ball of his foot. "Shall we go inside?"

"Lead the way." He seemed more amiable than in previous meetings and her suspicions grew. "When did the call come in?"

"Around 11:15pm. Neighbor heard the gunshots." He ascended the stairs. "Victim's been identified as thirty-two-year-old

Meredith Bowen." He pushed the door open and waited for Kate to pass through.

"And you say a note was found in her mouth? Same as before?"

"Yep. However, she was not shot in the head; well, it appears the perp attempted to do it, but missed. Got her in the chest instead."

"I assume we'll want to head over to the ME's office after this. I'd like to know if any sexual assault took place and, of course, get a look at the note. Make sure it's a match."

"I started to take it out of her mouth, but CSI went ape-shit, so I left it."

The reason she was called suddenly came into focus. Phelps was covering his ass. Making sure CSI didn't make any claims that he was tampering with evidence. By calling her out, he was solidifying his cooperation with the FBI. Having worked in San Diego's evidence collection department, it was no surprise why the crime scene investigators would object to his moving of any evidence. He should've known better, but his attempt came as no surprise and his actions afterward only confirmed her suspicions. Were the note to have mysteriously disappeared, she would not be here right now and this case would not be tied with the others.

She continued to study the apartment in search of anything that might jibe with what she already knew of her unsub. "It was after 11 when the 911 call came in from the neighbor?"

"That's right."

"Did you spot any forced entry?"

"No."

"So, Meredith Bowen knew whoever it was, most likely. Because who opens the door that late at night to a stranger?"

"Good point."

That was probably the first time he'd actually given her credit for something. She didn't like Phelps but needed more than that to get to the bottom of this and find the killer. "Do you know yet if she worked for Representative Copeland?"

"I'm not aware of it. The responding officer found her work badge, indicating she does work on the Hill under Congresswoman Pamela Carter."

"I bet if we dig deeper, we'll find she worked for Copeland too, no doubt."

"Look, Agent Reid, no offense, but your job here is to give us some fucking idea about who killed these women. Not how it relates to a particular individual or a particular job in politics. There's a killer out there and last I checked, the BAU was supposed to be the experts in profiling people like this sick fuck. How about you worry about that and I'll figure out the rest?"

Kate stopped and trained her sights on him. "What the hell is your problem? You've been less than forthcoming, dragging your feet with the sharing of information and right now, you're being kind of a dick. No offense, but I'm here to help and it's essential I understand the lives these victims had so I can ascertain who might have killed them. You've yet to share Janine Atherton's phone records. And now you're telling me that I'm not doing my job? Screw you. We've got three bodies and you're sitting here trying to pull rank? You really want to go there, detective?" She stepped closer. "You might not like me, but I'm damn good at my job. I'm not here to step on your toes or steal your thunder, or whatever macho bullshit you're dealing with. I'm here to find the killer. And you'd better believe I will." She brushed past him and marched outside, pacing at the bottom of the steps. "Fucking asshole!"

One of the officers approached her. "Ma'am? Are you all right?"

"How the hell do you stand working for that man?"

"Detective Phelps?" The officer smiled. "Because he's a man you don't want to get on the wrong side of."

KATE RETURNED HOME for a quick shower and a change, then she knew what needed to be done. On her return, Nick was finishing his coffee at the kitchen table.

"You're back? How'd it go out there?"

"How'd it go? Shitty. That's how it went. I am absolutely livid right now."

"I can see that. Why don't you sit down and tell me what happened?" He began to rise. "You want some coffee? Looks like you didn't get a chance to have any yet this morning."

Kate sat at the table and pulled the elastic band from her hair and ran her hands through it. "I'm telling you, Nick. Something's not right with that man. Detective Phelps."

He walked back with a mug in hand. "Here. Why do you say that?"

"Because this whole time, he's been keeping things close to his chest. Meanwhile, Pearson with the Baltimore office and the local guy he's working with have been moving forward and I'm sitting here twiddling my thumbs because Phelps refuses to give me anything."

"Well, he called you out this morning. That counts for something, doesn't it?"

"Yeah, to cover his own ass. He sure as hell wasn't cooperative. Just giving me breadcrumbs and I'm sick of it. How the hell am I supposed to do my job with a guy like that?"

"I realize he's probably the first detective you've worked with who hasn't been helpful, but I'm telling you, Kate, he won't be the last. Some of them are just that way. They look at us as usurpers. Like we have no business telling them what to do."

"But that's the thing. I'm not trying to tell him what to do. This is something else, Nick. I seriously think this guy is a bad apple."

"Okay, let's not jump to conclusions. Being uncooperative doesn't make him a bad cop, just makes him an asshole." He reached for her hand. "Sorry you're having to deal with this. Just the way it goes sometimes. What can you do to still get your job done without having to work directly with him?"

"I just came home to get cleaned up, then I'm heading down to the ME's office to see the body and if there are any prelim reports available. I have to get this profile. Three dead bodies, Nick. Two worked for Copeland at some point in their careers, and I can almost guarantee this one did too. Not that Phelps will look into it, though. It'll be up to me."

"The best thing you can do right now is like you said, talk to the ME. You don't need Phelps' permission to do that. Get what you can and then work to find out who this latest victim was. Where she worked, who she hung out with. You know the drill. Who says you got to consult with that guy? What you're doing isn't going to interfere with his investigation."

"Assuming he's actually conducting one."

"Right. But you can continue without him. And from what I'm seeing right now, that's probably your best option, at least in the interim. Phelps will start taking heat for these murders. His captain is going to want answers. There'll be a come to Jesus meeting for him sooner rather than later and you'll be the one who comes out smelling like a rose."

"You think that'll be before another woman is killed or after?"

"I'm not going to lie, there's probably a little bit of chauvinism you're dealing with too. And for that, I'm sorry. But like I said, it won't be the last time. And I think you probably know that."

"Thanks for the coffee. I'm going to go jump in the shower. You heading out?"

He nodded. "I shouldn't be late tonight. Call me later, okay?"

"I will." She kissed him. "Thanks for the pep talk. I kind of miss that."

"Me too."

ON HER WAY to the ME's office, Kate's cell rang with a much-anticipated call. "This is Agent Reid."

"Fraser here. Good morning. Did I catch you at a bad time?"

"No, sir. I'm glad to hear from you."

"Sounds like you're driving, so I won't keep you. I just wanted to let you know that I've moved forward with what we discussed. And I think you might be interested in what I found."

"Oh yeah?"

"I'd rather not go over it on the phone. Are you coming into the office today?"

"Yes, but not until later. How about we meet around 11am?"

"I'll be here. See you then."

"See you then." Kate pressed the end call button and looked at the road ahead. Maybe this day would turn out better than she had expected.

11

The body of Meredith Bowen lay on the stainless steel table inside the offices of the Medical Examiner. Kate had arrived in hopes of gaining further insight into the motives of this killer who had now taken three lives over the span of just two weeks. A fact that Detective Phelps seemed to dismiss, or simply didn't care about.

"Dr. Carr, I'm Agent Reid. We spoke on the phone earlier."

"Pleasure to meet you. Forgive me, I'm already gloved and ready to go or I'd return the handshake." He approached the table. "Where is Detective Phelps?"

"Back at the station, I believe, finishing paperwork. I'll be sure to forward your findings on to him as soon as we're through."

"Good. Okay, so the victim, as you know, is a 32-year-old, Caucasian female. Preliminary cause of death is a gunshot wound to the chest. It will take time for toxicology and DNA to come back. But what I can tell you now is that Ms. Bowen appeared to try to fend off her assailant." The doctor picked up Meredith's left hand. "Skin under the nails, which we hope will reveal the suspect's DNA, as well as a bullet graze to the scalp, which suggests a struggle or evasive measures on the part of the victim."

Skin under the nails was a careless move on the part of the attacker and this emboldened Kate. "So she opens the door, maybe recognizes the person, the attacker forces his way inside and tries to shoot Ms. Bowen in the head, which is in line with what we know about the unsub so far. Fails to connect, but in the ensuing struggle, fires into the victim's chest." Kate observed the victim as she spoke. "I'm seeing a slight gunpowder residue."

"That's right, meaning the shot was fired at close range."

"How soon do you expect labs to return?"

"I'll be honest with you, Agent Reid, it's a slow process. I understand the urgency and I will do the best I can to expedite the results."

"Thank you. Identifying the attacker is my top priority. Something I wish to do before he kills again." She checked the time on her phone. "Thank you for your time, Dr. Carr. I'll wait for your call."

"Good day, Agent Reid."

This news was encouraging, but the waiting game was a difficult one. And as Kate left the ME's office, there was still something else that weighed on her mind. Something that could offer insight into another aspect of this investigation. The time had come to see if Fraser would deliver on his earlier message. As she headed back toward the WFO, Kate made the call.

"Fraser here."

"It's Kate Reid. You still have time to meet?"

"I've got about an hour before I need to head into a meeting. Are you on your way back to WFO?"

"I am. I'll see you in about fifteen. Thanks." She ended the call, ready to make another she'd promised this morning. The line rang. "Hey, it's me."

"How'd it go at the ME's office?"

"No labs back yet, of course, but some good news: skin was left under the victim's fingernails."

"Then you'll have to cross your fingers the DNA belongs to someone with a record; otherwise, you'll be shooting in the dark."

"It's the best lead we've got right now. I'm on my way back to the WFO. I just wanted to check in. I'll see you tonight, hon."

"Bye."

Kate was hesitant to mention her impending meeting with Agent Fraser. Only insomuch as Nick wouldn't agree with her tactics. But she was her own woman, her own agent, and if this was what she needed to do, he was no longer her boss and she didn't need his permission. Dwight, on the other hand, might be concerned, but depending on what she discovered, it was possible he would ignore the how and focus on the why.

The building was just ahead and Kate pulled into the parking garage, finally making her way to Fraser's office. Another murder and Phelps was again dragging his feet. The reason for his behavior lay in wait for her now. "Knock, knock."

"Agent Reid, come in. Close the door behind you." As she took her seat, he wasted no time getting down to business. "I'm not surprised your taking issue with Detective Phelps' behavior. There are things here that would make me question where his loyalties lie. A couple of things to note first, he's been reprimanded on more than one occasion for sexual harassment of his fellow female officers."

"No surprise there, but not exactly what I was looking for."

"Bear with me. I'm just setting the stage. I have a few buddies at Metro PD who don't hold a great deal of favor for Phelps. And the more I got into it, the more I began to understand that he is a man who looks after himself. By all accounts, a good detective, but let's just say that if he saw you dying in the street, he'd probably walk on by unless it was in his interest to help."

"Okay. This all makes sense, but any indication that he might be less than scrupulous?"

"You mean, is he on the take?"

"To put it bluntly—yes."

"He has had run-ins with IA regarding misconduct. However, he's never faced any charges. He probably had a few friends who have vouched for him and got him off the hook."

"Or he's paid them off to do so."

"Possibly. But I think you're dealing with a man who could very well be running this investigation with his own best interest in mind. Not the victims'. That being said, I'd be careful. He's been with Metro PD for more than ten years. His roots are deep, probably stretching for miles. I imagine he'll do what it takes to protect himself."

"So it's time for me to handle this investigation on my own."

"I wouldn't necessarily say that, but if there were leads you wanted to run on, it might be best to run on them alone. For now."

"Thank you. You've been a tremendous help." She began to rise.

"Glad to do what I can for the Bureau. Our jobs are hard enough without having pissing matches with the local authorities. You let me know if there's anything else I can do."

"I appreciate that. I think I know what I have to do." She stopped and turned. "Oh, hey, if you see Caison, let him know I said hi."

"Will do. Take care, Reid."

NOT ONLY WERE toes about to be stepped on, they were about to be pulverized, but letting this investigation drag on any longer than necessary was both shameful and dangerous. First things first, Kate needed a complete profile, something Phelps had insisted was her job to finish, yet offered no material to make it possible. The time had come to solicit outside help in the form of a man she had hoped to work for in the very near future.

While she was instructed to wait to learn whether she had made it to the second round, this couldn't wait and if it jeopardized her chances, then so be it, though she suspected it would serve to bolster her standing, as she and Vasquez discussed.

Dwight's expertise did not lie in the psychological analysis of killers. That had been Georgia's wheelhouse, but her presence in these halls was long past. And he wouldn't object to Kate's going outside for help. So that was what she would do—on her own, without consulting a man who had thus far thrown obstacles before her. Armed with the inside track about Phelps, Kate would proceed without his knowledge.

She headed toward the fifth floor and marched straight into Dwight's office. "Can I talk to you? It's important."

"Sure. Everything okay?"

"Not really, no. I learned a few things about my contact at Metro Police."

"Detective Phelps."

"Yes. And based on what I discovered, I think it's best if I shoulder more of the investigation."

"And you've spoken with the detective about this?"

"Of course not. If I had, I would be in here with a different story because he would surely object. That being said, I'm looking to you for help—and permission."

Dwight pulled back in his chair and regarded Kate with growing concern. "Are you sure there isn't another way? I've worked with his kind before and there's usually some common ground."

"Not this time, Dwight. I realize this is something I don't have a great deal of experience in handling, but if we want to get our arms around this case and understand who we're dealing with, I believe this is the only way."

"Do you want me to talk to his captain? Have him reassigned?"

"I think he has a long reach and that it wouldn't make much difference, except to make things even harder for me. No, I'd rather just do what I have to do and worry about him after I get what I need."

"If this is what you believe must be done, then I'll support you. Hell, this is still our investigation, in part, so I don't see any harm if you need answers as to how you go about getting them."

"Thank you."

"I will warn you, be careful. This might bite you in the ass."

"Oh, I fully expect it to, but at least I'll find the killer." She disappeared almost as quickly as she had arrived. Back to her desk and back to work.

With the information she'd compiled to date, she had a good idea of the type of person they were looking for. Male, mid-to-late twenties. Caucasian. And probably someone in the political arena. This someone could be after Copeland perhaps for being fired or spurned in some way. The only thing that would dispute this was if the latest victim hadn't worked for Copeland at some point in her career. That was the first thing she needed to find out.

A database search for Meredith Bowen's employment records was her first priority. As Kate reviewed the information, she didn't spot any obvious connection to Copeland, a discouraging fact she hadn't counted on. But she was confident of her approach. Perhaps she knew him as a consultant or through an outside organization and not directly. According to her research, Meredith worked for

Representative Pamela Carter. That was who Kate needed to see for more insight into Meredith's background.

Kate grabbed her things. "Vasquez, I need to head out for a while. Working on this latest victim."

"Okay. I expect forensics to come back on Brenner as soon as this afternoon, but tomorrow at the latest. If I get it, I'll give you a shout."

"Appreciate it. Talk to you later." And she was out the door, once again, wasting no time on running on her own hunches. It was what she did best.

Kate jumped on the Metro and took it all the way to the Hill. Capitol South Metro station was the next stop. Her unexpected arrival might cause distress to Mrs. Carter and Kate wasn't sure she had heard about what happened to Meredith. If that was the case, she would have to be the one to break the news. Better her than Phelps, at any rate.

Security was tight, but after several minutes, she was allowed entry, even without an appointment. It was the one thing an FBI badge offered. People usually didn't stop her from going where she needed to go.

A young professional woman sat at a desk in front of an office Kate assumed belonged to the congresswoman.

"Excuse me. I'm FBI Agent Reid. Might Representative Carter be available to speak with me?"

The woman appeared concerned. "Do you have an appointment?"

"I'm afraid I don't, but it is very important I speak with her."

"Let me see if she's available." She picked up the phone. "Mrs. Carter, I have an FBI Agent Reid here to see you." Her eyes peered at Kate. "No, ma'am, she's not on your agenda but says it's very important she speak with you. Okay, thank you." She ended the call. "Mrs. Carter will be out in a moment. Please have a seat."

"Thank you." Kate's leg twitched while in the chair. She was wired and it was because she was on the right track. At least she had the backing of the guys in Baltimore and her own office. Without that, this would be much more difficult. However, it wasn't going to be a walk in the park either. What Dwight said resonated. She would have to take precautions. Even meeting with Mrs. Carter, she knew would get back to Phelps. And when it did, he would take it out on her in some manner. So she'd better get what she needed before that happened.

"Agent Reid?" A woman who looked to be in her late forties wearing a conservative blue suit approached. "I'm Representative Carter. Please, come into my office."

Kate followed her inside. "I'm very sorry I didn't make an appointment, but I'm afraid this was urgent."

"I'm assuming you're here regarding the death of my top aide, Meredith Bowen."

"Um. Yes, ma'am. I—I wasn't sure if you had been made aware of what happened."

"Unfortunately, yes. I received a call from the police this morning."

"Detective Phelps?"

"Yes."

This was a surprise, but it wouldn't derail Kate's efforts. "Of course. I am very sorry for your loss."

"Thank you. It is a terrible tragedy. Meredith was a wonderful young woman with an extremely bright future ahead of her."

"May I ask how long you had known her?"

"She came to work for me about a year ago, maybe a little more than a year." The congresswoman smiled. "She was so eager to learn the job. We will all miss her so very much."

"I'm sure. I don't know if you're aware, but I'm working with the detective on another similar investigation as well as coordination on another murder of a woman in Baltimore. All appear to have been committed by the same perpetrator."

"Oh my God. I wasn't aware of that. Is that why the FBI is involved?"

"Yes, ma'am. I work in the Washington Field Office under the resident BAU agent, Dwight Jameson. We were asked to assist, given that we're dealing with multiple jurisdictions, and of course, the nature of the crimes."

"I'm familiar with the Behavioral Analysis Unit. I'm sure you've seen your share of horrific crimes, Agent Reid."

"I have. But I'd like to talk to you about Meredith. We don't have much in the way of leads right now and are awaiting the labs, which, unfortunately, do take some time. So, rather than wait longer than necessary, I'd like to pursue a path I believe is worthwhile in helping to find her killer."

The woman almost broke down in tears. "I'm sorry. It just feels so surreal and to hear you say that—it's difficult."

"I'll try to keep this brief. I have done some preliminary work with regard to Meredith's previous employment. I was wondering if you might be aware of her background, particularly as it relates to working for or with another member of congress."

Representative Carter cocked her head slightly. "Not that I'm aware of. I'm the only House member she's worked for and as far as I know, she hadn't worked for any other member in the House or Senate. She was in the early stages of what could have been an amazing career." She paused and cast her gaze toward the ceiling. "However, I do recall her mentioning a time when she worked for a newspaper. Small one, nothing major. She had graduated with a journalism degree and started down that path for a while. It's likely she had contacts on the Hill at that time. Even with a small paper, she was incredibly resourceful and would've worked hard for a story. So, yes, I believe she would have known people around town." She pulled out her desk drawer. "I was going through her things this morning, actually, and cleared out her desk. What few personal belongings she kept here, I put in my drawer to be collected by a member of her family. I found this bundle of business cards." She handed them to Kate. "You might find something in here."

"Thank you, Mrs. Carter. This will be extremely helpful in the investigation."

"Please, it's Pam. Listen, I do have to attend a meeting, but if there's anything else I can do. Anything at all to help you, please don't hesitate to contact me. I'll do everything in my power to help you find whoever killed Meredith and those other poor women."

"I can't tell you how much I appreciate that, Pam. Thank you for this. And thank you for your time."

She began to show Kate to the door. "You find her killer, Agent Reid. Meredith deserves justice."

Kate nodded. "Goodbye, Pam."

IT HAD BEEN a worthwhile trip to the congresswoman's office. The bundle of cards Kate held in her hand as she sat at her desk was a physical version of the contacts in her phone, perhaps even more than that. Not many people kept business cards anymore, but Kate was lucky Meredith had.

"You're back?" Vasquez approached. "I didn't see you come in. How'd it go?"

"Good." She held the cards up.

"What are those?"

"Meredith Bowen's contacts. Her boss, the congresswoman, handed them to me. She kept them in her drawer at work."

"Well, shit. That's good news. You find out anything else?"

"Not really, no. But I believe I'll find something in here."

"And if you do?"

"Then I'll run on it alone. I haven't talked to Phelps since this morning. I don't know what the hell he's doing, and right now, I don't care. Right now, I'm going to sift through every one of these damn cards and find a path to Copeland."

12

The forensics report on the piece of material found wedged in Tasha Brenner's mouth had finally come. When the email appeared in her inbox, Vasquez opened it immediately. She'd been waiting on Agent Pearson in the Baltimore office to forward it. He'd given her a heads up that it was good news. Now she was about to see for herself.

Upon opening the file, she devoured the report, looking for whatever it was that was about to give them a much-needed leg up on this investigation. With three women dead, they had to get a handle on this because hell was about to be unleashed by way of the media.

"Reid, you have to see this." Vasquez peered into the bullpen and noted she wasn't at her desk. "Shit." This was too good to wait and she began to hunt for her partner. Her first stop, Jameson's office. "You see Reid anywhere?"

"No. Not in a while, why?"

"I think we might've gotten a break on the case and we need to get to Baltimore now."

"Try her on her cell. I have no idea if she's here or not. Last she told me, she was running on a lead herself."

Vasquez already knew what that lead had been. Kate was hell bound on two things—getting to the bottom of Copeland's involvement with these murders and exposing Phelps as a bad cop. In D.C., those were highly dangerous objectives and Vasquez feared it would throw her off the primary goal, which was to find the killer before he killed again. "I'll call her, thanks."

"Hey—anything I should know?"

She stopped. "Not yet. I'll let you know if this is significant." As she returned to the bullpen, relief swept over her. "There you are. I was just looking for you."

"I just got back. What's up?" Kate replied.

"We need to go to Baltimore and see Pearson. We've got a lead on the material left on the victim." Before Kate could respond, Vasquez was already heading toward the elevator. She stopped and turned back. "You coming?"

"Yeah." Kate jogged to catch up with her.

They stepped onto the elevator and Vasquez pressed the parking garage button. "You want to tell me where you were, or am I supposed to guess?"

"Chasing my tail."

"Sounds productive."

"Yep."

She continued to eye Kate. "Don't worry. I think we've got something here we can sink our teeth into."

"I hope so."

THE SHORT TRIP found their arrival at the Baltimore office ahead of schedule.

"Agent Pearson is finishing up a meeting. He'll be right out," the assistant replied.

"Thanks." Vasquez nodded to Kate to step away from the desk. "First thing we need to do is ask him if the detective he's working with has said anything to Phelps."

"I agree. The longer I can hold him off, the better."

"You really think you're going to get something on this guy?"

"I don't know, but he's doing more harm than good on this investigation and if I can accomplish more without him, then I will."

"But you haven't yet."

"A minor detail."

Agent Pearson approached. "Morning, Agent Vasquez, Agent Reid. Thanks for coming over. Follow me."

The Baltimore Field Office had been around almost as long as the WFO and housed far more agents. It also covered a larger population. Pearson continued toward his office. "Right through here. Can I get you two a coffee or water?"

"No, thank you. I'm fine." Kate sat down.

"Me too."

As Pearson continued inside, he returned to his desk. "Okay, so I know Agent Vasquez has viewed the report on the fabric. What are your thoughts, Agent Reid?"

"Well, I think it'll be important that we discover if the fabric matches what was found on the other victims. It's not a leap to assume it does. And, because time is of the essence here, I suggest we work on finding out where the fabric came from. Narrowing down a location is also critical."

"I'm already ahead of you on that one." Pearson typed on his keyboard for a moment. "Based on the forensics, the remnant came from an 1800 thread count bedsheet and the word written with a high-end brand of red lipstick."

"No DNA?"

"Just the victim's. We can still pursue the origins of the bedsheet remnant. And that's what I've been working on." He continued to type. "But wait, it gets better. This wasn't just any bedsheet. It's extremely high quality."

"This person has money?" Vasquez asked.

"I don't know about that. What I think is that we need to find the manufacturer, because I'd seriously consider the possibility that the remnant came from a luxury hotel."

"Couldn't it also have been from someone's house or even a retailer?"

"We can safely rule that out because the report indicated it had been washed with an industrial-type of detergent. I got a report on the chemical composition and with some digging, I discovered that detergent was made by a company called Sunburst Chemicals."

"Is that where we're going?" Vasquez asked.

"Yep. Let's get a client list from them and go from there."

With his head down, staring at the file in his hand, Nick continued toward Quinn's office. Upon reaching his destination, he noticed the door was open, but the office was empty. "Damn."

"You looking for me?" Quinn appeared next to him and made his way inside.

"Yeah. Do you have a minute? I had a chance to review the profile you put together on the New York case."

"Sure. Come in and have a seat." Quinn perched on the edge of his desk while Nick sat down. "What do you think?"

"I think this is great work. I definitely believe this will get us on the right track."

"Thank you. Look, I know this has been an adjustment—for all of us, but I hope you know that we are a good team and it just takes time to feel each other out."

"I get that and I have no problem with it. It's clear the three of you understand one another and are all on the same page."

"Good. And we want you to be on that same page too."

"Agreed. I assume the others have seen this?"

"No." Quinn pushed off his desk and walked toward his chair. "I thought you should see it first."

Nick began to nod both an approval and an acknowledgment for Quinn's consideration. "I see no reason to delay your research. Let' get it distributed and see if we can find this man." Nick began to rise. "I'll let you get back to it."

"You came here just to give me the nod of approval? You could've just as easily emailed me."

Nick turned awkward for a moment. "I could've, but I think it's important we share facetime. How else are we going to gain a full understanding of each other?"

"I see your point. But I assume this will be brought up in the meeting this afternoon before we head to the New York field office?"

"Of course. Like I said, though, I'm a firm believer in discussing matters face to face. I'd like us to get to the point where we can finish each other's sentences, if you catch my drift."

"I do. I'd like that too, Scarborough. Since you're here, I might as well update you on my progress with the applicants."

Nick's brows raised. "Oh?" He wasn't good at the whole sheepish thing—never had been. And it seemed Quinn wasn't buying it either.

"I think I'd like Agent Reid to come in and spend some time with me, when she can."

"She's working a case with the Baltimore office and local police in DC and Baltimore. I can't say when she'd be available."

"I'll give her a shout. Have her shoot over some dates, hopefully in the next week, that might work for her."

"Sounds good. Appreciate the update." Nick disappeared.

Quinn folded his arms and peered into the corridor. While he appreciated his boss' approach to team building, he was under no impression that Scarborough was there for any other reason than to check on whether or not Reid was still in the running. If this was what it was going to be like, perhaps he'd made the wrong call to bring her in again. Unfortunately, the only way to know for sure was to do just that. He was aware of the investigation placed before Agent Reid and he was anxious to discuss her findings to date. Her previous report revealed a great deal of aptitude on her part.

With his cell phone in hand, he made the call. "Hello again, it's Quinn. Did I catch you at a bad time?"

"A little. I'm sorry, but I'm right in the middle of chasing something down."

"Don't be sorry. It's your job. Listen, I won't keep you. Just wanted to know if you had a few minutes to meet here this week?"

"Of course. I'm in Baltimore right now. I could actually meet you this evening when I return. How late will you be in the office?"

"How about we meet for dinner?"

"Sure. That'd be great. I'll be back around 7, maybe a little earlier. Depends on what we find."

"Great. We'll pencil in 7:30 at Monroe's on 6th Street."

"Perfect. Thank you for the call. I'll see you tonight." Kate slid her phone back into her pocket.

"Who was that?" Vasquez asked.

"Agent Quinn at BAU Headquarters."

"Yeah, I know Quinn is at Headquarters. What did he want?"

"Wants to meet for dinner."

"That's a good sign."

"I think so. And, it'll give me a chance to show him what I've worked up so far on this case. It's the opportunity I've been hoping for."

"Congrats, Reid."

"I'd hold off on that. It's a process—he has assured me."

"I'm sure he has. Looks like he's doing this by the book. I wonder if Scarborough has anything to do with that?"

"Oh, you can bet on that. I won't hold it against him, though. This is on me and I got it."

"I know you do." Vasquez turned to Agent Pearson. "You ready to divvy up that client list?"

"I need to get hold of Ramos. He'll want in on this." He turned to Kate. "You want to make a call to Phelps?"

"Later. He's got his hands full right now."

Vasquez eyed her and pulled her back for a moment while Pearson continued toward his office. "Be careful. You don't want him to get wind of what's happening between you and Phelps. You'll be the one who looks bad and it might affect Quinn's decision."

"I'm watching out for that."

The list they'd received from Sunburst Chemicals was extensive and included hotels and resorts and some retail. It hadn't been quite the slam dunk they'd expected, but it was all they had right now while Kate waited on DNA from Bowen.

"What we really need is for the Department of Forensic Sciences to get their shit together and see if they get the same results on the other victims," Pearson added.

"More importantly, if we can determine the other pieces are from the same cut of cloth? We'll be golden." Vasquez stopped.

"You know, Reid and I should head back. We'll put some pressure on the forensics team and see how far out their results are. And, we can work on the names you've given us."

"Probably best. I'll start working on my list and recruit Ramos as well as a few of my team. The sooner we can figure out where this material came from, the better." He offered a greeting. "Appreciate you two coming out here today. It's nice when we can all work together." He smiled.

"You have no idea," Kate replied.

KATE STEPPED out of Vasquez's car. "Thanks for the ride. I'm going to head out to meet Quinn. Are you going back inside?"

"For a while. I'll start working the list. You go on. I'll be anxious to hear what Quinn has to say. I'll see you bright and early."

"Don't hesitate to call if you find something." Kate continued toward her car as Vasquez walked inside the WFO.

Having Quinn's opinion was no small deal. According to Nick, he was the best he'd seen. Of course, he probably wanted to forget about the last profiler he'd known not so long ago. Kate would reserve judgment.

She pulled out of the garage and checked the time. "Damn." With the press of a button, she waited for his line to answer.

"Hey, it's me."

"Where are you?" Nick asked.

"I'm heading to Monroe's for dinner with Agent Quinn. Are you still at the office?"

"Yeah. I'll be here for a little while longer. We've received some additional information that's proving useful, so I'm helping the team work through it. I didn't realize you'd had plans with Quinn."

"I didn't. He called me earlier and I suggested we meet for dinner since I was heading back from Baltimore kind of late. I figure it's a good opportunity and I don't want to pass it up."

"No. Definitely not. Go—enjoy. By the way, how did Baltimore go?"

"Good. We're getting closer. Looking for the origins of the fabric and Vasquez and I stopped in to see the progress our team was making on the forensics testing. They hope to know more tomorrow. So, fingers crossed, we'll start getting somewhere."

"You don't need luck, Kate. Just your sixth sense. Take advantage of this dinner with Quinn. Play up your strengths."

"I know the deal. I'll see you later tonight."

"I'll wait up."

She continued driving through downtown until reaching the restaurant. "Only five minutes late. Made better time than I thought."

The valet opened her door.

"Thank you."

"Here's your ticket, ma'am. Enjoy your dinner."

Kate walked inside the restaurant and headed toward the host when she spotted Quinn wave a hand toward her. She smiled and continued on. "Sorry I'm late."

"Not at all." He stood and greeted her. "Glad you could make it. Must've been a crazy day for you." He pulled out her chair.

"Nothing you're not accustomed to, I'm sure. I just spoke with Agent Scarborough. Says you all are making progress on your New York case."

"I think so. The rest of them are still working. I turned over my info late this afternoon."

"So you don't go out in the field at all?" Kate picked up the menu.

"I do sometimes. But mostly I get called to do profiles, which does require a decent amount of travel. I always visit the field offices and start building a rapport with the agents."

"That's a good way to do it."

"Glad you approve." Quinn turned to the waitress who had just appeared. "My guest has arrived."

"What can I get you to drink, ma'am?"

"House white is fine, thank you."

"And you, sir? Can I top you up?"

"Sure. Thanks. Gin and Tonic."

"Right away."

"I'm sorry, I didn't mean to suggest you needed my approval in some way." Kate felt flustered by his comment.

"I'm just giving you grief, Reid. Relax. This isn't an interview."

It sure as hell felt like one to her. "Right."

"So, how's your investigation going?" Quinn continued to peruse the menu.

"Feels a little start and stop, you know? But we're making progress." She wondered if now was the right time to ask for his advice on her profile. She had no idea what type of meeting this was, business or pleasure.

"That's how it usually goes, but you know that. You've got enough cases under your belt to understand how it works."

"I do, but seems like each one is different."

"They are and it's good you recognize that."

"Glad you approve." A smirk masked her face.

"Touché."

"So, Agent Quinn..."

"Call me Noah. We're not in the office."

"Noah. Can I ask, is this a social call or are we here to talk about the job?"

"You don't mince words, do you, Agent Reid?"

"It's Kate."

"Of course. Well, Kate, I guess you could say I'm trying to learn a little bit more about you. Your thought processes. Understand how you operate during an investigation."

"Okay. Well, that's good. Because I was hoping to get your opinion on what I've got so far in terms of a profile."

"I'll tell you what. Email me what you have. I'll read it now and give you a 30,000-foot view of what I see."

"Right now?"

"Sure. Won't take me long. Let me take a look. Food won't be here for a few minutes. I'll give you some quick thoughts. Will that do?"

"Yes. Thank you. That would be great."

"Good. Let's see what you've got, Kate."

13

Quinn finished reading the report as they reached the end of their meal. He placed his phone on the table. "I'm very impressed. But..."

Kate's heart dropped into her stomach. "It's not enough."

"Well, no, but I think you knew that. I'll tell you what." He checked the time. "Shit, it's almost 10. I'm sure you'd like to head home."

"No, what is it? What were you about to say?"

"You have time to go back to the office? I'd like to show you something that I think will help you over the hump."

"Yes. Of course, I'd love that." This was what she'd hoped for. Insight from the man who, in Nick's opinion, was the best in the field.

"Then we'll settle up and head out. If you're sure it's okay?"

"I don't have any other plans. I'd like to do this."

~

As she followed Quinn in her car headed for BAU Headquarters, she grew curious if Nick was still there and made the call. "Hey, it's me. Don't suppose you're still at the office?"

"Actually, I just left. Are you on your way home?"

"No. I'm following Quinn back to Headquarters. I was kind of hoping you'd still be there."

"What are you heading back there for?"

"At dinner, he asked that I forward the profile I created, and based on its current form, he offered to provide me with additional insight. So we're going to his office. I hope that's okay. I know it's late."

"Hey, whatever you need to do—you know that. If he can help and potentially offer you a break in this investigation, go for it. I'll see you when you get home."

"Thanks, hon."

"No thanks necessary. Just let me know when you're heading home so I don't worry too much, okay?"

"I will. Love you and don't wait up."

Situations had arisen in the past when Nick exhibited overly protective behavior and she'd wasted no time confronting him about it. That was all it took for him to willingly take a step back, reminding himself how he never wanted to be that way toward her. Sometimes it was just a man thing, sometimes it was more. But this time, there was no reluctance in his tone. A measure of relief that brushed aside any distractions. Because the time for distractions on this investigation was over.

The security gates were just ahead and Quinn passed through quickly. While the grounds never really closed, it wasn't nearly as busy as during the day when law enforcement from around the country came and went along with FBI staff and trainees. She almost missed her time here and thought about Will Caison. Meeting with Fraser the other day stirred memories of her crossing paths with Will some months ago. It had been a horrific time for the Bureau and the country and while much of the memories still remained at the forefront of the nation, the Bureau and the country continued on, as they always had.

"Badge please." The guard at the gate leaned toward Kate's window.

"Oh, sorry." She rummaged through her purse and retrieved her ID. "Here you go."

He scanned the ID and raised the gate. "Have a good evening, ma'am."

"Thank you." She continued through and followed Quinn toward the parking area nearest the BAU offices.

Quinn waited for her to exit her car. "You ready?"

"As I'll ever be." Kate followed him inside.

The elevator doors parted, exposing the expansive open space lined with cubicles and offices and a spectacle of advanced technology. If one were a fan of baseball, this place would be considered "The Show."

Kate continued to follow Quinn to his office, noting several staffmembers working diligently at their desks. "Thanks for doing this, Agent Quinn."

He held open the door to his office. "Technically, we are at the office, but please, it's still Noah. And we're on all the same team, aren't we? I'm here to help. Go on in and have a seat." He followed her inside and headed toward his desk. "Okay, first of all, let me say that what you've developed so far is good—very good. However, it's clear you've hit a hurdle."

"I have. We are working on the origins of the fabric scraps left inside the victims' mouths, but as of yet, we've only received information on one of them."

"Okay. And your report also states that you believe this individual to be male, Caucasian, and approximately twenty-five to thirty-five years old."

"That's correct."

"Aside from that description covering a broad range of individuals, it's also considered one of the most generic and obvious." He held up pre-emptive hands. "Now, before you go on, let me explain myself. While the majority of serial killers are exactly as you've detailed here, there is one glaring possibility that I believe has been overlooked."

"And that is?"

"Per your file, no sexual assault on any of the three victims appeared to have taken place."

"From what we know right now, that's correct."

"And, another contributing factor I see that is quite substantial and meaningful is the note. Now don't get me wrong. There are plenty of white male serial killers with Oedipus complexes and other 'mommy issues,' and so the use of the word 'whore,' in those instances, wouldn't be out of place. But in this case, because the killer wrote the note in what you believe is red lipstick?"

"Yes."

"Okay, red lipstick. Whore and red lips, one could venture to say, are synonymous. That's not to say all women who wear red lipstick are whores, but most whores wear red lipstick. At least, that's what we are led to believe through television, pornography, and even some mature video games. But I think I'm veering off-base here. Let me continue by saying this, I notice you suggest that the link between these women is their association with a political figure."

"That's right. However, I'm getting push back on that theory."

"In this town? I bet you are. That said, today you discovered the fabric was a scrap of high-end bedsheet."

"Possibly from a hotel," Kate continued.

"Okay, good. So, you have three women, shot dead, a scrap of high end sheet shoved in their mouths with the word 'whore' written in red lipstick. And—all three worked or were associated in some manner with a male politician."

"I haven't found the third connection yet to the politician, but I'm working on that."

"So let's just assume, then, that the third victim is also connected." He held her gaze.

Kate could see that he was trying to coax an alternate conclusion to her assessment and perhaps she had begun to see what he was getting at. It was an assumption that was very much outside the norm and a situation that rarely occurred in a serial murder investigation. It seemed not impossible, but improbable. "You don't think it's a man. You think it's a woman taking revenge?"

"Have you not considered the possibility?"

"I can see where you're coming from and, frankly, I hadn't concluded that as an option. But there's one thing that I discovered when I visited the crime scenes and viewed the victims during their examinations."

"And that is?"

"The trajectory of the entry wounds suggests the killer was taller and, in some cases, significantly taller than the victims, meaning it's likely the shooter was male." Kate noticed a smile appear on Quinn's face. She was right and he knew it.

"Well, that does make a difference. But I still maintain you should consider the possibility the killer is female. And, wasn't the first victim shot in her car? The angle of the entry wound would imply nothing other than the fact that the victim was sitting. Look, if nothing else, it's entirely possible you could be dealing with someone behind the scenes. Or worse, multiple killers. I know you've come across that before."

He'd done his research. And while she hadn't expected the

intrusion into her background so soon, it had to happen at some point in this process. That said, it was something she hadn't considered. She thought she had him and he just turned the tables.

Quinn pulled up a file on his computer. "Come around."

Kate approached the other side of his desk.

"This is an investigation I consulted on about two years ago."

She began to read aloud the summary he'd opened. "An often overlooked theory is that a woman has the potential to inflict horrendous pain upon her victims. This is a case where a man is not able to see beyond a woman's traditional role in the world. That of wife, mother, caregiver. Because of that, the capture and conviction of a female serial killer is rare indeed. However, what is not debated as much as it should be is the possibility that a woman could control another individual—a husband, a son, or lover—into committing brutal acts upon victims she seeks out for whatever reason, whether known or unknown to the one being controlled. This is the phenomenon I am currently exploring in the profile below." She turned her attention to Quinn. "You've considered this before?" Kate returned to her seat.

"Yes. However, we can't be sure that's what you're dealing with now. I'm simply showing you another possible avenue to venture down."

Kate nodded. "I hadn't considered this. To date, the cases I've worked have been fairly cut and dry in regard to the gender of the unsub."

"And in general, that's the case, but in reading your assessment, I'm able to draw parallels to this investigation you just read from."

"I can't thank you enough for opening my eyes. I'm still in the very early stages, but with three women dead, I don't have time to follow the wrong path."

"I'm not saying you're wrong. I'm just opening your eyes to the possibility you could be."

"Thank you. It means a lot to me that you took the time. It really does." She began to rise.

"I think I'd like to head out. Seems I've got a lot of work to do."

Noah showed her out. "Of course. And thank you for letting me impart some wisdom. Believe it or not, it's not something I get to do often. But, Kate, I do see a great deal of potential in you."

She stopped at the door and turned toward him. "Even though I could be chasing the wrong lead?"

"That's part of the process, so don't beat yourself up about it. You've been a field agent for the past few years. This is a new arena for you. I can tell you that I'll be tightening up the list of prospects again tomorrow. And just so you don't lose any sleep, you should know that you're still in the running."

Her relief was evident. "Thank you. Thank you very much."

"Goodnight, Kate."

"Goodnight, Noah." She walked out of the office and into the elevator and when the doors closed, the anxiety that had built up to that point was finally released. "Oh, thank God."

DETECTIVE PHELPS NOTICED the congressman enter the coffee shop. He raised two fingers on his left hand to garner the man's attention in the near-empty café. Copeland nodded and began his approach.

"What's so urgent you needed to get me out of my bed at 3am? I told my wife I was going to the gym before heading in to the office."

"Do you usually go to the gym in the mornings?" Phelps asked.

"No."

"Probably should've come up with another excuse, then." The detective sipped on his coffee. "That one's yours. Figured you'd want it."

"Thanks. So tell me, why am I here?"

"I got the Medical Examiner's report back on Janine Atherton about two hours ago. The ME called me first and said it was important that I review it as soon as possible. So I did."

"And?"

"I'm sorry, congressman, but I'm going to have to have you come in and make a statement."

"What? I thought we had an agreement?" Copeland leaned over the table and in a hushed tone began, "I paid you not just a lot of money to keep this as far away from me as possible, but have worked to gain the favors you've asked for as well."

"Then maybe you should've used a condom."

He pulled back, appearing embarrassed. "What? What the hell are you talking about?"

"I mean you left DNA behind and you just fucked everything up for yourself—and me. This is something you should've been upfront about."

"What a minute. Okay, so I slept with her, but how the hell would they know it was me? I don't have a goddam criminal record. Don't they have to have you in some sort of database to know who you are?"

"Yes. I suppose you don't recall the swab and prints they took from you prior to being sworn in as Virginia's Fifth District representative? What, you think that shit doesn't show up in our system? You're in the fucking security clearance database."

Phelps watched as Copeland's face drained of color. "You have to make a statement saying you were with her the night she was killed and that you slept with her."

"I can't. I can't do that. I'll lose everything. My wife, my family, my seat. There has to be something else you can do. Can't you hide the report? I mean, what's the point of having you in my pocket if you can't do anything for me?"

Phelps' face turned deadpan. "First of all, I'm not in your pocket. You're in mine. Secondly, I can't hide the goddam report. It came directly from the ME. His files. Not mine. Look, you'll have to come clean about your relationship with Atherton. There's no way around it. But that doesn't mean you killed her, right?"

"Yeah, I mean, no. I didn't kill her. I swear."

"Then you come in at 8am this morning—voluntarily—and make the statement. I'll do my best to keep a lid on it. This doesn't have to get out."

"But it will, won't it?"

"Depends on how much money you've got. I'll keep it quiet for as long as I can. The problem I see here is that the Feds are going to get this same report in a matter of hours. And I'll tell you, that pain in the ass Reid won't let this go." He sipped on his coffee again. "She won't blab her mouth off about it, but it does mean they'll grill the shit out of you about the other murders."

"I can handle that. I just can't handle the media getting hold of this. You have to stop that from happening. Swear to me you will."

"Like I said. I'll do what I can—but it's going to cost you."

14

When the ding of the elevator sounded, Kate felt the tremors from Dwight's weighty steps, which approached with noticeable haste. She turned in his direction before he reached her. "What's wrong? What's happened?"

"Did you see the ME's report?" he asked.

"Which one?" Kate turned back and began to search her computer.

"Atherton. I haven't seen it yet, but I just received a very interesting call from Detective Phelps."

"Phelps? Why did he call you?"

"I can speculate, but I'd rather read the report first. Phelps said Representative Copeland is going in at 8am to make an official statement."

"Then we should get down there now."

"Just hang on. Find that report. I want to know everything before we go down there."

"Here it is." She opened the file just as Vasquez made her approach.

"What are you looking at? Did you just get this?"

"Yes."

The three of them began to read the summary of the report and it seemed all had reached the same conclusion.

"We got him." Kate smiled and turned to Dwight. "We got him. We have to get down there now."

"I don't want you going in there thinking the congressman is guilty."

"Did you read what I just read?"

"I did. But just because they found his DNA doesn't mean he killed her. Come on, Kate. You know better than to jump to that conclusion. There's going to be more to this."

"Then let's get over to Metro PD and see what he has to say." Vasquez was already walking away but stopped short, noting neither was following her. "What are you guys waiting for? Let's go."

Dwight gave Kate that look she'd usually only seen in Nick's eyes. The one that told her she needed to reel it in. "We're coming," he replied.

As the two headed toward Vasquez, Dwight continued. "Look, I know you're gunning for this congressman."

"I'm not, but I'll tell you, he should've been brought in for questioning more than a week ago. And the only reason he's coming in now is because he knows he has no other choice."

"Maybe, but do *not* overstep your bounds. This is still Metro's case and Phelps' case. We're here only to consult."

"Okay, I got it."

THE TEAM ARRIVED SHORTLY before Copeland's scheduled statement, and it appeared Phelps had been expecting them.

"Thanks for coming down on short notice. I know how busy you guys are," Phelps began. "The congressman will be here in a few minutes. Why don't we go back to my office?" He reached to Kate and gestured for her to lead the way. "Agent Reid."

She walked along the corridor, trying to assess what Phelps' slant was going to be once Copeland arrived. The conversation she'd had with Quinn also sprang to mind and she realized her observations of the congressman could be vital. Would he fit her initial profile of the unsub or Quinn's idea of who was behind the murders?

Phelps closed his door. "Before he gets here, I'd like to establish some ground rules. I get that you all are the Feds and you can pretty much take over this investigation, especially considering it now appears to involve a member of congress."

"That's not why we're here, detective," Dwight replied. "We read the ME's report. We understand that there is physical evidence that Mr. Copeland was with Janine Atherton."

"That's correct, and Mr. Copeland is respecting the investigation by offering up his statement."

"But the fact of the matter is, it's taken Copeland almost two weeks to come in and it appears the only reason is because of the forensics." Kate noticed Dwight's dagger-like look and changed her tone. "Regardless of how long it's taken, we can now at least rule out the congressman as a suspect. That has to be done if we wish to pursue other leads."

"I couldn't agree more, Agent Reid." Phelps' line buzzed. "Detective, Mr. Copeland is here to see you."

"I'll come and get him. Thank you." He turned to Dwight. "If you all would remain here, I'll bring him back. It's best if we do this in here and not in an interrogation room. I don't want the man to think he's being placed under arrest."

"Whatever you think is best, detective." Upon his departure, Dwight turned to Kate. "Agent Reid, if you're having difficulty remaining impartial, then maybe you should let Agent Vasquez and me handle this."

"No. I'm fine. I apologize if I overstepped. I'd like to stay— please."

"Don't make me do something we'll all regret," he replied.

Within minutes, Phelps returned with the congressman. "Mr. Copeland, I'd like to introduce you to Agent Reid, Agent Vasquez, and Supervisory Special Agent Jameson. They're helping us find Janine's killer."

"Good morning. I didn't expect an audience."

"Mr. Copeland, it's imperative we understand your relationship with Ms. Atherton so that we may continue to work toward excluding those she knew as possible suspects and look for her true killer." Dwight offered his hand.

"Thank you, Agent Jameson."

"Please, have a seat. This shouldn't take long." Phelps guided him to the chair and returned to his desk. "As you know, you're here because you and Janine attended a fundraiser the night of her death and according to the medical examiner's report, it appeared you two were intimate on that occasion as well. And so we'd like to ask you some questions as it pertains to that."

"Okay."

"And just for the record, you're here voluntarily and are not considered a suspect, but a person of interest in the investigation."

"I understand."

Hiding his anxiety seemed a chore as Kate watched him fidget in his seat and his eyes dart back and forth. Maybe Dwight was right.

Maybe she shouldn't be there because all she wanted to do was to watch him squirm, confident he was hiding something. "Excuse me for a moment." She wandered the halls until spotting a break room and once inside, Kate took inventory of her priorities as she peered through a window and onto the busy street. She had convicted this man before he even opened his mouth. A fatal flaw in someone who wore a badge. Once a champion of justice, she was not affording the congressman the same approach. But the worst part of all was that it wasn't because of him directly, it was Phelps and how he'd been skirting around her since she came on board. Assuming the two of them were operating together seemed logical but what if she was wrong?

If she couldn't get her act together, Dwight would throw her off the case and that would not only jeopardize the investigation, it would jeopardize her chances of working for Quinn because he would find out.

Kate returned to the office where Phelps was already engaging Copeland in a series of questions. Dwight cast a wary eye as she closed the door behind her. "I apologize for the inter-ruption."

Phelps nodded to her and redirected his attention to Copeland. "As you were saying, you and Janine were at the fundraiser and you left about twenty minutes before her departure."

"That's right."

"How do you know when she left? Did she contact you?" Kate was contravening but couldn't help herself in this instance.

"Yes. We are—were close. She indicated to me that she wanted to leave and I said that was fine. And so she did."

After yet another scathing glance from Dwight, Kate finally pulled back and watched as Phelps threw soft-ball questions at the congressman. Still, she observed him and still, he was nervous. Probably for the political life he was about to lose.

"Okay, Mr. Copeland. I think that should cover everything." Phelps began to rise. "Please call me if you think of anything else."

"I will, detective. Thank you." Copeland turned to Kate. "Agent Reid." He offered his hand.

"Sir. Thank you for coming down." She returned a reluctant handshake.

They waited for Phelps to escort the congressman out and it didn't take long for Dwight to pounce on Kate once again.

"You mind telling me what the hell is going on with you?"

"I'm sorry. I shouldn't have said anything at all. We're observers and that was my only job."

"You're damn right. In case you've forgotten, that man is a member of congress, not some thug on the streets being hauled in to flip on his boss."

"You think he deserves a pass because he's a politician?" Kate's anger began to rise.

"Okay, we aren't going to get into this here." Vasquez stood between them. "Let's just get back to the office and we can discuss it further."

It was a rare occasion when Dwight and Kate would disagree, but on this one, she knew she was in the right. Phelps was a dirty cop and was protecting Copeland as evidenced by his questions. But she couldn't prove it—not yet.

THE TENSION WAS PALPABLE, yet no one spoke on the drive back to the WFO. Kate knew she'd messed up and it would be up to her to apologize. It wasn't a position in which she'd often found herself, but Dwight deserved an apology.

Once they'd made it back inside, the words Kate had expected to hear came almost the second they stepped off the elevator.

"Reid, can I speak to you for a moment?" Dwight didn't stop and instead continued toward his office.

Kate turned to Vasquez. "Guess I deserve this."

"Hold your ground. I think you might be right on this one. Come find me when you're done."

"Yep. Thanks." Kate continued while Dwight had already disappeared beyond the corridor. When she arrived, he stood at his door.

"Have a seat." He closed the door behind her.

"Look, I know what you're about to say..."

"I don't think you do, Kate. You see, I've always been on your side. Always. I know the shit we deal with in the field and the sickening crimes we're expected to solve."

"Then why are you..."

"Let me finish. Whatever is going on between you and Detective Phelps needs to stop—now. I get he's an asshole. Anyone with eyes can see that. But that doesn't mean you can dismiss his role in his own goddam investigation."

"But this isn't like the others we've worked on. I mean, this guy dodges my calls, doesn't give me all the information. Did you know I had to get Janine Atherton's phone records myself because Phelps wouldn't forward them to me? And now there's this whole weird relationship between Copeland and Phelps. Did you listen to those questions? Are you kidding me? He was the last guy to see Janine alive, left DNA evidence behind, and never once does Phelps ask if he was the one who killed her. Kind of an important thing to establish, don't you think?"

"It doesn't matter what we think. Our job isn't to indict Mr. Copeland. That's Phelps' job, should it come to that. Our job is to help him find the person responsible for killing all three women and regardless of their past dealings with Copeland, I think you can see that the man is not a killer. Let alone the fact that he has alibis for his whereabouts when the other women were killed. So, I'm only going to say this one more time: back the hell off Phelps and do your job, Agent Reid. I get that you likely won't be here for much longer, but I will. And I'll be the one to suffer the wrath of the Metro Police if you sour that relationship."

Kate went slack-jawed and it took her a moment to realize it. Never before had Dwight spoken to her this way. Of course, never before had she ever given him cause to. "I'm sorry. I was unprofessional and I apologize. You warned me and I kept on."

The tension in Dwight's shoulders seemed to release. "Kate, this just isn't like you and so I realize that you truly believe something else is at play here, but until you find out what it is and whether it involves the congressman and or Phelps, I implore you —stay in that man's good graces. If he's in the congressman's pocket, your life is about to get infinitely more complicated and with what else you're trying to accomplish right now, I wouldn't test fate."

"What am I supposed to do in the meantime?"

"Get what you can from Pearson in Baltimore, from Vasquez, and I'll do what I can on my end to liaise between the two of you if necessary. But do not ruffle his feathers or Copeland's until you are damn well ready."

"Okay. I won't." She began to rise, tail tucked between her legs.

"Kate, I'm saying this for your own good as well as mine. How likely do you think Agent Quinn is going to be to bring you on if you've had a scuffle with local police that had the potential to damage an active investigation?"

She only stared back at him.

"I'm not trying to be an asshole. I'm trying to watch out for you —just like I always have."

"I know." She headed back to her desk where Vasquez waited

with what appeared to be bated breath. "I'm not fired or anything, if that's what you're waiting to hear."

"I didn't think you'd get fired. Look, I understand where you're coming from with this, but I bet whatever Jameson said to you, he's probably right."

"So you think I should back down too?"

"Yes and no. You just need to remember that you've already started down your own path, without Phelps, and I'll help you with that."

"Thank you." On her desk were the business cards Meredith Bowen's boss turned over. This was information Phelps knew nothing about. "Hey, I've made some progress on a few of these contacts, but you think you could give me a hand on a few more?"

"Those belonged to the latest victim?"

"Yeah. I need to know if she knew Copeland and how. Jameson can't shoot me down if I have legitimately connected the three victims to the congressman. At least, I don't think he can."

"Then hand over some of those puppies."

THE CONGRESSMAN THREW his keys on his desk and dropped into his chair. His office at home was the only place he believed he could go right now. Because if he went back to the Hill, he feared people would ask where he'd been. Officially, it was a personal appointment that didn't show up on his calendar, but if he was forced to lie about his whereabouts, that would make matters worse. Instead, he called Phil and told him he wasn't feeling well. So now he sat at his desk at home and dropped his head into his hands.

He had to start preparing for the inevitable. Phil was already doing most of the leg-work, but it would be up to him soon enough to start taking the hits. Copeland wondered who would be next and prayed it would not happen again, but the odds were against him.

He turned on his computer and began to search through his files, his contacts, emails, and anything else he could find to figure out if someone was doing this in retaliation. Who had he pissed off lately, besides his constituents? And did he really believe someone was killing these women to exact revenge? Seemed like a far-fetched plot straight out of a political thriller, but this was Copeland's life, the life of his family and something very bad was happening. As he carried on his search for someone, any one of his associates who could do such a thing, his emotions got the better of him. Not just for the loss of those innocent young women, but for all it was about to cost him.

"Hey? You're home?" The petite and slender woman in khakis and a button-down blouse appeared at his doorway. "I thought I heard the door. I was upstairs." She continued inside.

"Sue? I thought you'd be at school with the kids today."

"Not today. I volunteer on Wednesdays and Fridays. Today's Tuesday." Her brow furrowed as she drew near. "Are you okay?"

"Yeah, yeah, I'm fine. Just, you know, this whole thing with Janine and all."

"Oh, honey, I'm so sorry you're having to go through this. She was a good person and I'm sure a very good employee."

"She was."

"Do the police have any leads at all?"

He shook his head.

"That's just awful. It's still just so hard to believe." Sue folded her arms and cocked her head in sympathy. "Can I get you anything? A coffee? Have you had breakfast?"

"Um, yeah. I'll take a coffee, actually. Thank you, sweetheart."

"Will I have the honor of enjoying you home with me today, then?"

"I think so, yes. If that's okay."

She placed her hand on top of his. "Of course it is. I'm always here for you, just as you are for me. I'll be right back with some coffee and we'll have a nice talk."

"Thank you." He watched her leave and whispered, "I'm so sorry."

15

The correlation between Copeland and the latest victim, Meredith Bowen, appeared to be within reach. Hours Kate had spent sifting through contacts and the day had nearly come to an end when she came across the business card of a city councilman. The time had come to follow this and see if it led to Copeland, or if she really was on the wrong track and had developed some personal dislike for both the congressman and Detective Phelps, as Dwight had suggested, while a killer remained on the loose.

"I've got to run out. Probably won't be back." Kate grabbed her things.

"Where are you off to?" Vasquez pulled away from her research into the purchase of the material. "You find something?"

"Not sure yet. That's what I need to figure out. See you tomorrow?"

"Yeah, okay. Hey, let me know if it's something, yeah?"

"I will. Let Jameson know I left?"

Vasquez nodded.

Within minutes, Kate was on the road, heading toward the city of Manassas, about thirty minutes from D.C. Meredith Bowen was associated with this councilman in some way and when she'd made the call, the woman on the other end of the line wouldn't officially confirm Meredith's employment, instead suggesting Kate put in a formal request for information. And that was what she would do, along with using her skills to collect unofficial information in the process.

There was a reason for not making mention of this to her new boss and old friend, Dwight. He'd already made it clear for her to stay on her current path and finish her profile of the killer, but in her mind, this would accomplish just that. She still couldn't quite convince herself that it was Copeland who was responsible, in fact, the more she dug into the case, the less that seemed to be true. However, that didn't dismiss her hunch, and it was a strong one, that he had played some part in the murders, even if unwittingly so. And once she could establish a firm connection of all three victims to Copeland, Phelps wouldn't be able to ignore it and neither would Dwight.

On arrival, she approached the information desk at the city hall. "Excuse me." She retrieved her badge. "FBI Agent Kate Reid. I'm here to make a formal request for information concerning an ongoing investigation. Can you direct me to Councilman Hilgard's office, please?"

The man peered at her credentials and seemed to understand this was a matter of some importance. "Yes, ma'am. His office is down the hall and to the right. His assistant should be there to guide you."

"Thank you for your time." She continued along the corridor and reached the door labeled with the councilman's name and entered. "Hi, I phoned earlier regarding an investigation I'm working on. FBI Agent Reid. Was it you I spoke with?"

"Yes. Agent Reid. Hello. You're here to place a formal request for information?"

Kate moved closer and wore a concerned expression. "I am, but I was hoping you also might be able to help expedite the request or maybe offer something less formal that would help me find the person I'm looking for."

"I can try, but as I said on the phone..."

"I understand there's only so much you can do. But as I'm sure you can understand, this is a matter of urgency."

The middle-aged woman with the pixie haircut cast her gaze around as though she was being watched. "Well, why don't you tell me what you need and I'll see what I can do."

"Thank you so much." She retrieved the business card. "I came across this card. It belonged to a woman named Meredith Bowen."

"I'm familiar with Ms. Bowen."

"Unfortunately, she was murdered a few days ago."

"Oh my God. Oh my God, that's awful."

"Yes, it is. And that's why I'm here. It's very important that I understand what her relationship was with the councilman. Did she work for him? Was she a consultant? And, the relationship the councilman had with Representative Copeland. From what I gather, the congressman also served on this council a number of years ago."

"That's right. I'd only just come on board, but yes, Mr. Copeland served on this council from 2008 to 2011, when he decided to run for Congress." The woman began typing on her keyboard. "Let me see what I can find in the records."

"What records would those be?"

"Well, I have the meeting minutes, votes, agendas; pretty much everything pertaining to the council. If I recall correctly, Ms. Bowen presented before council a few times in the past. Let me see if I can find out when that was." She looked at Kate, who was standing over her desk. "You might want to take a seat. This could take a while."

"Oh, sure." This was exactly why she drove all the way down here because meeting face to face was always the way to get things done. That was what a lot of people failed to understand in this day and age when communication was almost exclusively via email and text messaging. Sometimes, face time was the best way to get something that might be outside the proper channels. An important lesson she learned from the man who recruited her.

"Okay, I found her name on three agendas over the course of two years. One in 2010 and two others in 2011. After that, she came on board to work for the councilman to facilitate coordination between the other districts."

"So Ms. Bowen worked for the councilman after 2011?"

"Well, during 2011 through 2015, according to her employment records." She eyed Kate. "Which, by the way, I'm not supposed to tell you."

"Of course."

"Anyway, she quit in 2015. Don't know what happened after that."

"She went to work for Representative Carter."

"Oh? Well, that's fantastic. Good for her." She appeared to immediately regret her comment. "I mean, it was good, but she's not here anymore."

"No, ma'am. Can I ask, the instances she presented to council, was Mr. Copeland in attendance?"

"Let me see. Yes. I see his name on the list of attendees."

"Were you aware of any other professional or maybe personal dealings Ms. Bowen had with Mr. Copeland? Lunches, calls, anything of that nature?"

"I really can't say."

"Are you sure? It's extremely important."

"Can't you ask the congressman?"

"Well, yes, however, I want to be sure I get an impartial answer. Unfortunately, Ms. Bowen can't speak for herself on the matter."

The woman appeared to consider Kate's request. "I just don't know how much I can say. I don't have a lot of firsthand experience on this issue."

"Can you tell me who does?"

She shot another look back and forth and again seemed to consider her choices. "Listen, I don't want to get anyone in trouble, but it's also a real shame that poor girl is gone. If I were you, I'd talk to Councilwoman McManus. I can give you her number."

Kate knitted her brow. "And she'll be able to shed some light on Ms. Bowen?"

"Yes. She was much closer to the situation than you might think. And I'm afraid that's all I can do for you, Agent Reid."

"Situation?" Kate decided not to push the assistant any more. "You've been more than helpful, ma'am. Really. Thank you." She took the sticky note with the name and number on it. "I'll contact her." Kate began to walk away.

"She's just down the hall. You could try popping in."

A smile appeared on her face. "I'll do that. Thank you so much."

"I hope you can get justice for Ms. Bowen."

"So do I. You have a good day." Kate left the office and continued in earnest along the lengthy halls of the city building in search of Councilwoman Jen McManus. She would not leave without answers. Putting together these puzzle pieces were key to finding the killer, she was sure of it, and Kate was not a woman who took no for an answer.

Upon spotting the councilwoman's office, she entered to find a small reception area where two people sat at workstations. "Good afternoon. I'd like to talk to Ms. McManus. Is she available?" Kate held out her badge.

A young, smartly dressed man eyed the badge. "Is she expecting you?"

"No. But it's important I speak with her. Can she spare a few minutes of her time?"

The man picked up the phone. "Ms. McManus, there's an FBI agent here to see you." He paused while listening. "Agent Kate Reid of the Washington Field Office, according to her credentials. Of course. I'll let her know." He ended the call. "She'll be right out. Can I get you something to drink while you wait?"

"No, I'm fine. Thank you, though." No sooner had Kate answered the question did the councilwoman appear from her office. "Ms. McManus? I'm Agent Reid. Can I speak to you for a moment?"

The councilwoman eyed her assistant before turning to Kate. "Certainly. Please, come in. This is rather unexpected. How can I help the FBI?"

Kate stepped inside and waited for her to close the door. "I'm investigating the death of a woman by the name of Meredith Bowen. And by the look on your face, you knew her?"

"I did. I haven't spoken to her in some time. Not since she went to work on the Hill. What happened to her?"

"She was shot in her apartment a few nights ago."

"Oh my God." She turned away. "How can I help?"

"I've been looking into Ms. Bowen's friends and contacts and it appears she had met or in some way had known Representative Grant Copeland. Are you familiar with him? I believe he served as a member of council here until 2011."

"That's right, he did. And yes, I know him. May I ask, is he a suspect?"

"No. Not at all, ma'am. I'm just looking to see who Ms. Bowen socialized with to get a fuller picture."

"Well, I can tell you, she wouldn't have socialized with the congressman."

"What makes you say that?"

"Is this off the record?"

"Of course."

"Grant Copeland is an egotistical, womanizing son of a bitch and most of the women, in this office at least, stayed as far away from him as possible."

"I see. So, did Ms. Bowen know him?"

"Oh, yes. I haven't spoken to her since she left here, but she and I shared more than a few lunches where Grant Copeland was the main topic of conversation."

"In what way?"

"Well, I'll tell you," She shook her head. "He tried to get his tentacles around her—and me, for that matter, but I held more power over him as a council member than she did as a staffer. The harassment lasted for some time and, in fact, I know it was the reason she left."

"Did she ever file a complaint? Did you?"

"Oh no. That's not how it works here. You deal with it and either move on or accept it. After a while, he stopped going after me because I think he knew what was at stake. But he kept on with Meredith. I guess I should've said something, but you know, well, I didn't. I guess there's no excuse for that."

"I understand that situation can be difficult to handle." Kate tried to empathize, but really, had never faced that sort of problem. Plenty of others, but sexual harassment wasn't one of them.

"I think once Grant decided to run for the House, things changed. She stayed on a while longer, but left about 18 months or so ago, working somewhere, I don't know, but we kept in touch via email and the occasional call. In fact, a member of the press approached her during his first campaign. Someone she'd known back in her journalism days, I guess. But he point-blank asked her if Grant had ever made unwanted sexual advances."

"And she said no?"

"That's right. I guess the reporter sort of let it go after that. I don't really know, but I figure he must've because I never saw anything about it in the papers. My God. Just doesn't seem real. I can't believe she's gone." She peered at Kate. "Does Grant know?"

"We have talked to him regarding other concerns. I can't say if he's aware of this or not."

"I bet he's not been very forthcoming with information on whatever it is you're looking for."

"Not exactly. In fact, I'm only here because I was speaking to Congresswoman Carter. Ms. Bowen worked for her after she left here. And through a series of contacts, I ended up here."

"I can say with a fair amount of confidence that Grant Copeland is not capable of murder."

"I don't believe he is either, Ms. McManus."

"Please, call me Jen."

"Jen. But in order for me to find the killer, I need to have a full understanding of Meredith's life. Her friends, her social life. I need to know who she was." Kate was hesitant to mention the other women because, as it was, she would likely see a letter of censure come her way if word got out about her inquiry, especially without Metro PD's knowledge.

"No, Grant's not a killer. He's an arrogant misogynist, but not a killer."

"Are you aware of any other of these types of relationships Mr. Copeland had like this? Any other staffers that you know of?"

"I'm not aware of any. However, I'd be fooling myself if I didn't believe there were plenty of other women out there who faced the same thing from him during his illustrious political career. I suspect if any of them came forward, he wouldn't have a political career to speak of."

"Sounds like that would be the case." It was the light-bulb moment she was waiting for. That was the key. Someone was either working to expose that side of the congressman, or working to keep it quiet.

"Agent Reid? Are you okay?"

"Yes, sorry. I was just thinking about something else."

"I'm afraid I don't have much else to tell you on the matter. I wish I did. I wish I'd kept in closer contact with Meredith." She teared up. "I'm so sorry she's gone."

"Can I ask you a final question?"

"Shoot."

"Given what you know about the congressman, do you feel he aspires to higher office?"

"Grant Copeland? Absolutely. If that man thought he could be president, he would go after it with everything he had. Hell, for all I know, he will."

Kate stood. "Thank you for your time, Jen. I can't tell you how much you've helped me. And Meredith."

"Oh, okay." She stood and walked toward the door. "If I think of anything else, I'll let you know." Kate was heading through the door when she continued. "Agent Reid, will you let me know when you find whoever was responsible for taking Meredith's life?"

"Of course I will. Goodbye, Ms. McManus—Jen."

16

S ue Copeland peered into her back garden while she washed her coffee mug in the sink. The afternoon caffeine pick-me-up was necessary in order for her to see the day through. Since the troubles began for her husband, she hadn't been sleeping well and in fact considered making an appointment to see her doctor. But for now, the coffee helped, but it did nothing to silence the thoughts in her mind. Her concern for Grant and his future weighed heavily on her shoulders—his too, she could see it. It seemed as though he was keeping the worst of it from her and had been playing down the potential damage this would cause when the story broke.

The familiar tone of the doorbell reached her ears and pulled her attention to the moment. Placing the cup in the drying rack, Sue wiped her hands on a kitchen towel and began walking toward the foyer. No butler or housemaid in this home. She preferred to see to the daily running of her own home and was a fan of solitude. That was due, in part, to Grant's job, which often found him in the public eye. And in part to her own personality trait. With the children almost grown, it was her time to reclaim herself and she preferred to do that alone.

Upon reaching the door, she peered through the side window draped with a sheer curtain panel. She opened the door, her face masked in concern. "Phil? What are you doing here? Grant's at the office."

"I came here to see you. Do you have a minute?"

"Of course. Please, come in." Sue stepped aside while Phil entered. "Can I get you something to drink? I think the coffee's still warm."

"No, thank you. I'm fine." He was already heading toward the living room. "There's something we need to talk about."

"So you said." She sat down on the chair opposite him. "I suppose this has to do with the investigation into Janine's death."

"Not just hers. There've been others."

"What others? Who worked for Grant? He hasn't said anything about this to me."

"That's because the other two victims didn't work for him directly. At least, not anymore."

"Well, who were these people? Did I know them? My God. I don't understand what's happening. Is someone after Grant? Phil, what else don't I know?"

"Look, Grant doesn't know I'm here. I need information that he doesn't want to share."

"What information? From what I gather, you know far more than I."

"Sue, I need access to his personal laptop. The one he keeps here at the house. Can you give me that?"

"Yes. I suppose so. But why? What do you think you're going to find?" Her voice began to fail.

"I don't know. I just need to cover all the bases. You understand? My job is to protect Grant—and you. I can't do that if he's keeping things from me."

She considered his request and noted the sincerity in his eyes. "Okay. I'll log in." Sue walked into Grant's office at the end of the hall and booted up his laptop.

Phil followed her inside. "I know what you must be thinking..."

"That my husband could be lying to the both of us?" She entered the password.

"I don't know anything for sure." He moved closer and examined her features, placing his hand on her shoulder. "I know how afraid you must feel right now. I'm here to make sure you both stay on the right side of this."

"Might as well sit down, I guess." She stepped aside and folded her arms in anticipation of what he might find.

"I'd feel better if you let me do this alone. I know what I'm asking, but if and I mean, *if*, I find anything, I'd rather see it before you do."

"Fine." She left him alone and waited for several minutes in the kitchen. What was she going to tell Grant about today? She supposed that would depend on whether Phil discovered anything. "Damn it. I can't just sit here." She made her way back into the office where Phil still sat in front of the laptop. "Anything?"

"No. Not that I can find." He closed the lid and stood. "I'm sorry to have put you through this. Believe me, I am."

"It's okay. I understand, I guess. You're trying to protect him." She noted his approach as he stood inside her personal space. He was so close, she could smell his cologne that mixed with the minty scent of his breath.

With his index finger, he tucked the short brown strands of hair behind her ear. "Everything's going to be okay, Sue. You don't deserve to go through this and I'll do what I can to mitigate the damage."

"You've always been there for us." She stepped back slightly to reestablish her space. "I appreciate your concern."

"I'd like to ask a favor of you before I go."

"Yes?"

"I'd like to ask that you not tell Grant I was here today. It'll only make him question my loyalty and that's the last thing any of us needs right now. I need to know that you'll keep this between us."

"Of course I will." An uneasy smile formed on her lips. "I'll show you out." Sue moved into the hall and toward the foyer, feeling the steps of the man behind her. "Grant knows you're loyal to him, but I promise I won't mention anything about today. I know how difficult it must have been for you to make the choice to come here without his knowledge." She pulled open the door.

"I want for nothing except to know that you're safe. You and Grant." His eyes bored into her as he again placed his hand on her shoulder, sliding it down until he reached her hand. He raised it and pressed it against his chest. "This, too, shall pass, Sue. I just need a little time."

She nodded and gently pulled away her hand. "Goodbye, Phil." She watched him step beyond the threshold and turn a final time to acknowledge his departure. He stepped into his car and soon disappeared beyond the end of the drive.

KATE'S ENTHUSIASM about uncovering a link between Copeland and Meredith Bowen had given her the courage to approach Quinn once again. Given their previous discussion, she wanted his thoughts and now walked through the halls of the BAU Headquarters and headed straight for his office. "Excuse me, Agent Quinn?"

"Reid? I wasn't expecting you." He pulled away from the file on his desk.

"I should've called first. I'm sorry. I can come back another time."

"No, don't be ridiculous. You already made the drive. I have to assume you have something important on your mind. Come in."

"Thank you. I do have some news." Upon taking her seat, she began with her enthusiasm no less tempered. "What we discussed the other night—well, I wasn't really sure how to proceed except that I knew I needed to find a connection between the latest victim and Grant Copeland."

"And did you?"

She nodded. "I did. Apparently, Meredith Bowen was the recipient of what appeared to have been several unwarranted sexual advances on the part of Mr. Copeland."

"While she was in his employ?"

"No. She never worked for him directly. And this was some time ago, while he was still a councilman."

"You now have proof that he knew the three women who are now dead. The final victim, while not having worked for him, knew him."

"That's right."

"So, tell me, Reid, what are you going to do with this information? Does it lead you to conclude Copeland is your unsub?"

"No. Not at all. I've been toying with the idea that it could be one of two scenarios and I wanted to bounce them off you. Firstly, and this one I think is the most likely, I figure someone's out to get him."

"That doesn't narrow down much in the way of a suspect, does it?"

"Well, no. But hear me out. I'd like to consider the possibility that it could be a political enemy."

"Copeland would've had to make some hellish enemies to kill off three women he'd known." He regarded Kate carefully. "Dig deeper. A political enemy would almost certainly damn himself and any future career were the truth to be exposed. A far too risky proposition."

"Even if said foe hired someone to do the job?"

"I believe so, yes. And especially if it was a hired hit. Because that means the hired killer was motivated by money and not loyalty. And you still have to consider that whoever is doing this knows of Copeland's affairs. That's probably information he hasn't possibility shared."

She sighed and considered her other proposition. "Then it's someone who's trying to keep the truth from being exposed. Someone who's trying to protect Copeland."

Quinn nodded. "A more likely situation, in my mind. But who would be willing to go to prison for murder to protect the congressman? It would have to be someone fiercely loyal."

"Who felt protected in some way," Kate added. "Like if it were discovered, he or she would be safe from prosecution."

"Who do you think is safe from prosecution? That's a stretch to suggest."

"Not if the person thinks the cops will help hide the truth."

"And so we get back to Detective Phelps."

"Maybe." Kate was beginning to feel frustrated. "I thought I was on the right track, but as you say, it would be a stretch."

"Yes, but I wouldn't say you're completely out in left field. I'd say to look inside Copeland's inner circle. And, as we discussed previously, I'm inclined to believe the killer could still be a woman. I wouldn't rule out Mrs. Copeland. She stands to lose the most if her husband's past comes back to haunt him. Disgrace, humiliation, and his income."

"You think I should question her? On the basis of what?"

"Exclusion. Simple as that. You're looking to exclude her from any involvement so that you can continue to search for the killer. And I would put it in those terms. Go see her, if you can without backlash from the detective. Get a feel for what her marriage is like. What she's like. You do that, and you'll know if you're on the right track."

"I'm supposed to see Phelps later this afternoon. He has the forensics back on Meredith Bowen. Of course, he didn't divulge any of the results. I suppose if DNA had come back on the skin under the nails, he'd have arrested the person already. Made himself look the hero. So I just don't know what I'll find when I get there."

"Whatever it is, it'll be more than you know right now."

She nodded with greater confidence than when she arrived. "Yes. Thank you, Agent Quinn."

"I didn't do much. Just showing you different perspectives. That's probably the most important thing we can do in this job. Don't wear blinders. Look at all possible options."

"I appreciate your help and I'm sorry to barge in. I'll be sure and call next time."

"Don't worry about it. It's a pleasure working with you, Agent Reid. And, I'd like to continue this as part of the interviewing process. Why don't we plan to meet up as often as you need to? I'd like to help if I can."

"Absolutely. Thanks again. I'd better head out." Kate left his office, head down and determined to figure out if what she had meant anything at all.

"Kate?" Nick appeared from around the corner. "I didn't know you were coming here today."

"Oh. Hi. I was in my head just then. Um, yeah, it was spur of the moment. I needed to bounce some ideas off of Agent Quinn regarding the investigation. He just said we should meet as needed to help us continue forward on this one."

"That's a good sign." He moved in closer. "You going to be home for dinner tonight? Thought maybe we could go out to eat."

"I should be, but I'll let you know. I'd like to go out." She smiled. "I'll talk to you later."

"Okay." Nick shoved his hands in his pockets and watched her leave.

FOR MORE THAN TEN YEARS, Sue Copeland let Grant and all his so-called advisors tell her how to dress, how to behave, what to say, and what to think. Well, that would stop now. And her first plan of action was to see for herself what Phil had been looking at on Grant's laptop.

She marched into his office and turned on the computer. Phil had trust in her and that would work to her advantage now. She doubted he would've gone through the trouble of clearing the computer's event log and that was where she would start looking.

There had been a time in the not too distant past when she began to feel a lack of trust for her husband. She was well acquainted with his behavior and so she'd learned how to keep track of what he was doing on his computer. And of course, he trusted her implicitly, so he had not suspected she would ever consider viewing the contents of his computer herself. And while she hadn't felt compelled to do so in quite some time, today was not one of those days.

Sue opened the control panel and the event logs. Each location Phil had visited had been logged in. What files he'd accessed, if he'd accessed the internet and if he'd made any changes to the programs—added or deleted anything.

When the logs loaded, she examined the information. From what she could see, Phil accessed Grant's email contacts, viewed his personnel files, which contained a few higher-ranking individuals and were also password-protected. Even Sue didn't have that password and doubted Phil was able to view it. And finally, he'd gone online, presumably to view Grant's browsing history. That was the first place she would start.

Once the browser opened, she checked the history. Nothing unusual. He had visited investment sites, government sites, and others that appeared inconsequential. Nothing there. Except there was one other place she could check and that was the temporary internet file history. Upon opening the file, she'd found it had been erased. Nothing was in the temp file, which should have, at the very least, shown what Phil had opened. That was red flag number one.

Exiting that system, Sue began to view Grant's contact list. Still, nothing seemed unusual, with the exception that she hadn't known most of the people on it. Instead, she would view the files he'd accessed. "Damn it." Grant's email was the last place she'd wanted to check. The problem was that it would automatically download any new emails and that might raise concern once Grant used his computer again. Still, would he even notice? Probably not and so she decided it was worth the risk.

Upon opening the email account, it behaved exactly as it was supposed to and began downloading recent emails. It wasn't until the final email downloaded that she grew concerned. Sue clicked on the message that was from a woman by the name of Karen Hildebrand. She didn't know the name and there was no subject line. But immediately, her hackles raised.

"*I told you not to contact me again. You need to let this go and I will not be harassed. Don't make me hate you, Grant.*"

She scrolled down farther as it had been a reply to an earlier message. That message had been sent only an hour ago. It was possible Grant had logged into his personal email from his office computer, but he rarely did so. Sue continued to read the message.

"*I don't think you're safe. You should go and stay with a friend or family outside of D.C. Please—I know how things ended between us, but I'm telling you this for your own good. Please reply so I know you got my message. I'm so sorry.*"

"What the hell is this?" Sue eyed the office as if the answer would simply present itself to her, but no. It would not and she would have to figure this one out on her own. Who sent this message? "And who the hell is Karen Hildebrand?"

17

The Metro Police station was in sight as Kate pulled alongside the front of the building where a few metered spaces were open. The day was drawing to a close and coming here wasn't her first choice, however, keeping up appearances of agency cooperation was paramount. A ding on her record were Phelps to complain of a lack of support would only serve to damage her future plans. Still, she couldn't help but wonder if he would fully share the findings of the forensics report on Meredith Bowen, or would pick and choose what he revealed. There was no doubt the detective was doing his best to keep her out of the loop. And trying to prove that would be the hard part. But for now, she had a way forward and would need his cooperation in order to succeed. Something she would get, one way or another.

Inside, Kate approached the lobby desk and before getting the chance to introduce herself and why she was here, the man she'd seen before appeared to recognize her.

"Agent Reid. You here to see Phelps?"

"I am, yes."

"I'll call him right up, ma'am."

"Thank you." If only Phelps was so cooperative instead of behaving like a self-important prick who was almost certainly taking money to help keep Copeland's name out of the press.

"Reid. Come on back." Phelps arrived but scarcely stopped before turning on his heel and heading back toward his office.

"What a warm welcome," she whispered under her breath.

"Thanks for stopping by. Let me show you the report and you can be on your way." Phelps retrieved the file and tossed it onto his desk, sliding it toward her. "Meredith Bowen was shot in the chest, as you know, but it appears to have been at near point-blank range, meaning..."

"Meaning gun powder residue."

"That's right. I'm already working on a trace of the weapon from the shell casing found on the scene. Interesting that we hadn't found casings near the other victims, which suggests the killer is getting sloppy. Also, the graze to her head left telling signs of a struggle."

"Any DNA reports?" She continued to view the file. "I understand the ME found skin under the nails."

He appeared concerned she had been made aware of this fact. "Nothing yet. All we've got are the forensics. No labs. As soon as I get those, I'll forward you the info."

He was keeping something from her. Perhaps he already had the labs and didn't want to share what he knew. It would be easy to get to the truth. She'd already seen Dr. Carr and making a call would be the only way to know for sure. If that was the case, Kate would have the upper hand and Phelps would be out on his ass.

She peered up at the detective. "Can I ask you something?"

"Go ahead."

"Have I done something to offend you?"

"Sorry?"

"I feel as though you'd really prefer if we weren't involved. I'm just trying to figure out why."

"Look, it's nothing personal, Reid. I just don't like it when the Feds come and start sniffing around my investigation. I know what I'm doing and I don't like being second-guessed. Sorry if that offends you."

"I'm not here to second-guess you, detective. I'm here to offer a profile on the unsub and get you what you need to find the person responsible."

"Last I checked, you still don't have a complete profile."

"That's because I'm still waiting on labs and forensics. I've shared with you what I know so far."

"Yeah well, what you have describes just about every perp I've got on the books, Agent Reid. I'm not trying to piss you off or shove you aside. I'm just trying to do my job."

"So am I." She returned to the file and continued reading. That was when she spotted it and had to read it again. "Did you read this in its entirety?"

"I did." He approached her. "Why? What'd you find?"

"The trajectory of the bullets that struck the chest and the graze is almost identical to the shot fired at Tasha Brenner. According to Agent Pearson, Brenner stood from her bed to defend herself and the killer placed her where she was discovered."

"And?"

"And that suggests the person was taller than both of these women. That we know this person must be at least 5'10" to 6 feet tall?"

"Sounds about right. I'm sorry, am I missing something here? This adds nothing new to your assumptions. You already suggest the killer is male. One would assume the male to be taller than his female victims."

"Yes, but now it appears conclusive. And now we can narrow down the field when talking to the people in their circles. Don't you think this is something I would find important to my profile?"

"Yes. Which is why I invited you here this afternoon. Look, I'm starting to feel as though it's you who has the problem here, not me. You're defensive, overbearing, and frankly, you don't have nearly enough experience to be doing this sort of work. I was doing this job when you were still in braces."

The argument was about to escalate, and he had a point. He was the one who invited her to view the report. She was in the wrong in this instance, as much as she didn't want to admit it. Her prejudice against him had become transparent and she was about to jeopardize everything. What she was saying was not new and yet she wanted desperately to find something he was withholding from her. "I apologize. I will add this information and, hopefully, we'll get DNA back on the skin samples, which I'm sure you'll pass along to me as soon as you get them. That could be the answer to everything."

"You think I'm not well aware of that?" But before he could finish, the arrival of a woman standing in the doorway drew both of their attention away from the current circle jerk of conversation and prevented Kate from digging a deeper hole.

"Mrs. Copeland?" Phelps approached her. "What are you doing here, ma'am? Is everything okay?"

She cast a glance to Kate and then back to Phelps. "I was hoping for an update on the investigation into Janine Atherton."

"Come inside, please." He took her gently by the arm. "I'm not sure you should be here, ma'am. I had promised your husband's chief of staff I would do everything in my power to keep him out of the papers while we're investigating these terrible crimes. Your being here could threaten that."

Kate wondered what power he had wielded to do such a thing and how much it had cost Copeland.

"I'm not trying to jeopardize anything. I just—I just need to know." She looked at Kate. "I'm sorry, but who are you?"

"Agent Kate Reid. FBI." She stood and offered her hand. "Nice to meet you, Mrs. Copeland."

"Are you helping the detective?"

"Yes. My team and I are working with Detective Phelps and the authorities in Baltimore in a connected investigation."

"I see. Yes, I—I had heard there were others." She turned back to Phelps. "Detective, this has begun to take its toll on my husband. He doesn't know I'm here and I would appreciate it if you didn't tell him. Are you any closer to finding the person responsible for killing those women?"

"We are getting closer, yes."

"Is there anything I can do to help? Anything you need at all?"

"No, ma'am. Just keep doing what you're doing. Your support for the congressman is what's needed most right now. I appreciate your offer, but you should really go. Reporters are always hanging around and for them to spot you, well, it would not do us any good."

"Of course. I understand. I'm sorry to have bothered you." She again looked at Kate.

"Why don't I walk you out? I was just leaving anyway." Kate approached her, noting a sideways glare from the detective. "Thank you for the information, detective. I'll be in touch." Kate ushered Mrs. Copeland away.

As they walked outside, Kate considered if Mrs. Copeland had wanted to reveal something and that on noticing an FBI agent, she opted to hold her tongue, doubtful of the impact on her husband. This could be a blessing in disguise. Revealing something about her husband might fall on deaf ears if it had been only Phelps in the room and she might not have had this chance. The time was now to ask the question proposed by Quinn and convince Mrs. Copeland that Kate was there to help her. "Ma'am, can I ask you a couple of questions regarding your husband?"

"Of course."

Just as they reached the end of the walkway, Kate stopped her. "I can see that you want answers as it relates to the tragic deaths of those who knew the congressman."

"Yes. Of course I do."

"That said, I'd like to ask you something very personal and I, in no way, mean any offense." She waited a moment for any objections and when none came, Kate continued. "Were you aware of any transgressions made on the part of your husband in the recent past?"

"You mean do I know if my husband cheated on me?"

Kate nodded. "I'm sorry to ask, but it's relevant to the investigation because I believe..."

"You believe he was sleeping with Janine Atherton."

This wasn't exactly as Quinn proposed, but Kate had to run with it now. "I do, ma'am. Evidence suggests..."

"My husband is a good father, I'll say that about him. But our kids are almost grown and well, were he not in the public eye, I doubt we would still be married. Not that that's what I would want, but Grant has and always has had a wandering eye. I believe he was having an affair with Ms. Atherton and I also believe she was not the only one."

"Do you have any proof of their relationship?"

"No. I don't. Do you?"

Kate couldn't reveal the facts of the DNA report as it could threaten the investigation. "What about the others?"

"The other victims? I can't say because I don't know who they are. That's one of the reasons why I was here. I'd hoped to get clarity on that issue."

"Is there anyone on your husband's staff who might know anything? A confidant?"

Mrs. Copeland turned away. "I can't remember where I parked."

"I'm sorry to have to ask you these things. I'm sure it's difficult to hear."

"Are you married, Agent Reid? Do you have children?"

"No—on both counts."

"Well, let me just tell you that it's far more difficult than you might think. Especially being married to a politician. I've stood by my husband for many years, watched his career soar, and I've been willing to overlook certain character flaws. But if he is in any way responsible or caused the deaths of those girls, I'll be the first to make sure he's held accountable. So, as far as a close staff member, yes. His chief of staff, Phil Vega. In fact, Phil came to see me earlier today, another prompting for my visit here."

"What did he want?"

"To look at Grant's computer."

"And did he?"

She nodded. "He said he didn't find anything, so after he left, I decided to have a look. I've done it before, though not in a while. I guess I thought I was past that stage. I was wrong. I'd seen an email from a woman who didn't want anything to do with Grant. And the real reason why I came today is that I believe that woman should be warned that those who've crossed paths with Grant seem to be paying a high price for their association."

"Can you tell me the name of this woman? Mrs. Copeland, if you think someone is in danger, please—let me get word to her. Let me protect her."

"Isn't that a little outside your wheelhouse? I was planning on saying something to Detective Phelps, but I get the feeling Grant may have gotten to him already. I've seen it before. But I don't see that in you."

"I can help this woman, whoever she is."

Mrs. Copeland reached into her handbag and retrieved a slip of paper. "This is who the email came from. I'm afraid I don't know who she is or where she lives, but I suppose you'd be able to find that out somehow."

"Thank you. Yes, I'll be able to track her down. Mrs. Copeland, you might have just saved this woman's life."

"I don't know if she was involved with my husband or not, but she doesn't deserve to die, if that's what's happening here. God knows what the hell is going on." She raised her hand to shield her eyes. "I see my car ahead. I really must go now. You won't tell anyone it was me who gave you the name?"

"I don't know what's going on either, Mrs. Copeland. I wish I did. But this will remain between us. Thank you again. And if you need anything at all. If you feel as though you are no longer safe, please call me. I mean that." She handed her a business card. "Any time. Day or night."

"I will. But I don't believe for one second Grant killed those women and I don't believe I am in any danger. If I did, I would've packed up my children and left already. Goodbye, Agent Reid."

Kate watched as she headed toward her car and drove away. She retrieved her cell phone. "Hey, it's me. Can you run a name for me? Karen Hildebrand. I have an email address. I'll text it to you. If you can't track down a location or phone number, we might have to email her." She paused. "It's possible she's the next target. We have to act quickly."

～

AGENT VASQUEZ TURNED AWAY from her desk at the arrival of her partner. "Karen Hildebrand. 28, single, no kids, lives in Alexandria in a two-bedroom brownstone. Should we go talk to her?"

"Absolutely." Kate nodded. "We should swing by Jameson's office and let him know." She led the way.

"Afternoon. By the look on your faces, something's happened. What's going on?"

"I ran into Mrs. Copeland while I was meeting with Phelps at the station. He received additional forensics information, though no DNA yet. Anyway, to our surprise, the congressman's wife appeared in his doorway. Phelps tried to get her to leave and after a somewhat tactless effort on his part, I offered to walk her out and she was more than willing to discuss her husband's history."

"Reid called me a short time ago and gave me a name. Said it came from Mrs. Copeland and that it's possible this woman might be in danger. I ran the name and got her address. We wanted to head there now."

"Where is she?"

"Alexandria."

Dwight grabbed his keys and phone. "Good. I'm coming with you. You can fill me in on the drive."

KATE PEERED through the windshield as they approached the home. "I think this is it."

"Do we know if she's there?" Vasquez leaned forward from the back seat. "It's after six. She might be."

"If she's not, you got a cell phone number, right?" Dwight asked.

"No. Just email, but I do have a work number. We can try

that." Vasquez stepped out. "We're here now, so might as well give it a shot and hope for the best."

Kate stepped out of her car and waited for the team to join her on the sidewalk. "So, are we just going to tell her that her life's in danger?"

"First thing we need to understand is how she knows Copeland and gain insight into what's been going on between them in recent days and we'll go from there." Dwight started up the steps to the door and pressed the intercom. Several moments passed when he looked to his team and tried again.

"Yes?"

"Ms. Hildebrand, I'm Agent Jameson with the FBI. We'd like to have a few words with you regarding Grant Copeland."

Another span of silence and then the door clicked open.

"Let's go." Dwight led the way into the entrance where another door awaited. He knocked.

"Can I see some ID, please?" The voice of Ms. Hildebrand sounded through the door.

"Of course." Dwight pulled out his badge and held it in front of the security lens. "Agent Dwight Jameson. I'm here with Agents Reid and Vasquez. It's very important we speak to you, Ms. Hildebrand."

She opened the door. "Come in. What is it that you want?"

Kate wasn't expecting the curt response. "We won't take up much of your time. We just need to ask you some questions, Ms. Hildebrand."

"Of course. I'm sorry. It's Karen. Please, have a seat in the living room. You'll have to forgive me. I've been somewhat stressed out today. And, my house is a mess."

"It's fine. I understand." Kate sat down next to Vasquez. "We'd like to speak with you regarding an ongoing investigation."

"Somehow I expected you would show. You or the cops. This is about Grant Copeland?" She appeared frail and shaken.

"It is, yes. Have you been in contact with the congressman recently?" Kate was cautious of just how much to reveal at the moment.

"Unfortunately, yes. Though it sort of came out of the blue. I hadn't heard from him in quite some time. Then he just sends me an email about..." She looked uncertain.

"Karen, please continue. We'd like to understand your relationship with Mr. Copeland," Dwight replied.

"Relationship? That ended long ago, which was why his email was such a surprise to me."

"What was in the email?" Vasquez urged her.

"I guess you could say it was a warning. I don't know how else to take it."

"A warning? What was he warning you about?" she added.

"Well, he said I could be in danger. I assume that's why you're here? He must've said something to you? You did mention an investigation involving him?"

"There is, but no. He was not the one who referred us to you. In fact, it was Mrs. Copeland who'd seen the email exchange earlier today."

"Oh my God."

"Before we get too far ahead of ourselves," Kate began, "can you tell me when your relationship with the congressman ended?"

"It was, geez, more than a year ago. Around the time he began his bid for re-election. He was the one who ended it. Cleaning up his little messes before hitting the trail. He's always the one who ends it. I guess that's the way it works with a married man." She turned away. "I can't imagine what you must think of me."

"You'll get no judgment from us, Karen. How did you meet him?" Dwight asked.

"We travel in the same circles; well, we used to until I got out."

"Got out?"

"I quit politics after he and I split up. It's all such bullshit, you know? Full of games and lies and deceit. I thought I could make a difference, but I was wrong."

"And when it ended, there were no hard feelings?" Kate continued her line of questioning.

"No. I was pissed for a while, but I never threatened to tell his wife or anyone he knew, for that matter. I just wanted to be done with it and move on with my life. And I had until I got that email. Freaked me out."

"I'm sure it did." Kate looked to Dwight for permission to tell her why they were there. When he nodded, she continued, "There've been some developments regarding women who had crossed paths with Mr. Copeland."

"You mean others who he had affairs with?"

"Mainly, yes, with one exception. But, my point is that three of these women have died."

"Jesus. Like murdered?"

"Yes."

"And what? You think I'm next? Oh my God. Are you serious? So his email was right? He told me to get out of town. I thought it was some political mess he was trying to cover up or something. What am I supposed to do?"

"That's why we're here," Dwight added. "I think we should get you someplace safe until we know more."

"You don't know who killed them, do you?"

Kate shook her head. "With your help, you could get us a step closer, but we do ask that you come with us tonight so that we can keep you safe." She noticed the woman, who was only a few years younger than her, tremble with fear like a child. "I'm sure this must be a shock to you and I'm sorry for that. But, Karen, it's important we get you out of here—tonight."

18

An old-fashioned gas-style lamppost was the only illumination in an otherwise shadowy area near Lincoln Park where Phelps waited for Copeland to arrive. The time had come to warn him of what was about to happen. No amount of money was going to keep this out of the press any longer, nor would it offer protection from scrutiny, a fact that had emerged the moment Copeland's wife decided to visit the station earlier in the day, while a reporter who often loitered in search of a story noticed her arrival.

Phelps spotted headlights approach in the distance and when the car pulled alongside his own on the quiet road, he knew it was the congressman. Upon approach to the driver's side window, he rapped the knuckle of his index finger against the glass. Copeland rolled down his window in response and Phelps began, "'Bout time you showed up."

"Sorry. I got held up at the office. As I'm sure you can imagine, it's been a difficult time for my staff. We aren't getting much work done at the moment." He opened his door and placed one foot on the sidewalk.

"Don't. There are cameras around here. Best to keep your face hidden. You know your wife came to see me today?"

As he closed the door again, Copeland replied, "I didn't know that. Why?"

"Asking questions about the investigation. And her timing couldn't have been worse. Agent Reid was with me reviewing the Bowen file."

"Shit."

"Shit is right."

"What'd you do?"

"I tried to calm her nerves. Then Agent Reid showed her out. I spotted them talking outside for a few minutes. Don't have any idea what they talked about because Reid left right after that."

"Damn it. You summoned me just to tell me that? What is it I'm supposed to do? Jesus. I don't even know why the hell they went after Meredith. I never slept with her. I'm starting to lose my shit, Phelps. And now this?"

"What are you supposed to do? You're going to get your wife in line because I'll tell you what, Agent Reid isn't your only problem. A bottom-feeder was hanging out at the station, spotted her, and came to me and started asking questions."

"You mean a reporter?"

"Yes, a goddamn reporter. This isn't going away, Copeland, and the time's come for you to get a handle on it. I've done everything I can do, but your wife just screwed us, big time." Phelps surveyed the area for any bystanders. "Look, be ready 'cause shit's about to hit the fan."

"What the hell are you going to do about this, Phelps? Huh? You think I'm going to let you leave me flapping in the wind?"

Phelps' eyes turned dark and his expression hardened. "Are you threatening me?"

Copeland seemed to shrink back. "No. I'm just... I'm just trying to find a solution to this. Do you even have any idea who the hell you're after? Who the hell is trying to destroy my life?"

Phelps retrieved a cigarette from his pocket and placed it between his lips. With the lighter's flame flickering at its end, he continued, "Here's what you're going to do." He inhaled until it caught fire and continued to talk. "You're going to come in tomorrow and make a statement."

"I already did that."

"Listen carefully. You're going to make another statement. This time, you need to reveal how you knew those women. Look, we have no evidence to suggest you were involved in any way with their deaths. You have alibis. And we can prove you were at the hotel when Atherton was killed. That's the good part."

"And the bad part?"

"I doubt the media or the public will care about that. But you won't be arrested."

"For God's sake. This is going to ruin me."

"Your concern for the victims is touching."

KATE TUCKED the sheets in between the couch cushions. "There you go. I hope this is okay for you."

"It's perfect. Thank you, Agent Reid."

"You're welcome, Karen, and please call me Kate. I understand what you're going through more than you know." She placed a reassuring hand on her shoulder. "You're safe here."

In that moment, keys sounded in the lock of the front door, capturing their attention.

Nick entered the apartment. "Hello. I didn't know we were expecting company." He continued inside and greeted Kate with a kiss on the cheek. "Who's your friend?"

"This is Karen Hildebrand."

"Nice to meet you, Karen. Nick Scarborough."

"I told her she could stay here until we can make other arrangements. It was too late to secure accommodations."

"Okay."

The confusion on his face imposed the need for further explanation and Kate would have to call for a sidebar. "Will you excuse us for just a moment?" She gestured toward their bedroom and Nick followed.

"What's going on?" He folded his arms across his chest.

"She's in danger. It's a long story, but we believe she could be a target of the same person who killed the other women."

"We?"

"The team. I had an unexpected meeting with Mrs. Copeland. It turns out that the congressman sent Karen an email stating she could be in danger."

"Are you serious? He sent that via email? Didn't think to warn her in person, or maybe the cops?"

"Now you see what I'm dealing with? But yeah. His personal email, by all accounts."

"Copeland must assume that whoever's after these women is after them because he had affairs with each one."

"Seems so. Although Meredith Bowen, the latest victim, doesn't appear to have had any physical relationship with him. He harassed her, according to her acquaintances. I'm aware this isn't protocol..."

"You and the team did what you thought was best to keep that woman safe. I wouldn't second-guess your decision. I didn't when

I was there and I won't do it now. If you think she's in danger, she can stay as long as it takes."

"Thank you. I don't want to tell Phelps she's here. He'll skewer me."

"Based on what you've told me, that seems probable. What's your plan then?"

"Set up surveillance on her house. I want to know who comes to visit."

"That's what I would do. You need help getting that set up?"

"No. Dwight's already on it."

"Good. And what about Phelps and Copeland?"

"Now that I've been able to establish a clear connection between all of the victims and Mr. Copeland, I'm going to ask for an arrest warrant."

"You're going to arrest a sitting congressional representative? On what charge? You said you were certain he wasn't the killer. Kate, you might want to rethink your strategy. I just said I wouldn't second-guess you and here I am. But the reason I say that is you get him spooked like that. Arrest him. The press will hound you and this will be all over the news."

"And I might scare away the real killer?"

"You're confident it isn't Copeland, right?"

"Right."

"Then it's entirely possible whoever it is will high-tail it the hell out of Dodge. There'll be too much heat and any more women out there who've gotten tangled up with Copeland will be exposed. That might be what you want. I don't know. The problem is, you still don't have a motive. Whose agenda do these murders serve?"

"Then what? I don't know if there are more people out there like Karen. If there are, and someone else knows it, I can't protect them. I still have no DNA evidence on anyone other than

Copeland and that doesn't prove anything. I can't find the owner of the cell phone who made all those random calls to the victims. It was likely a burner. I'm running out of options, Nick."

"What does Dwight say?"

"He agrees we should look into Copeland's inner circle. According to Mrs. Copeland, his chief of staff, Phil Vega, is the man in the know. He's given a statement to Phelps. He's been cooperating. And, he made a visit to the wife today and checked out what was on Copeland's computer."

"Did he find anything?"

"That's how we found Karen."

"You run a background check on this Phil Vega?"

"Alicia's working on that as we speak. She's supposed to let me know tonight what she comes up with. It's just—this is all stuff that should've been done already. If one more person dies because Phelps was protecting the congressman..."

"Just keep doing what you're doing. Sounds like you already found your way forward. You don't need my advice, except I will say this. Arresting Copeland on the grounds that he had relations with those women isn't going to fly. Being a philanderer isn't illegal in this country. Well, it might be some states, but you catch my drift."

"I do. I'm just eager to get the truth from him about his affairs and any others he's hiding and I have a feeling he won't willingly offer it. I'm sure he knows more than he's letting on. Or maybe Vega does. After I hear back from Alicia, she and I will make a trip to see him. Depending on what we find, I'll go from there."

"You got it under control, Kate. Just don't screw up where a congressman is concerned. I'd be hard-pressed to say your career would survive it. By the way, what's Quinn's take?"

"He's opened my eyes to things I hadn't considered."

That's kind of the point, right?"

"It is. I'm trying to remain cautiously optimistic, as they say, about the position. I hope he'll make a decision soon."

"Me too. I could use you at my side again. Don't get me wrong, I've got a great team, but with you there, we would be unstoppable."

KATE REACHED for her cell phone, which rested on the nightstand. With squinted eyes, she tried to focus on the caller ID until she realized it was Alicia. "Hey," she said in a raspy tone tempered with concern. "You what?" Kate shot up in bed. "Where are you? Okay. I'm on my way."

Kate jumped to her feet and pulled on her clothes.

"Everything okay?" Nick asked.

"Sorry to wake you. It was Alicia. She's surveilling Phil Vega. I have to go meet her."

"Why?"

"Something she found. Listen, can you make sure Karen stays here? Don't let her leave."

"Okay, but I have to go to work too." He checked the time. "In three hours. Shit. It's two in the morning, Kate."

"I know. Just, please, just don't let her leave. I'll call you later. Go back to sleep." She leaned over the bed to kiss him.

THE STREETS WERE quiet as it approached 2:30. Kate's impending arrival brought with it growing anticipation. The reason behind Vasquez's decision to stand watch had to be significant.

She spotted her partner's car ahead and killed the headlights, rolling to a stop. Before stepping out, she called her. "I'm behind you."

"Good. Hop in."

Kate exited her car and quietly entered through the passenger door of Vasquez's. "Okay. I'm here. Tell me what you found."

"I did some digging and made a few calls. Checked into Vega's history, like we talked about."

"And?"

"Before Vega went to work for Copeland, he worked for another politician. The man Copeland initially defeated when he was elected as a councilman. I realize that's not exactly earth-shattering news. But what is, I think, is the fact that the man he defeated is still in contact with Vega. And just so happens to now be a congressman himself."

"Recent contact?"

"Like last week."

"Okay. How do you know this? Did you get his phone records?"

"I got Vega's, yes. Requested it relative to the current investigation. No big deal, right?"

"Right."

"But this guy, this former political opponent of Copeland's is reaching out to Vega again for a reason. And I think that reason is he wants Vega to get dirt on his boss."

"So Vega tells his old boss about Copeland's string of infidelities. Gives him the dirt to what? Blackmail him?"

"Given what's happened, it doesn't appear blackmail was enough for this man. At this point, I'm leaning toward the notion that he wanted them dead."

"To frame Copeland." Kate nodded. "But he's got solid alibis. I don't know, Alicia. I mean, any kind of scenario like this is going to ruin Copeland's career no matter what, so why kill the women?

And that doesn't explain why you're here, watching Vega's house."

"When I got the phone records, I tried to piece this together. And yeah, Copeland's got alibis, but what if Vega doesn't? He's been cooperative, very, from what I gather. Look, I know this is a shot in the dark, but I came here for a couple of reasons. I wanted to know if he was going to go to Karen Hildebrand's house, first and foremost. Or to another potential victim's. I can't fathom a reason behind killing these women, but that doesn't change the fact that they're gone. Kate, I think Phil Vega is in contact with the killer—maybe even directing him on his former boss' behalf."

"That must be why he wanted to know what was on Copeland's laptop. Looking for more potential victims. Like the email warning Karen." Kate considered the idea. "This fits with my initial theory. What about Mrs. Copeland? Could she be in danger?"

"I think he's going after anyone who Copeland himself would want silenced, if he was so inclined. This goes way beyond black-mail. Whoever's behind this wants to see Copeland get the chair. That's why I'm here. I need to keep a tail on him. We have to know more about Vega. Something doesn't smell right and this case is starting to flounder."

"Then I'll stay with you."

"What about Karen?"

"She's at my place. She'll be fine there until we figure this out. Have you called Dwight?"

"No. I probably should."

"He should know what you found. We need more, though. What about getting a warrant to search his house?"

"Possibly. But I don't think what we have right now is enough to get one. That's why I want to follow him for a while."

"This is good work, Alicia. Here I've been chasing my tail

trying to pin this on Copeland and Phelps, but what you've done... You could be right about this and I should've seen it sooner."

"I might not be right, and you know, this hard-on you've got for Phelps, I'll be the first one to tell you that I think it could've clouded your judgment. Don't get me wrong. I have no doubt Copeland and Phelps are working together in some form or another, but the killer is who I'm after. And none of us thought it was the congressman."

As the sun began to rise, Kate and Vasquez waited in her car, expecting something that hadn't yet happened. And for the past few hours, Kate replayed what was said over and over in her mind. This whole time, Vasquez had been the one who maintained focus, not Kate. And if it hadn't been for the unexpected run-in with Mrs. Copeland, Karen Hildebrand could well be dead and Kate would still have believed it was Grant Copeland's fault. Maybe it would have been, but the killer was still unknown. And regardless of Quinn's insight, Kate had followed her own path, which was leading nowhere. What right did she have to continue to pursue the position at BAU Headquarters? She was no profiler.

"What do you want to do now?" Kate asked.

"Shit, I don't know. I'd like to get into his house."

"Too risky with him inside. Now, Phelps might be able to do something, but I don't think we'd get away with it."

"Where's your sense of excitement, of confronting danger?"

"Somewhere back in Florida, I think." Kate recalled her brash and unpredictable behavior on the Blackwater investigation that eventually led to her first official kill.

"We can still keep a tail on him today. He'll have to leave for work soon, I imagine." Vasquez turned to Kate. "What do you think?"

In that moment, Kate's cell phone buzzed with an incoming text. She viewed the message. "Shit."

"What is it?"

"It's Phelps. Says some reporter ran with the story. It's on the front page of the *Post*."

"That means it's going to be everywhere in a matter of hours."

"Yep. Which means we're screwed." She looked to Vasquez. "I guess it's time to tell Phelps what you discovered and hope he wants to pursue it."

"He'll destroy this case. You know that as well as I do."

"He's not going to get the chance. In fact, I suspect he'll be on his best behavior now. Oh, I bet he'll start cooperating. Might be the best thing that could've happened."

"Then let's get down there and show him what we have on Vega."

"What *you* have on Vega. You did the legwork. Not me."

19

It was too late. The front lawn was crammed with reporters. The congressman backed away from the window and dropped the bedroom curtains. "It's happening. Sue, what are we going to do now?"

"You're going to work, just like any other normal day. If you deviate from your routine, they'll pounce and we both know that."

"I suppose you're right. You're always right." He drew nearer to her while she sat on the bed. "I'm so sorry to put you through this. I can't imagine what you must think of me. What the press has reported."

"You think I believe anything they say? I've been around this town long enough to know better than that. This has nothing to do with you and everything to do with a murderer who killed your friends and colleagues."

"Do you think someone could be after me?"

"After your seat, yes. Working to destroy your political career, absolutely. And I won't stand idly by while that happens." She handed him his tie. "Put this on and go to work."

"What will you do?"

"Same as I always do."

Grant tied his tie and smoothed back his hair. "Wish me luck while I venture out into the wolf pack."

"Hold your head high, my love. You've done nothing wrong." Sue kissed his cheek and walked him to the front door.

He pulled it open and the horde converged on his doorstep, snapping photos, screaming questions at him. He turned to Sue a final time. "I'll call you later, honey." The first step was the hardest, but Grant advanced toward his car, bobbing and weaving through the crowd.

"No comment," he replied to one reporter before stepping in his vehicle.

Once the engine revved, they began to step away and allowed him to leave his driveway. And then like wolves, they focused their efforts on Sue until she finally closed the door.

As he pulled onto the road, Grant called the only other person he trusted besides his wife. "It's me."

"How bad is it?" Vega replied.

"About a dozen or so at my doorstep."

"Jesus. You're coming in now?"

"Yes. Are you there yet?"

"No. I'm just about to leave, though. I'll call to see how bad it is at the office. We might want to bring you in through the rear entrance today."

"I don't want to do that. I need to push through them so they know I've got nothing to hide."

"But you do, don't you? It's going to come out, Grant. There's nothing we can do to stop it now. The insinuations are already rampant. I'm afraid it's over."

"I refuse to believe that. I didn't kill those women."

"Doesn't matter. What matters is the relationships you had with them."

"Hey, look, I never screwed Meredith Bowen."

"No, you harassed her. And that's much worse." His sigh came through loud and clear. "You'll have to resign and the sooner the better. Should I prepare a statement?"

Sue's words reverberated in his mind. "Hell no. I'm not giving in to them. We need to make it clear these deaths had nothing to do with me or my history with them. I can't believe what you're telling me right now. I thought you of all people would stick this out with me."

"Let me work on a statement. We have to say something. I'll see you in a little while and we'll talk more. Goodbye."

Phil peered through his kitchen window and spotted the cars across the street that had been there all night. They were already watching him, but he didn't know what they knew or if they knew anything and were just there to scare him. The problem now was that they would follow him. But perhaps the way around that was to go into the office as usual, then get a ride out. Copeland's office was going to be slammed with reporters and he stood a halfway decent chance of getting out of there unnoticed so long as he wasn't in his own car.

He walked into the hall bath and straightened his tie and returned to the kitchen window a final time before leaving. "What the hell?" The cars were gone and his wish had just been granted.

With expediency, he fled his apartment building. It was urgent he get to her at all costs. Vega made the call while he drove. "It's me. Can you meet me at La Costa's near H Street in twenty minutes? Great. I'll see you then."

∼

ON ARRIVAL at the coffee shop, he spotted her sitting at a table, a cup of steaming coffee in her hands as she took a sip. A subtle wave of his hand and he approached her. "Thanks for meeting me on such short notice."

"That's fine. I figured with what's going on that you'd want to talk. Is he okay?"

"No. But you might be able to help him. How about you finish that up and let's take a drive. I don't want to talk here."

"Yeah, sure. Okay." She finished her drink and stood. "Let's go."

Vega led the way outside and opened the passenger door of his car for her. A quick read of the area and he stepped inside. "I know a place that won't have any eyes or ears. We can figure this out together."

She nodded. "Thanks for doing this, Phil. It means a lot to me and I know Grant would appreciate it too."

Within several minutes, they'd arrived at Vega's preset destination.

"This is the place?"

"Yes. Is this okay?"

"I guess so. Looks abandoned."

"Exactly why I chose it. Come on. Let's go in."

Vega pushed open the door that led to the lobby. "This place has been abandoned for a while, but they're about to tear it down. Follow me; this unit's open." He looked back at her. "What's wrong?"

"Nothing. Just don't think we should be here. Isn't there some-place else we can talk?"

"We need to ensure complete seclusion. Especially in light of the story that came out this morning."

"Right." She retrieved her cell phone. "Maybe I should just text my office and let them know I'm running late."

"No." Vega nearly slapped the phone from her hand. "No texts. Not until we're done. Can't risk it." He noted her growing fear. "Look, I know these are extraordinary circumstances, but with everything that's been going on, it has to be this way. I'm trying to help you. You understand that, right? Haven't I always been there to help, especially where Grant is concerned."

"Yes. Of course you have. I'm sorry. Let's just figure this out and get a story together. I know you have his best interest at heart."

"Go on in." A final check of the area and he closed the door, securing it behind him.

∿

"We should've kept a tail on him." Vasquez pulled into the Metro PD station. "We risk losing the only lead we have."

"If this story hadn't come out, I'd say you might be right, but I think he'll want to stay close to Copeland today," Kate replied. "If what you say is true, he'll want to keep Copeland in his sights. Right now, let's focus on getting Phelps up to speed on what you found out about him. It will make a difference."

"What about Baltimore?"

"Of course Pearson will want to be updated, but what we need to remember is, Vega's here in D.C. Unless something else goes down in Baltimore, Pearson can't do much for us."

They stepped out of her car and entered the station, which was already teeming with the press.

"Welcome to the circus." Kate held the door for her as they approached the front desk. "Is Detective Phelps here?" She displayed her badge.

The officer pointed toward the hall. "In his office. Go on back before you get hammered by these assholes."

"Thanks." She headed into the corridor with Vasquez and approached Phelps' office. "We need to talk."

"I figured you'd show. Close the door."

"Vasquez received evidence that Copeland's chief of staff, Phillip Vega, was in contact with Copeland's political opponent on several occasions in recent weeks." Kate jumped right in because any more time dedicated to this man was time better spent elsewhere.

"So."

Vasquez appeared stunned. "So? So given what's happened, don't you find that the least bit concerning?"

"In what way? People in Washington talk to one another. Last I checked, that wasn't a crime."

Kate stepped toward him and hovered over his desk. "Look. Whatever deal you have going on with Copeland is over. You understand? If you don't bring Vega in, then I will. And, I'll bring in the guy he's working for too. That's one congressional official and two members of the House. You want a circus? I'll give you a damn circus."

"The fuck you think you are?" He stood from his chair. "You aren't running this investigation, I am. I decide who to question. You and your team at the FBI are consultants, so you'd better check your ego, missy."

Heat rose in her cheeks and her heart beat faster in her chest. "I'm going to recommend charges of obstruction be filed against you. You want to play this game, you chose to piss off the wrong person. Don't think for one minute I don't see through you, Phelps." She stared at him, waiting for a response, but none came.

Vasquez reached for Kate's shoulder. "Come on. We're wasting our time here."

"That's right. Go on, pretty lady. Listen to your sidekick."

Kate stopped in her tracks.

"Don't. You'll only make it worse." Vasquez nudged her to continue until she finally gave in.

VEGA CONTINUED INSIDE the derelict apartment unit. "Thank you for trusting me. We can fix this."

The young woman was put together well, but her frayed nerves were beginning to show through the polished veneer. "So how should we handle this? What can we do to minimize the damage to Grant? I'm so sorry he's tangled up in it. I can't imagine what he must be going through right now."

"I think the only way to solve this is to rid ourselves of the problem in the first place."

"What do you mean?"

He took hold of her shoulders and forced her to a nearby chair. "Have a seat."

"What are you doing? Phil, you're hurting me."

"I'm sorry it has to be this way, but you brought this on yourself."

Her eyes reflected the fear that he instilled in her. She seemed to understand now the purpose of their meeting. "Please, Phil, don't do this. You don't have to do this."

"You fucked him, Wendy. You fucked him when you knew he was married and had a family and none of that mattered to you."

"You think Grant is innocent in this? Do you even know the kind of man you work for? What an arrogant son of a bitch he is?"

"The truth comes out now, doesn't it? Grant can't do any more favors for you here, can he?" Phil retrieved the gun tucked in his belt. "I won't pretend he doesn't share blame in this, but he'll get what he deserves soon enough. You should thank me for sparing you the public humiliation you would've endured once word got out. The others would thank me too, if they'd had the chance. Except maybe Meredith. She was an unfortunate result of another of Grant's misdeeds, but then, she had been a tease, even tried that shit with me once."

"Oh my God. You're fucking crazy, you know that?" She tried to jostle around him, but he wouldn't release her. "Let me go. I swear I'll scream."

Vega pointed the gun at her forehead. "You won't have time." He stepped back and fired, flinching as her blood and brains spattered across his face. He continued to hold her arm as she fell limp and he lowered her to the ground.

She lay still, eyes wide and staring up at him as though she were in a pool of water, drowning. He grabbed his briefcase and retrieved the plastic bags in which to place his now blood-stained clothes. A fresh shirt and pants were neatly folded inside along with something else. The scrap of fabric that had become his own personal signature. A fitting one at that. With the red lipstick, he wrote the word that held all the meaning it needed. Each of these women had earned it, even Meredith Bowen and maybe especially her.

Vega folded the soft and luxurious piece of bedsheet and approached her again. Kneeling down, he pressed on her chin to open her mouth and with two fingers, pushed the fabric inside as far as he could. Upon stepping back to examine his work, he realized she looked like a squirrel hiding a nut. While the thought made him smile, this was no laughing matter. It was a job and the job was done.

With meticulous care, Vega placed his soiled clothes into the plastic bags, along with the paper towels used to clean his face. The abandoned building had no running water, but he had planned for that too. Bottles of water assisted with the cleanup, but he would leave her here for the police to find. It would likely be a few days, he hoped. The building wasn't scheduled for demolition for another week. For now, though, Vega would go into the office and prepare a statement for Copeland and play the good and loyal chief of staff he was supposed to be.

~

No sooner had the elevator doors parted was Kate marching in haste to Dwight's office. Vasquez trailed close behind.

"Just calm down, Kate. I know you're pissed, but don't go in there making demands to Jameson. He won't go for that and you know it." Vasquez grabbed her in the hall. "Kate. Stop. Take a breath."

"Can you believe that guy? Who the hell does he think he is?"

"He's the lead investigator on a case we're consulting on. Look, the way he handled that was shitty, but if you want to get him thrown off, or get the entire department thrown off, then you need a valid reason and you need to deliver that reason with a cool head."

"You're right. I'm just seriously pissed off."

"I know you are. And you have a right to be. That condescending prick deserves the boot. Let's go in there together, present our case, and see what Jameson has to say about it."

"Yeah. Okay."

Just as they were about to make their way inside, Dwight charged out of his office. "What the hell just happened? Get your asses in here, both of you."

"Phelps is refusing to question Copeland's chief of staff, Phillip Vega, even after we presented him with new information." Vasquez was the first to jump into the fire.

"I just got a call from his captain. He says you two were planning on getting him thrown off the case and that we would be taking over. Is that true?"

Kate folded her arms. "Yes. It's true. He needs to get the hell out of the way so we can do our goddamn jobs. I'm telling you, he's hiding something big and it's going to cost us this case. We're going to lose our only lead. It's bad enough the *Post* ran that story, but now we have to deal with Phelps' obstruction? I can't sit by and watch that happen, Dwight. I won't."

"You have any idea what kind of shit storm you just stirred up? Now I got to go in there and talk to his captain and kowtow to him. For someone who's trying to get hired on at BAU Headquarters, you sure as hell are kicking up a hornet's nest over this detective."

She threw her arms in the air. "What am I supposed to do? He's ignoring recommendations, stalling on sharing evidence and statements so I can complete a profile to help him. He has left us with no choice. Vasquez got a lead on this chief of staff and I'll be damned if we're going to let it go cold." Kate turned on her heel and started out the door.

"Reid?" Dwight shot a look to Vasquez before following her into the corridor. "Agent Reid, wait."

She stopped and whipped back around. "What?" Realizing who she was addressing, she closed her eyes and inhaled. "I'm sorry. You didn't deserve that."

"You're damn right I didn't. Kate, I understand your frustration. Believe me, I've been in your shoes before and I'm sorry as hell you have to go through this. It was bound to happen at some point in your career."

"What should I do, Dwight? Vasquez and I have been busting our asses trying to stop this killer before he kills again."

"But that's the problem, Kate. That's not your job. Not this time. And I'll be honest with you. I think Vasquez is the only one trying to find the killer. You've been too busy trying to bring down Phelps and Grant Copeland."

"I know they're tied together. I swear they are. And now you're telling me I have to let this go? Just sit by and watch Phelps ignore the facts?"

"Confronting him wasn't the way to go. Let me talk to his captain and try to smooth things over. I'll tell him we'll take a step back and let his people do what they think is best. But I will voice my concerns over this Vega situation. If the captain chooses to ignore me, then there isn't much I can do about that. At least our asses will be covered."

"I don't want to just cover our asses, Dwight. Regardless of what you think, I want to stop this killer. If Copeland's the type of man I think he is, he's got more women in the wings and we'll need to find them before the killer does."

20

The arrival of Phil Vega at Copeland's office on the Hill went largely unnoticed. The staff was too busy dousing the many fires that raged as a result of the front-page story in the *Post*. In fact, they were so preoccupied, no one noticed the speck of blood that clung to his cheek. It wasn't until he caught a glimpse in a mirror on the way to see his boss that he wiped it away. And there was something else he noticed too; the face that peered back at him was that of someone he no longer recognized.

"There you are. Christ, where have you been?" Copeland approached him. "We need to get out in front of this. Do you have that statement ready? And I don't want any of your bullshit resignation talk." He waited for an answer. "Phil? What the hell's going on with you? You said you were going to work on a statement. Where is it?"

"I was held up. I'm sorry. I'll have it to you in the next thirty minutes."

Copeland regarded him with growing concern. "What's going on? You look—unnerved. Did something happen?"

"No. I'm just trying to figure out how we get past this."

"Right. Okay, just get something together as soon as possible. We're being hounded by the press and I don't know how much longer I can hole up in here."

"Of course. I'll get right on it."

Copeland watched him leave with mounting worry. He leaned on Phil in times of distress, but this was far worse than any of them had ever experienced. This was a career-ending story and now it seemed his right-hand-man had felt the same.

With his cell phone buzzing in his pocket, Copeland returned to the moment, though it was no less troubling. "Yes."

"You and your boy better get down here now."

"Like I said before, we've already given you statements. What more is there?"

"I've got a lobby full of reporters. Captain is up my ass asking questions about why the Feds want me thrown off the investigation and you're asking what more?"

"You're the one who offered me assurances and you're the one who failed to live up to them, even after we came to an agreement."

"Tread lightly, Congressman. If you don't come down to the station, you'll leave me with no choice but to bring you in. Think of how that will play out in the media."

"I need some time. My chief of staff is drafting a statement now. Can you at least give me an hour?"

"You have one hour. If you're not here, I'll send someone to come and get you."

"You know, Phelps, for a man in your situation, demands ought to be doled out with a modicum of respect."

"I could say the same about you. I'll see you in one hour."

The line went dead and Copeland stared at his phone as though he could reach through it and put a chokehold on this man whom he wished he'd never engaged. If word got out he'd paid him to help silence the increasing questions about the murders, Copeland would be drawn and quartered, regardless of his innocence.

He marched out of his office and through the maze of corridors leading to Phil. "Is it ready?"

With his eyes fixed on his computer, he began, "Almost. I'm polishing it up now."

"Good. We have an hour before we have to go to the station."

"Why?"

"Phelps is demanding it."

"Are we under arrest for something?"

"No. But if he isn't seen as trying to move the case forward, including our voluntary arrival and subsequent statements, it's going to make us and him look increasingly guilty."

"He should be focused on finding the killer. Not indicting us on the public stage."

"As much as I'd like to agree with you, if we don't do as he asks, he'll send someone here to get us. That's the last thing we want. Voluntary cooperation is the way to play this and I think you know that."

"I'm printing off the statement now for your review. Then we'll go. We'll do what the detective wants. I don't agree with it, but if you think it's best, then that's what we'll do."

"Good. I'll grab it, mark it up, and then head out."

As Grant left his office, Phil understood the time had come to bring this to an end. Finish what he had set out to do. Copeland's career was over, but Phil wanted much more than that. He wanted to make him pay for what he'd done.

~

THE TEAM APPROACHED the Metro Police station and Dwight began, "I'll let you do the talking, unless you want me to step in."

"No," Kate said. "I'd rather take it from here. The pressure you put on his captain obviously worked. Phelps said the congressman and his chief of staff would be here by eleven." She checked the time. "It's 10:45 now. And by the looks of the place, my guess is they'll come in around back."

"Yeah. They won't make it past the front doors." Vasquez headed into the halls of the station with Kate and Dwight in tow.

"Your guys here yet?" Vasquez peered inside Phelps' office.

"Any minute. So glad you all could make it."

"I'm sure you are," Kate replied. "I don't know if you've met Agent Jameson. He's the resident BAU agent at the Washington Field Office."

"I've spoken with your captain about the investigation and the growing tension between our two departments." Dwight offered his hand. "I'm hoping I can help get us back on track."

"Look, I want nothing more than to find the person responsible for the murders of those women, but I'm telling you, you're barking up the wrong tree. Copeland is no more guilty of killing them than I am. All I've been trying to do is keep us on the scent of the real killer."

"I agree, but can you say with any confidence that his chief of staff is just as innocent?" Kate added. "Especially given what we brought to your attention earlier?"

"I guess we'll find out soon enough."

"You are going to get Vega to submit DNA, right?"

"For what reason?"

"For the reasons I've already laid out. I realize we're still waiting on Bowen's DNA, but it will come soon, and when it does, we need to have Vega's on file. At the very least, to exclude him as a suspect, since it seems you've exonerated him, same as you have Copeland."

"I imagine his attorneys will want a say in that matter," Phelps added.

Kate was at her wit's end and was nearly ready to confront him once again, but when an officer peered inside, he diverted her anger.

"Sorry to interrupt. A body's been found in an abandoned apartment building on 5th."

"Get Leighton on it. That's his area," Phelps replied.

"We did and CSI showed up. They found something in her mouth and a blood-laden thumbprint on her shoulder. We're running it through the system now, but we know the victim's name is Wendy Montrose."

"And?"

"The material had the same word written on it as the others. Looks like this one's yours." He began to step away, but stopped short. "Oh, and, it appears she knew Representative Copeland."

"And you know this how?"

"Her cell phone was recovered and the call history showed Copeland's name several times in the past few days."

"Who has that phone now?" Kate directed her attention to Phelps before the officer could answer. "If Vega's number is on there too... How much more do you need, detective?"

TIME HAD PASSED and still no Copeland and no Vega. Kate considered the likely scenario that neither would be appearing at the station. "I think it's safe to say you missed the boat on this one, Phelps. They aren't coming. Now we have another dead body and no idea where they are."

"I'll make some calls to his staff. I'll find them," Phelps replied.

"You and I both know they're long gone. What we don't know is did they both go voluntarily or was Copeland coerced? Our time's up, Agent Jameson. How do you want to handle this?"

"We'll have to defer to Detective Phelps."

"I'll go to Copeland's office and I'll send an officer to his house." Before he could continue, Kate interrupted.

"We'll go to Vega's house. And, if you're okay with it, sir, I'd like to ask Agent Quinn to come along with Vasquez and me. If Vega's behind this, then any help Quinn can offer at this point will be welcomed, especially in light of the fact we don't know where Copeland is."

"Do you have an issue with that, Phelps?" Dwight asked.

"No. Do what you need to do and I'll do the same." He holstered his weapon. "Just keep in contact." He began to leave but stopped short. "This wasn't how it was supposed to go, Agent Reid. Despite what you think of me, I wanted to catch the killer, same as you."

"Guess you didn't do your job, then."

"I suppose not, but then, neither did you." Phelps disappeared into the corridor.

"That was helpful." Dwight peered at her as he brushed by. "Ask Quinn to meet us at Vega's house."

"Smooth." Vasquez patted Kate on the shoulder. "Come on. Let's get going."

Dwight was on his cell outside when Kate and Vasquez reached her car. He ended the call and turned toward them. "Phelps is currently on his way to Copeland's office. He called them, but they said the congressman left with Vega. No one knows where they went."

"Why is he wasting his time going down there, then?" Kate

asked. "He should go to the building where they found the newest victim."

"He is. He's turning around now. For Christ's sake, Kate, he's not the damn enemy here, okay? Let him do his job."

"That's what I thought he was doing. Whatever happens today, I'll find out the truth about him. Then I'll wait for your apology." She pressed the remote on her Explorer and slipped into the driver's seat. "You coming with us?"

Dwight entered the passenger seat while Vasquez slipped into the back. "You'd better hope you're right about him, Kate."

"I am." She pressed the ignition button and pulled away.

"I should've stayed there this morning," Vasquez said. "I had eyes on him and I let him go."

"It's not your fault," Dwight replied. "No one had anything on him until he pulled a disappearing act that made him look guilty of something."

"We did, but no one wanted to hear us." Vasquez caught Kate's eyes in the rear view.

"What about Quinn?" he continued.

Kate kept her sights on the road ahead. "I called him on the way to the car. He's meeting us there."

The silence that prevailed along the way hardened Kate's resolve, but there was no mistaking a price would be paid for her behavior. Dwight was a fair man, but she'd pushed it too far. Her handling of the situation was unprofessional at best and insubordinate at worst. She wondered what effect it would have on her working for Quinn, should he make the recommendation to bring her aboard. Kate had risked her career on this detective whom she was compelled to see fall. What it would do to the Bureau's relationship with Metro PD was unknown, nonetheless the consequences would reverberate through the WFO for some time.

"That's his place, up ahead." Vasquez pointed toward the driver's side.

"I think that's Quinn's car." Kate pulled up behind him. "He's still inside it."

"Wait." Dwight reached for Kate's arm. "What if Vega's here? We should call Metro for backup."

"If he is, I don't want to spook him if he has Copeland with patrol cars racing up the street. We have no idea if either of them have weapons." Kate eyed Dwight and saw the dismay in his expression. "I'm sorry. I'm not the one in charge and I'm overstepping—again."

"I just wish I knew what the hell was going on with you. This isn't who you are. But unfortunately, we don't have time to discuss it." Dwight stepped out.

Quinn must've noticed their arrival and stepped out of his car and waited for them to approach. "What's the plan, Agent Reid?"

"This is SSA Jameson. It's his call."

"Agent Jameson. We've spoken on the phone. Pleasure to meet you in person. I'm SSA Quinn. BAU Headquarters. I believe I know your previous boss."

"Yes, of course. Forgive me for being short, but we should go and see if Vega's inside."

"And if he is?" Quinn began to follow as they moved forward.

"I'll have no choice but to bring him in by force. He failed to arrive at Metro PD for questioning. Doesn't put him in a very good light."

Quinn turned to Kate. "I'm not sure I need to be here, Agent Reid."

"I disagree. Once we get inside, I hope to find the fabric used on the victims, or anything that might point to his collusion with Copeland's rival. Or maybe even Copeland himself. Something we still haven't ruled out. That's why I asked you here. Your insight is very much needed here today."

Vega's apartment unit was on the first floor and on approach, Dwight knocked on the door. "Phillip Vega, FBI. Open the door." Seconds passed with no answer. He knocked again. "FBI. Open up."

Kate shook her head. "Time to get inside."

"Without a warrant?" Quinn asked.

"I was on the horn with the judge this morning," Dwight said. "He's signing it now as we speak."

"I didn't know you..."

"It's my job, Reid. In case you forgot." Dwight knocked a final time and when there was again no answer, he drew his weapon. "Stand back." He turned to Kate. "You have anything you want to say?"

"Nope." She took a step back.

Dwight pulled the trigger and busted the lock. Holstering his weapon again, he pushed open the door.

Light shone through the veiled front window, but not enough to get a look at the place. Kate turned on a lamp in the front room. "We know he was here at least until 8am, which was when Vasquez and I left and headed to the station after getting the call from Phelps."

"You were here? Why were you staking out his house?"

"Agent Vasquez found evidence Vega had been talking to one of Copeland's political adversaries, a man he'd run against early in his career. We thought it could mean Vega was tracking down these women and relaying that information to this person. But what we didn't know was if he was responsible for their murders. We traced several calls over the past few weeks from this man to Vega. That was our first clue that he might be working to sabotage Copeland's career by exposing his infidelities."

"And murdering them?" Quinn added.

"I don't know." Kate eyed him before returning her attention to the living room.

"What are your thoughts on Vega?" Dwight asked Quinn.

"Considering another body's been discovered and neither Vega nor Copeland are anywhere to be found, I wouldn't rule out the connection. My concern is who is really pulling the strings. As I've told Reid from the beginning."

"By the sounds of it, this political rival is pulling the strings," Dwight said. "Which leads me to assume Vega is getting a shit ton of money or this person is blackmailing him for something."

"That's definitely a possibility. I'm going to check out the bedroom." Quinn continued into the hall and turned in to the only bedroom in the apartment.

"And you want to go work for him?" Dwight said.

"I thought I had a handle on this profile, but after talking with him, he opened my eyes to the possibility I could be wrong. I'm not entirely sure I am wrong, but I'm open to his opinions. That's why I asked him to come here and give us his thoughts."

"Whatever you say, Kate. This needs to come to an end. Doesn't matter how we get there, just so long as we do." Dwight continued to search the kitchen.

"Reid?"

Kate heard Quinn shout from the back.

"Better go see what he wants," Vasquez said. "I'll keep looking in here."

Kate continued into the hall toward the bedroom. "What is it?"

"Take a look here." Quinn stood in front of Vega's dresser.

"What'd you find?"

"Do you know if Vega has a girlfriend?"

"I have no idea. I haven't been allowed to speak to him directly. Only Phelps has."

Quinn pointed to the bed. "You said Vasquez was here throughout the night. Do you know if she saw anyone come in?"

"No. She believed he was alone."

"Both sides of his bed appear to have been slept in."

"That could've been from another night. Maybe the guy doesn't make his bed every day."

"Maybe not. Still, it appears as though he did have a visitor in recent days. Just a point to consider." Quinn opened the dresser drawers. "He's very neat, otherwise."

"Couldn't that speak to his character? Like maybe he's obsessive."

"Possibly. I'm still looking for something more definitive. We need something that will point to..." He stopped.

"What? What'd you find?"

Quinn pulled out a picture at the bottom of his underwear drawer.

"Oh my God." Kate stood next to him and peered at the picture. "You could be right about someone pulling the strings."

"And not your political adversary."

As much as Kate wanted to believe she had gotten this one right, Quinn now held evidence to suggest otherwise. "No. Looks like she could be our Svengali."

21

The elite Unit 4 team waited in the conference room for their new senior unit agent to arrive. A briefing on their crime analyses was scheduled before one of the members, Eva Duncan, was to be called on as an expert witness in an upcoming trial.

"Sorry I'm late." Nick Scarborough entered and took his seat. "Got held up in a meeting."

"No problem. Duncan was just about to fill us in on her testimony strategies for the Figueroa trial on Monday." Levi Walsh was the team's investigative analyst who provided suggestions to law enforcement regarding threat and critical incidents. He offered insight into investigative perspectives. And it seemed he was still withholding judgment on his new boss.

"I spoke with the entomologist and got him lined up to assist Duncan with expert testimony." The second most senior agent on the team, Cameron Fisher, worked almost exclusively with the National Center for the Analysis of Violent Crime (NCAVC) field coordinators to facilitate requests from law enforcement nationwide. He also brought in the experts needed to work forensics when necessary.

"So we have everything needed to get to trial," Nick added as he glanced around the table. "Where's Quinn? We need his profile on the offender's behavior. Anyone know where he is?"

"I haven't seen him, but I know he finished his report. I got the email earlier today," Duncan replied.

"Last I heard, he got a call from the WFO on a case they're working." Walsh turned to Scarborough. "Your old stomping grounds."

"I'm aware of their current investigation regarding the congressman."

"That blew up this morning, I heard," Walsh continued. "He must've gotten called out to give them a hand."

"I'll give him a shout. In the meantime, sounds like you all have this under control. I appreciate your expediency and I'm sure New York appreciates the help. I'll let you all get back to it." Nick began to leave.

"Scarborough?" Walsh stopped Nick in the corridor and jogged to catch up. "Do you know what's going on with Quinn's job opening?"

"As far as I know, he hasn't made a decision yet but is narrowing down the field. Why?"

"Look, I don't want to be an ass, but word is your girlfriend is in the running for the job."

"And?" Nick immediately jumped into defense mode.

"And, we're all wondering, if that happens, how it will affect your ability to run the team."

"It won't."

"You're new here. You're very well respected, but you're still new. And frankly, we don't know your style yet. We're all concerned about this. We'd just like to be kept in the loop."

"I understand. Quinn will have to decide which way to go. All I can do is offer assurance that I have absolutely nothing to do with his decision. It's his and his alone. If it comes down to it, and Agent Reid is selected, it won't get in the way of anything we're doing. There will be no special treatment. Nothing. I've worked with her for the past few years at WFO and it was never an issue."

Walsh held Nick's gaze. "Okay. I hope, if it comes down to it, that you're right. None of us wants this team compromised in any way."

"That won't happen. I'd better go make that call to Quinn. Make sure he doesn't need anything from us." Nick paused a moment. "Thank you for letting me know the concerns of the team. And—I am listening." He carried on toward his office.

Their concerns were valid, but he had no real way to prove to them that it wouldn't be an issue. He knew it wouldn't be, Kate knew it wouldn't be, but only time would prove that was the case. And that was operating under the assumption she was going to be chosen for the position. An uncertainty in any event. One which he hoped Quinn would put to rest sooner rather than later. Perhaps that would happen if in fact Quinn was in the field with Kate and Dwight. Something he was about to verify.

In his office, Nick made the call. Kate's line rang, but there was no answer. "Damn." He dialed Quinn's number and again, and the line rang. And again, his voicemail picked up. Nick figured something important was happening and he had but one option left. This time as the line rang, Dwight answered. "Hey, it's Scarborough. I heard something was going down with the investigation you're working on."

"You heard right. We're in the middle of it now."

"Is Kate with you?"

"She is. We're searching the chief of staff's apartment right now. He and his boss have disappeared. They were supposed to show up at the Metro PD station this morning. Neither of them did."

"Sounds like you're in the weeds. Hey, is Quinn there too, by any chance?"

"Yep. Kate's been working with him on developing the profile for the case. When this came up, she called on him and he offered to help us find these two."

"Good. Thanks for letting me know. I'll let you get back to it. Hey, if there's anything I can do."

"I know. I got to go."

Nick looked out over the grounds of Quantico from his office window. He'd begun to feel like an outsider. The people on his team hadn't yet placed their full faith in him and he no longer had a say in Kate's professional life. It was an adjustment to be sure, although he knew it was the only way to ensure she traveled down her own path to success. Not one he set out for her.

COPELAND STARED at the man in whom he had placed his confidence. But it was beginning to appear as though that man might bring about his downfall and perhaps had perpetuated the entire scenario as it was currently unfolding. "Why aren't we going to the station? We agreed this was the best way to defend the accusations."

"You agreed. Not me," Vega replied.

"Where are we going, Phil?"

Vega kept his eyes on the road. "This has to stop now, Grant. And I think you know that."

"What has to stop? Phil, you're starting to worry me. Where are we going?"

"You'll recognize it soon enough." He eyed Copeland. "And

don't bother reaching for your cell. This will all make sense soon enough."

The next several minutes elapsed in silence. Copeland needed a strategy and a way out of whatever was about to happen. The blinders were off and he now viewed Phil as the enemy, something he wished he had picked up on sooner. Now it might be too late.

"We're here." Vega pushed the gearshift into park and looked through the driver's side window. "She'll be out in a minute."

"Who? Who will be out in a minute? Phil, what the hell are you talking about? I don't understand what's happening here. We're supposed to be working together to get out of this chaos."

He turned to Copeland. "I asked her to come here."

"Who?"

Vega only smiled as he returned his attention to the coffee shop that they were now parked in front of. He checked the time on his phone. "Any minute now." Upon glancing through the window once again, he spotted her. "Right on time."

Copeland's face went pale when he saw her. "What is she doing here? What the hell have you done?"

Sue Copeland smiled as she spotted Vega rolling down his window and continued her approach. "So, what's the rush? Why did you..." Her eyes shifted to Copeland and back to Vega. "Phil, what's going on?"

"Get in."

Her brow furrowed in confusion.

"Now!"

"Don't, Sue. Just go. Run."

"Get in the goddam car, Sue."

She looked at her husband and opened the rear passenger door. A final moment of reluctance before she slid into the backseat. "What's going on, Grant?"

"It's time you learned the truth about your husband. I'm going to show you the kind of man you married."

"You realize by not showing up at the station, Phelps is going to get nervous," Copeland began. "They're going to come after us, Phil. Are you sure this is how you want to do this?"

"You left me with no choice. This is all on you."

As they drove through the streets of D.C., heading somewhere neither of the Copelands knew, Sue reached for the handle on her door. She looked to Grant, who must've felt her stare and turned back. When he shook his head, almost imperceptibly, she released the handle and closed her eyes.

"Phil, you have to take us to the station. Clear up whatever this is because it looks bad. You understand that, right?"

"Don't worry, Grant. We're almost there."

KATE SPOTTED the Copeland house ahead. "I think that's it there."

"Okay," Dwight said. "I don't see any cars on the drive. Maybe Phelps' officer hasn't arrived yet."

"Or he did and discovered no one was here. We'll just have to see for ourselves if Sue Copeland is home," Kate replied.

"And if she knows where her husband is." Vasquez turned to Quinn, who was also in the backseat. "I hope your theory is right. If not, we're losing ground on Vega and the congressman."

Quinn stepped out and joined the others on the sidewalk. "Agent Jameson, after you."

Dwight took the lead and started toward the front entrance. The late afternoon sun was behind the house and cast a shadow on the entry, making it difficult to see any movement inside through the sheer curtains. He rang the bell.

While they waited, Kate's cell phone buzzed in her pocket. "Reid here."

"It's Phelps. We know where the fabric came from. The remnants left on scene all came from the same place. Detective Ramos in Baltimore said he was trying to get hold of your Agent Pearson to let him know but couldn't reach him, so he called me."

"Where did it come from?" Kate asked.

"The Regent Hotel near DuPont Circle. I'm heading down there now. Where are you?"

"Following a lead on Mrs. Copeland."

"What lead?"

"We found a picture of her—just her—in Vega's bedroom. We don't know the extent, if any, of her involvement, or if she's a target, but we're checking it out."

"Got it. If she's there, take her to the station, then meet me at the hotel as soon as you can. I'll head that way shortly."

After Phelps ended the call, Kate felt as though he was finally willing to work with her. It was entirely possible this was due to the fact that whatever deal he'd struck with Copeland had all but incinerated the moment he didn't show up at the station this morning. Kate knew this was Phelps covering his own ass, but if it meant some sort of cooperation on his part, she wouldn't reject it.

"Doesn't appear anyone's home," Dwight said. "We don't have a warrant and could be treading on some dangerous ground if we get in without one. This is still the home of a United States congressman."

"That was Phelps. They got a match on the fabric found on the victims and its origins. It came from the Regent Hotel."

"That's not far from here," Dwight replied.

"No. He's heading there soon. We can't be sure if Mrs. Copeland is safe, but she's not here. Do we get PD to issue a BOLO?"

"I think that's wise. In the meantime, we can be at the hotel in a matter of minutes. I say we head there now. Could be surveillance footage that'll confirm our suspicions. I'm surprised Phelps volunteered this information. I thought you were convinced he was an asshole."

"He is an asshole. But now he's an asshole who's trying to save his job. I know he was helping Copeland and I won't let that go."

"I didn't think you would."

Vasquez turned to Quinn. "She's determined. Right or wrong, that's who she is."

"I'm beginning to see that."

PHELPS STOOD outside the hotel beneath the porte-cochere as Kate pulled up. He meandered toward them and opened her door. "'Bout time you all got here. Any luck at the Copeland house?"

"No one was home." Kate stepped out as the others joined her. "What'd you find out?"

"Come see for yourself." Phelps made his way inside and headed toward the front desk. "Can I speak to your manager again?"

"Yes, sir. I'll call him up now," the woman replied.

Phelps turned his attention to the team. "So I had the manager search his system for if and when Copeland might have checked in."

"And?" Kate asked.

"He did. Several times in the past year."

"Okay. I get that would raise eyebrows, but congressmen travel, stay in hotels, and attend late dinners where it would easily explain why he would have been here," Quinn said.

"You're right. But like I told Reid, the fabric found in the victims' mouths came from this place. The bedsheets. So, you tell me, professor, you think that's a coincidence?"

The manager approached. "Detective Phelps. I see the rest of your team have arrived. If you'll all follow me. I'd like to keep this discreet, as I'm sure you can understand."

"Of course," Kate added.

"Mr. Copeland, or rather whatever name he had chosen to check in under, always requested this room. I knew it was him because I recognized him. Never said anything, though. Not my business. There are plenty of things I see around here and I've learned to keep my mouth shut." The manager retrieved his key to open the hotel room door.

"And when did he last check in?"

"About two weeks ago."

Kate looked to Vasquez. "Around the time Janine Atherton was killed." She continued inside. "Thank you. We'll let you know when we've finished searching the room."

"Of course." The manager left them to do their job.

"Phelps, you have the forensics report in hand?" Kate asked.

He retrieved his cell. "It's on my phone. Here. Take a look. The images match these bedsheets. At least in part. Most of the fabric was covered in the victim's blood, but as you can see here and here, the sheen and the cream color appear to match. And, according to the client list Sunburst Chemicals provided Baltimore, this hotel is their largest account." Phelps pulled down the covers to expose the sheets on the bed. "And the timing works out."

"Did you ask the manager if the cleaners noticed any damage to the bedding? Did they have to replace the sheets from this room in the recent past?"

"I haven't asked him much yet. Was waiting on you people to get here. This is your investigation, if I recall." He eyed Kate. "I thought you'd want to run it."

She dismissed his backhanded comment. "We should get a statement from whoever noted the damage. When and how bad it was. And of course, on what day. What about any surveillance?"

"They won't have any inside the rooms," Dwight said. "Halls, elevators, restaurant. That's about it."

"Right. We should get the footage from the days that Copeland was here. Someone could've followed him and also waited for Atherton. And, we find him with any of the victims, we've got not only him, but we can try to identify other potential targets."

"When you say we've got him, that only means he was cheating on his wife, not that he killed those women," Quinn added. "As you've said, Phillip Vega is your number one suspect. I think we need to be on the lookout for footage of him."

"What about the woman in the abandoned building, Wendy Montrose?" Vasquez looked to Phelps. "What's going on there?"

"They transferred the body to the ME's office. I haven't been down there to see it yet."

"I should stay here and review CCTV footage," Vasquez continued. "Detective, you should go to the ME's office. And wasn't there a thumbprint? Your people might've gotten a hit."

"I'll go," Kate said. "Quinn can come with me, if that's all right with you, Agent Jameson. Then Phelps can focus on the prints from forensics and you and Vasquez can stay here."

"Fine by me. Detective?"

"Got no problem with splitting up. We should cover all our bases right now. If it turns out that the print belongs to Vega or Copeland, it's best we find out now and continue to track them down."

Kate eyed Phelps once again. "And Mrs. Copeland. She's still missing."

22

Dusk had begun to creep over the horizon when they arrived at the Office of the Chief Medical Examiner. Kate pulled into the parking lot and cut the engine. "Thanks for coming with me and for earlier today. I know you've got other things on your plate right now, but I appreciate your willingness to help."

"This case is far more pressing than anything I'm working on at the moment. I want to help. And, I prefer to see my candidates in action."

"So I'm being graded?"

"Sort of." Quinn opened the door. "You ready?"

"Absolutely." Kate stepped out and headed toward the entrance. "I hope to hell we find something useful. With Copeland and Vega on the run, it's hard to say who's holding who hostage."

Quinn approached her. "Could be neither."

Kate pushed inside and approached the desk. "Dr. Carr,

please. He's expecting us." She held out her badge. "FBI Agent Reid and this is Special Agent Quinn."

The man pressed a button and a buzzer sounded on the door behind them. "Go on through."

The two entered the sterile corridor and Kate began, "Tell me, do you miss the daily grind of being in the field?"

"Sometimes. I do get out every now and again. Case in point. So it's not like we're all stuck behind desks. It's just not quite the same as it is for you. Why? Do you think you'll miss field work?"

"Yes. Sometimes. But then Agent Scarborough says working behind the scenes has been somewhat liberating for him. Although he'd been in the field far longer than I and had seen far worse."

Quinn stopped her in the hall just before they were about to enter the autopsy room. "I understand he saved your life."

"Yes. He and another colleague." She wouldn't reveal the identity of that person. Quinn was still an unknown.

"I'm sorry to hear your life had been in danger but grateful you had help. Please don't take offense when I say that one of my biggest concerns in bringing you on board is knowing your personal relationship with my boss. And that he would ultimately still be your boss too."

"I understand and it's nothing I haven't been faced with before. ASAC Campbell had those very concerns, but eventually, he came to understand that I'm my own person. I've carried my own weight and have never needed to lean on Agent Scarborough." Kate regarded him. "But you're still not convinced? What do I have to do to prove to you that Nick Scarborough isn't pulling my strings? That I'm not riding on his coat tails. In fact, I would prefer, if you still hold reservation, that I withdraw from the running. Frankly, I don't want Agent Scarborough's reputation sullied nor do I want to see my own reputation, which I have worked exceedingly hard to build, be questioned."

Quinn nodded. "Let's go inside."

Kate had no idea if she'd won the argument or raised more questions in his mind. And right now, maybe none of that was important. She was doing just fine with Dwight and Alicia by her side, on her team. Perhaps she'd placed too much import on this position. She'd experienced a freedom she hadn't known before Nick's departure from the WFO. And there was no denying it felt good. Kate would not be the subject of water-cooler conversations. It had taken her too long to dispel those very same conversations when she'd first come to the Bureau. Listening to everyone assume she was only there because Nick wanted it. Campbell had finally put those rumors to rest and to face that again—well, it just wasn't something Kate was prepared to do.

"Good afternoon, Agent Reid, or is it evening?" Dr. Carr offered his hand.

"Quickly approaching evening, I believe." She returned his greeting. "Thanks for sticking around. This is Agent Quinn, BAU Headquarters."

"Headquarters? Don't see you guys around here often. Pleased to meet you."

"Same here, doctor. No. We aren't often out and about like our friends at the Washington Field Office. So tell me, have you found anything that might help us catch the person who killed this woman?"

The doctor stepped around the table where the young woman lay covered in a white sheet with only her head and neck exposed. The bullet hole in her forehead had been cleaned and the skin around it purple from the blood trapped between her skin and her skull. He reached for an evidence bag. "This is the fabric that was discovered in the victim's mouth."

"Same as the others," Kate added.

"It appears so. It's going out shortly for analysis. But as I understand it, you have information on its origins."

"We do, but confirmation will still be necessary on this one," Kate replied.

He returned his attention to the body. "I was able to retrieve bullet fragments in the victim, which I believe is the first time something was left behind."

"There were casings found at the scene of the previous victim," Kate began. "But to my knowledge, the trace isn't yet complete. Unfortunately, these victims are appearing faster than we can get our test results. Which is one of the reasons why we're here now. I'm afraid our time has run out. We now have a potential hostage situation."

"I see. I'm very sorry to hear that."

"Any signs of a struggle? Similar to our last victim with the skin under her nails?" she continued.

"Doesn't appear to have been a struggle. More like the victim was caught off guard and simply murdered where she stood. There is still the issue of the thumbprint." He raised the woman's shoulder. "It's only partial, but it is my understanding that it may be enough."

"Detective Phelps is checking on that as we speak." Kate moved closer to the body. "We have to find something tying her to Congressman Copeland or his staff. I'm sure you've been reading the papers."

"I try hard not to, but this one does seem to be all-consuming at the moment. And that the congressman is at the heart of the matter."

Quinn moved next to Kate. "If we don't find him soon, I fear we won't find him at all."

SUE COPELAND STOOD inside the living room. "What is this place?"

"You should ask your husband. He's very familiar with it." Vega turned to Copeland in anticipation of a response.

"Grant?"

"It's my apartment."

"Your apartment? What are you talking about?"

"He's telling you this is the place where he brought his women, most of the time. Sometimes they stayed in hotels, sometimes they came here, depending on what was most convenient, I imagine."

"How did you get the money for this place? I don't understand."

"You want to tell her, or should I?"

Copeland regarded Vega with growing anger. "Donations. I used some campaign donations from my last election."

"Oh my God."

Vega approached her. "This isn't the man you married, Sue. He's been cheating on you for years. He bought this place. You have no idea what he has become. And I'm here to show you."

"For God's sake, you think I didn't know what he was up to? Not about this place, but about the other women? You think I'm a complete fool? Jesus, Phil, what the hell have you done?"

"You knew he was fucking around on you and did nothing? Said nothing?"

"You think I'm the first politician's wife to be cheated on? I knew what I signed up for from the very beginning. My God, Phil, did you kill those women because Grant was screwing them?"

"I had no choice. He was destroying everything I built. He was destroying you."

"You built?" Grant lunged toward him. "I'm the one who was

elected, not you. Who the hell do you think you are? You killed them? Janine?"

Vega pulled his weapon and pointed it at Grant.

"No!" Sue screamed out. "Don't. Please. Don't."

"Why do you care after what he's done? I was trying to protect you. Don't you see that?"

Copeland peered at him. "How could I have missed it? Something that is now so utterly obvious. You're in love with her. You're in love with my wife."

"I have something to show you." Vega continued to point his weapon at Copeland. "Go. Both of you. Or I swear, I'll shoot this son of a bitch right in front of you, Sue. Do as I say now. Go sit down."

Sue cast her gaze between the two of them and appeared ready to heed Vega's warning. "What is it you want me to see?"

Vega moved toward the couch and retrieved his laptop, placing it on the coffee table. He booted up the computer. "Sit down. Both of you." With the laptop running, he opened the files and a video began to play.

Sue and Grant Copeland watched as the images displayed on the screen. It was the apartment they were in now.

"You put cameras in here?" Grant looked to Vega. "You're fucking sick."

"I warned you to stop. That it would not only destroy your marriage, but also your career. But you didn't listen and now four women are dead."

"What do you mean, four? Phil, who was it this time? Whose life did you take as a way to what? Get back at me?"

Sue watched as the video played. It was Janine Atherton and she was in bed with her husband. The sounds of their lovemaking made her cringe and look away.

"Look at what he did to you. He humiliated you," Vega said. "And this is just the tip of the iceberg. There are so many others."

"Stop. Turn it off—please. How could you turn against us, Phil? How could you do this to me? If you are in love with me, then why put me through this? Did you really believe I could ever forgive you for murdering innocent women?"

"Innocent? Is that what you think they were?" Vega shook his head wildly. "They were whores. And I made sure everyone knew it. They were just as much to blame as Grant and they got what they deserved. And now it's his turn."

"You can't keep us here. They'll figure out where we are," Grant said.

"Probably, but it's not like I thought I'd get out of this unscathed. The point now is to make you suffer as much as you've made your wife suffer. I have loved you, Sue. For a very long time and I'd hoped you'd see who Grant really was. I guess maybe you did, but didn't care."

"I did care, but not enough to destroy my family. Ruin my children's lives and burn down Grant's career. He could've gone so much farther and you've annihilated that now. If anyone has destroyed me, Phil, it's you."

❧

THE MEDICAL EXAMINER pulled the sheet over the victim's head. "I'm sorry, but that's everything I have right now. I wish I had more."

"So do we," Kate replied.

"What do you think we should do now?" Quinn folded his arms and considered her like a teacher guiding his student.

"Find Mrs. Copeland. Find Vega and the congressman too. What else can we do?" She retrieved her cell. "Thank you again,

Dr. Carr. We've still got a lot of work ahead of us." Kate pushed through the door and made the call. "Where are you? Nothing yet from the ME's office. Anything on CCTV? The prints?" Kate's eyes widened as she looked to Quinn. "You did? That's good. Some good news. Sure, we'll head back to the station now." With renewed confidence, Kate slipped the phone back into her pocket. "Vasquez says they got Copeland and Vega on surveillance from the hotel. Vega was seen going into the room with a suitcase after Copeland checked out. Came out a few minutes later. It was reported that day that sheets had been taken from the room."

"That doesn't help us find either one of them."

"No. But it's safe to assume who the murderer is and I bet the prints will match too. It's Phillip Vega."

THE METRO POLICE station was still swarming with reporters. Word spread quickly that the congressman hadn't shown up to get a statement on record. And it was no longer a local story. In Washington, with a political climate as volatile as this one, everyone wanted in on the deal. The national stage had been set and the time had come for Kate to jump into the fray.

"You're here. Good." Phelps spotted Kate and Noah Quinn in the doorway. "Get inside and close the door. The rest of your team are here too."

"Any luck on your end tracking down Vega?" she asked.

"Not yet. I've got people searching his known hangouts, his house, parents' house. Any place we can think of where he might hole up with the congressman. And, we did get prints back. It confirms what we already know."

"That it's Vega," Kate replied. "And what about Mrs. Copeland? Any sign of her yet?"

"No," Vasquez said. "It's looking like she may be with them, either voluntarily—or not."

"What about Karen Hildebrand? Is she safe?" Kate looked to Dwight.

"I reached out to her via Scarborough. She's safe."

"Thank God. What about any others?"

"We did see another on the CCTV footage. I've asked our people to run the images through FACE in hopes of getting a positive ID," Vasquez began. "I did have an interesting call from Pearson regarding Tasha Brenner. She wasn't captured on video with Copeland. Though that's not a surprise considering the length of time that had passed since their relationship. I think it's now safe to say Vega knew where she lived and waited."

"Why's that?" Kate continued.

"Pearson said he and Ramos cleared the man she'd been with earlier in the evening. His prints turned up on a bottle of beer in her living room. Given what we know about Vega now, I figure he broke into her house and did the deed after that guy left." Vasquez looked to Phelps. "There is one thing. Do we know if the Copelands have just the one property? Is there a vacation home we don't know about where Vega might be?"

"We aren't aware of any additional properties." Phelps returned to his computer and began typing. "But I can search and find out for sure."

"What about a BOLO on Vega's car or Copeland's?" Kate began pacing the room. "Someone has to have seen them. Are your people on the lookout?"

Phelps shook his head. "I'll get one issued now." He nodded to an officer standing near.

"What the hell? That should've been done hours ago when neither showed up here."

"I got it handled, okay, Reid? Just back the fuck off."

Dwight stepped in. "That's enough. We don't need any infighting right now. Not when there could be more lives at stake."

Kate appeared disgusted. "Unbelievable. You do realize the gravy train is off the track, right?"

"Excuse me?" Phelps moved nearer to Kate. "What the hell did you just say to me?"

"You heard me. You're a real piece of work. You think we don't all know what you've done?"

Phelps refused to let go of her gaze. "Agent Jameson, you'd better call her off. I think her leash is a little too long."

"Reid, get the hell out of here," Jameson replied. "Don't make me do something we'll all regret."

"Come on. Let's get some coffee. There's still a lot of work to be done." Vasquez took Kate by the shoulder and led her out of the room.

"I'll go with them. Let you two hash this out." Quinn followed.

Kate tossed back a bottle of water in the breakroom where Vasquez remained by her side. "Can you believe this? He didn't even think to put out a BOLO? Are you kidding me with this?"

Quinn arrived to find them consoling one another. "You can sit here and be pissed, or you can do something to find Sue Copeland and make sure she's safe."

"And that would be?" Kate replied.

"I'd suggest asking a colleague to search the DOT cameras for Vega's car or either of the Copelands'. Don't need a BOLO for that."

There was one person Kate could ask who could get this information with little effort. "I'll make the call." She pulled her phone from her pocket and placed it against her ear. "It's Agent Reid. Listen, I know I said I wasn't going to ask for another favor..."

HAVING DECIDED there was no other solution than to recruit Agent Fraser once again, Kate, Vasquez, and Quinn headed back to the WFO, leaving Dwight to handle Phelps. It was probably the only way Kate could ensure she'd make it through the night holding on to her job. Perhaps having Quinn along wasn't the best decision she'd ever made. He was seeing a side of her she hardly knew existed, the impact of which remained to be seen.

"Thanks for doing this, Fraser. What'd you find?" Kate stood at his desk while the others hovered near.

"Looks like Vega's car has been on the move for much of the late morning and into the afternoon. DOT cameras caught him heading into Fairfax. That was around 1pm."

"Three hours after he missed the appointment at the station."

"Yep," Vasquez replied. "And we have to assume he went there to collect Mrs. Copeland."

"Right. When we checked the house, no one was home. And that was at around, what, 2pm?"

"Around that time," Quinn added. "Was he spotted anywhere after that?"

"Yes. They picked up his car again heading onto Massachusetts Ave."

"That's on the way back into D.C. He wouldn't be stupid enough to come back here, would he?" Kate asked.

"Depends if he's got a place to go," Quinn continued.

"Can you run a property tax check to see if Vega owns anything in the vicinity?"

"Sure." Fraser eyed Kate. "So he's the guy you're all after?"

"Almost certain."

"And what about the congressman?"

"We can't confirm his direct involvement. Though I suspect, if we're to find one, we'll find the other and get our answers."

"Okay, so according to county property tax records, Vega just has the one property, at least in his name."

"Can you check Copeland? I was booted out of Metro PD before we could find out."

"Sure, give me a second here. Okay, yeah, so Copeland's got the house in Fairfax. No. I'm sorry, Reid, I'm not seeing anything else in his name."

"Damn it. They wouldn't come back here without a place to go." Kate looked to Vasquez. "Any ideas?"

"What about a company?"

"A company?"

"Yeah. That Copeland might have ownership in. If he has one, it's entirely possible he could've purchased a property in the company's name."

Kate smiled and looked to Quinn. "She's good." Upon returning her attention to Fraser, she continued, "Can you run a check with the corporation commission for any ownership details on Copeland?"

"I'm on it."

They waited in silence for Fraser to get what they needed.

"Bingo. Agent Vasquez, you were right. Copeland is the managing partner of an LLC. That LLC owns a condo Downtown. You want the address?"

23

The city lights shimmered through the apartment window as Sue Copeland remained on the sofa, gun pointed at her, and sitting next to her cheating husband. As if that was the worst thing that could happen to her. What was worse was that she'd begun to watch Phillip Vega unravel before her eyes. A man who had professed his love for her and insisted the reason behind the murders was for her own protection. To show her the kind of man her husband really was.

However, Sue had already been well aware of who Grant Copeland really was and how his behavior had worsened over the years. Seemed the more political power he gained, the more power he wielded over those who worked around him, particularly of the female persuasion. And she was not blameless in his transformation. The money and the prestige she had greatly coveted. Her blind eye refused to acknowledge what was happening. And it seemed the greatest impact had fallen upon Phil Vega's shoulders.

"You can't keep us here," Sue began. "You have to realize they will find us. You say you love me, and the best way for you to show it is to let us go and surrender yourself."

The television played in the background as Phil watched the news. "It's too late for that. They've all but convicted Grant of the murders."

"I didn't kill them!"

Phil raised his weapon. "Maybe you didn't pull the trigger, but they're dead because of you. Don't kid yourself."

"So what now, Phil? Look, I know I'm the cause of this. I get that. But Sue, she's got nothing to do with my conduct. She doesn't deserve this. You did what you set out to do and that was to humiliate me in front of my wife, in front of the world. It's over now."

"The only thing that's over is your career, Grant." Vega returned his attention to the news broadcast. "The people are tired of corrupt politicians. They're tired of them assuming they are above the law. What I did will be seen as heroic."

"Are you insane? You murdered innocent women. You'll be seen as a monster." Grant looked upon his one-time friend and advocate. "I never would've believed you were capable of such things."

"Nor I of you, Grant. Yet here we are."

Sue watched the two exchange jabs at one another, working on a solution to this nightmare. "The only thing you can do now, Phil, is to let us go. Grant will not be free from persecution, but you stand a chance at escape. That's what I want for you. To be free of our lives and our choices." She felt the glare from her husband's eyes. "If you go now, there's still a chance you'll get out. There's no mention of roadblocks on the news. Not yet. Don't squander this opportunity."

"What the hell are you saying?" Grant eyed her with confusion.

Phil appeared to consider her argument. "Maybe there is still a chance. I—I never wanted to hurt them. But they shouldn't have done what they did. And when I saw him trying to warn one of them on his computer, I got even angrier."

"I know. In fact, I saw it too and went straight to the police. That's when I knew his cowardice had no bounds. Imagine, sending an email to someone with a warning that her life could be in danger." Sue inched closer to the edge of the sofa, almost within arm's distance of him. She caught the look of shame on Grant's face before returning her attention to Phil.

"You went to the police?"

"I had to. I did it to protect you. You see, I couldn't be sure what was happening. I do care about you, Phil, very much. But this isn't really about those women, is it?"

He shook his head, turning his gaze down to his feet. "I love you, Sue. And that love made me do things—bad things—and I see how it has hurt you. I see that now."

She reached across the space between them, resting her hand on his knee. "It's okay. I forgive you. The country will forgive you."

Phil watched her hand and turned slowly to meet her eyes. He began to nod. "I'll go. Then you two can leave and go to the police. Just please, give me a little head start."

"Of course we will." Her hand slipped from his knee as Phil stood. She fixed her eyes on his weapon as he lowered it to his side. A quick look to Grant and he seemed to understand what it was she was doing. The muscles in her stomach tightened and her pulse raced.

When Phil had returned fully to his feet, she stood. A smile laced with feigned compassion arose on her lips. She moved closer and was now only inches from him. "Can I at least say goodbye? I'll miss you. I'll miss our talks. If only I'd known sooner how you really felt." Sue pressed her lips onto his and as he surrendered to the warmth of her body, her arms raised as though she was about to embrace him. And when she felt confident his guard was down, she ripped the weapon from his limp hand and pushed hard against him. He stumbled back and fell over the chair from which he'd just stood.

Shock masked his face as he eyed the gun now firmly pointed at his head. "What are you doing? Why are you doing this? After everything you've said to me?"

Sue's only response was in firing the weapon, striking Phil in the cheek. He wailed in pain until she fired again, this time, striking him in the forehead. No more sound emerged.

"Jesus Christ!" Grant was on his feet, eyeing Phil on the ground and the woman who had shot him. His wife. "We have to get out of here."

"Why? This was self-defense. And that's what we'll make clear, you understand? I just stopped a killer. It's the only way we get out of this with our freedom and reputation intact."

The arrival of Kate and her impromptu team to the apartment building was stopped short by the presence of the man who'd worked hard to keep his investigation close to his chest.

Kate stepped out and quickly approached him. "What are you doing here?"

"Got a call of shots fired." Phelps lit up a cigarette. "We found them. Copeland and his wife are being treated for shock but are otherwise unharmed." He pointed to the ambulance. "Phillip Vega is dead."

"Dead?" Vasquez approached with Quinn trailing behind.

"Yep. Sue Copeland shot him. Claims self-defense and by the looks of it, I'd say she's probably right about that. So I guess it's over."

"Why didn't you call us?" Kate asked.

"No time. Sorry about that. Your boss is here, though, inside, so have a word with him about it if you want."

Kate wondered if her jaw was actually on the floor or it just felt that way. The likelihood that all three were here was the easy part to understand, but to have Copeland's wife be the one to take Vega down. Not that any woman wasn't capable of such a thing, but it seemed—contrived. Too clean. Like the congressman wanted it that way to take the heat off himself. "Can I talk to the Copelands?"

"Be my guest." Phelps blew smoke near her face as she walked past him.

She waved the others over and Vasquez and Quinn caught up to her.

"What are you going to say to them?" Vasquez asked.

"I'm going to ask them what happened. I need to hear it directly from them. I don't trust anything Phelps has to say." She noticed Quinn's disappointment. Like she should take the detective at face value and accept that it was over. And the killer was dead. But this wasn't over. Not for her.

"Excuse me, Mrs. Copeland? We met earlier in the week at the police station. Agent Reid."

Sue was draped in a blanket, even though it was a warm summer night, and held a bottle of water in her hands. "Yes?"

"I'm so sorry about what's happened. I can't imagine what you and your husband have just gone through." She could but was really trying to play up the empathy card. What was even more concerning was that Vasquez peered at her as though trying to figure out what game Kate was playing. This wasn't a game, but perhaps because of Phelps, she'd suspected everyone of lying and covering things up.

"Thank you."

"This is Agent Vasquez and Agent Quinn. As you know, we've been assisting the Metro Police and Detective Phelps on this investigation. In fact, it was only a short time ago, we discovered your husband owned an apartment in this building. It seems the man who brought you here was very smart."

"He was a family friend." Sue began to cry.

"Please. If you need to get statements from us, can it just wait? My wife and I need to go to the hospital."

"Of course, Mr. Copeland. My sincerest apologies." Kate nodded and stepped away from the ambulance.

"What is going on, Kate?" Vasquez asked.

"Something's not right. I mean, I figured they'd be here. We all did, but..."

"But what? That woman saved her and her husband's life. The man who killed those women is dead. You should be relieved. I know I am."

"What is it, Reid?" Quinn began. "What's got you bothered about this?"

Kate peered back at the couple, who were now being escorted inside the truck. "Did you happen to notice any signs of a struggle on her or the congressman?"

"They were wrapped in blankets," Quinn replied.

"Yes. But she was very calm."

"What are you getting at?" Vasquez continued.

"No agitation, no visible signs of a struggle to get the gun." Kate appeared dismayed by the theory developing in her mind. "So Vega just handed it to her? Said, here you go, shoot me?"

"After the brutal attacks on the women, the note; it doesn't seem to fit the profile." Quinn cast a brief glance at the ambulance that began to pull away.

"No. It doesn't," Kate replied.

"You're forgetting that he was a family friend. He must've felt guilty and pained by what had happened. He must've regretted what he'd done," Vasquez said.

"We can sit here and postulate all night, but what we need to do is get inside and take a look at the apartment. Talk to the CSI team about their theories as to what happened. Talk to Jameson. We can talk to the Copelands later. Hopefully, before the media gets to them," Kate said.

~

THE ELEVATOR DOORS parted on the eighth floor of the high-rise building in downtown D.C., an exclusive area that housed many government officials and wealthy lobbyists.

"That looks like the place." Kate gestured toward the unit with the opened door and several officers standing in the hall. She took the lead and made her way toward one of the men in blue standing in the doorway. "Special Agent Kate Reid." She flashed her badge. "We're working with Detective Phelps on this investigation."

"Who you here to see?"

"The lead CSI investigator."

The officer pointed toward the living room. "He's over there."

"Thanks." Kate walked inside.

"Don't touch anything."

She peered back at the officer as though she wasn't already well aware of that fact. "Yeah, thanks."

"Cut him some slack. He's just a kid," Vasquez said.

"Can I help you?" The lead investigator eyed the federal agents.

"FBI. Reid, Vasquez, and Quinn. Can we ask you a few questions?"

"The Feds, huh? We've already got one of you here, some-where. Anyway, shoot."

"We've actually been working with Detective Phelps. So that's him? That's Phillip Vega?"

"Yes, ma'am. They'll be loading him onto the truck soon."

"What can you tell us about the incident itself?" she continued.

"You mean, how'd he get shot?"

"Yeah."

"I haven't seen a statement from the victims yet, but we can glean at this point that she took a shot at his face, hit his cheek. Blew off damn near half of it. Realized he wasn't dead, then managed to get one off in his skull. That did the trick."

She looked around the room. "Nothing damaged. No signs the victim struggled to gain control of the weapon?"

"None that I can see just yet. According to the detective, the guy was a family friend. Mrs. Copeland must've convinced him to give up his weapon. Until we talk to them, it's just conjecture."

"Yeah. Listen, thanks for..." Kate spotted the laptop on the table. "Any idea who that belongs to?"

"Nope. We need to bag it and tag it, though."

"Agent Reid, I think we're at a standstill until we can speak with the Copelands." Dwight approached from the hall. "We should let these guys do their jobs."

"Of course. Thank you for your time."

"No problem."

They headed toward the front door and made their way outside.

"What are the odds we can get our hands on that laptop?" Kate stopped on a dime. "What about getting a subpoena for the Copelands' computers?"

"Why do you want to subpoena the victims' computers? Especially considering one of them in a United States congressman," Dwight asked.

"Part of the investigation. Like you said, Vega was a family friend who, I'm sure, was in constant communication with the family and Mr. Copeland, considering his position. We need to know if Vega left any indications of what he was planning or if the communications seemed disturbing in any way."

"I'd say that would be a reasonable request," Quinn began. "Problem is getting around Phelps to do it."

"See, I don't think so. I think he'd be more than happy to close out this investigation. They got their man. Let Copeland deal with the political fallout, if any. I mean, he's the victim, right? There were only a few people who knew of the affairs. And most of them are dead."

"Except Mrs. Copeland. We assume she knew, right?" Vasquez appeared to understand what Kate was getting at. "And there's the congressman, but I imagine he'll take as much of that to the grave as he can."

"That's where I think he'll get help from Phelps. Which leaves us to get to the bottom of Sue's motivations and whether or not she knew of the transgressions or if Vega told her. She certainly knew about Janine Atherton. I can't speak to the rest." Kate turned to Quinn. "You're from headquarters. Can you pull this off? Can you get us a subpoena for that laptop and whatever is in the Copeland residence? It has to happen soon, especially if Phelps has anything to say about it."

"Jameson will have the same pull as I do."

"I'd venture to say, given the confrontations of members of my team and Metro's lead investigator, Reid might be right on this one," Dwight replied.

Kate held his gaze. "Can you help us or not?"

"Why don't you get Scarborough to step in? He's the senior unit agent. I work for him, in case you don't remember."

Kate didn't want to have to rely on Nick for anything and

certainly not to grant favors for her, even if it meant she could get to the truth. If there was a truth to reveal. And this had begun to feel as though Quinn was testing her again. He was being far too reluctant. "I'd prefer not to involve him."

He eyed the people standing before him. "Fine. I'll make the call now. See what I can do. No guarantees."

THE HOUR WAS APPROACHING MIDNIGHT, but the warrant finally came through. Kate stood outside the Copeland residence with her phone against her ear. "We're here. Quinn pulled it off. We're getting ready to go inside now."

"Don't forget, this is your deal. You own it, no matter the outcome."

"I know. I don't know when I'll be home. We're going to take the computers, but that's all. I'll have to go back to WFO after that."

"Don't worry. Do what you have to do. I would."

"I know that too. I'll call you later. Bye." Kate ended the call as Quinn approached.

"You ready to do this?"

"Any word from the Copelands?"

"Their attorney is on his way. Copeland made sure his ass was covered."

"I'll bet he did." She turned toward the headlights that shone in her eyes. "Speak of the devil. Unless you're expecting someone else?"

"No. That must be the attorney. He's got the key to let us in."

"Nice change of pace not to have to break down someone's door," Kate said, laughing.

"That takes me back."

"Oh yeah? Where were you assigned after the Academy?"

"New Mexico, if you can believe that."

"Really? I hail from San Diego, outside Eureka, originally."

"I know. I reviewed your file, remember? I know a lot about you, Agent Reid." Quinn stopped talking as the Copelands' lawyer approached. "Thank you for coming down, sir. I'm sure you can understand the urgency."

"No, not really, but I'll have a chance to argue it in court. You have a lot of nerve doing this, especially when the congressman and his wife are in the hospital. Bet that won't look good for the Bureau."

"This is for the Copelands' protection. Nothing more."

The lawyer headed toward the front door, key in hand. "Uh huh. I'm sure. There you go. Uh, one thing, though. Nothing leaves this house without my approval."

"We are authorized to remove computers and laptops."

"That's right. And that's all you're going to take."

Kate brushed past the man and into the home that was pitch black. She found a switch in the foyer and a chandelier illuminated. "You guys ready?" She turned back to see Quinn and Vasquez trailing while the lawyer stood firmly in front of the door. "I'll go upstairs." She made her way to the second floor and began searching the rooms. "Found one," she shouted below and unplugged the laptop.

Two more rooms would complete the sweep of the upstairs. Kate headed back down. "Only got the one."

"I found one in the den. Probably Copeland's," Vasquez replied.

Quinn emerged from the living room. "Nothing on my end. These must be the only two here. Unless there's a secret hiding place."

"What about the congressman's office?" Vasquez asked.

"That's off limits. Government secrets and stuff. No way we'll get anything there." Quinn returned to the foyer. "If that's it, we should go and see what we've got." He headed toward the door. "See? That didn't take long. The Bureau appreciates your time."

The attorney stepped aside to let them pass and locked up the home. "Anything you find will also have to be submitted to me and my team for review. You understand that?"

"Yes, sir. Goodnight." Kate stepped into her car and keyed the ignition. "I sure as hell hope there's something here. I have a feeling my ass is on the line."

Quinn caught her gaze in the rearview as he sat in the back seat. "It is."

24

A few stragglers lingered at the WFO upon their return, among them, Dwight and ASAC Campbell, both of whom were conversing in the dimly lit bullpen when the elevator doors opened.

"We're not alone." Kate looked to Vasquez. "I have a feeling this is now a high priority for the Bureau."

Campbell spotted their arrival and a notable look of concern shrouded his face. "I hope you all know what you're doing. I thought you were one to toe the line, Reid, but it appears I might have been wrong in that assumption. You realize the pressure you've just put on this department?"

"I'm simply doing my job, sir. Covering all the bases and I didn't think that would be a point of contention."

"Oh, it isn't for me, but it is for Headquarters. You've stirred the pot getting a warrant to retrieve the personal files of a member of congress."

Kate carried on toward her desk as Quinn and Vasquez followed and remained silent in her defense. She'd already made it clear this was her call and they would not be held liable for anything that came of it. But knowing Vasquez, that was never going to happen.

"With respect, sir, we found some items of concern in the suspect's home and we're merely following up on their origins," Vasquez said.

"Such as?"

"Phillip Vega kept photos of Mrs. Copeland in his home, signifying their relationship was more than what it seemed."

"Or perhaps was a one-sided attraction," Quinn added.

"That's it? You got a warrant based on that?" Campbell looked at Dwight. "This could blow up on us, Jameson. I need you to keep a lid on this because if it does, I'll have not only the director on my ass, but we'll both be testifying before a congressional committee and we know how that will turn out." He headed into the corridor. "Keep me updated on your progress. I don't care what time it is—just do it."

Quinn watched him leave. "Seems a likable guy."

"Actually, he is, but he has a right to be concerned. We all do. Let's go set this up in the conference room and see what we can find," Kate replied.

In the early morning hours, the team and welcomed consultant, Quinn, huddled around the Copelands' laptops and Vega's home computer, which was confiscated by Phelps and finally turned over at the insistence of ASAC Campbell. Despite his warnings, he wasn't a man to leave his team flapping in the wind.

NICK FLIPPED through the television stations, unable to settle on anything. His mind raced as he waited to hear from Kate. It was approaching 3am and still no word. Not since she texted him that they'd returned to WFO. But this was not his investigation, although one of his own team was assisting. The last thing he wanted to do was step on Kate's toes, or Dwight's.

The past several weeks, he'd worked hard at separating himself from the WFO—from Kate and Dwight. And it hadn't been easy. All in the name of getting Kate to Quantico where he could again work with her. Something he missed so very much. But sitting here, away from the action, an administrator, of sorts. It was a difficult concept for him to wrap his head around. He enjoyed his new position; the prestige that came along with it and, of course, the money. Retirement was well within his sights now and a good retirement at that. He'd already given fifteen years to the Bureau. What was another five or more? Now he didn't have to confront, on a regular basis, the evils, the demons, and monsters that had so often haunted his dreams. The monsters he didn't catch and the demons who died in his presence and sometimes as a direct result of his actions. That was the reason he desired change. But now that he had it, was it enough?

Nick walked into the kitchen and opened the cupboard above the stove and peered at the bottle of Jack Daniels that was still half-full. Perhaps he would find sleep if he could quiet the thoughts that spun in his head. Would it permit him to stop thinking of her and what she was doing? Why couldn't he let her be who she needed to be?

The answer stared back at him as plainly as the label on the bottle. Kate was becoming someone who didn't need him anymore. Not in the way she had in the past. The tenuous beginnings of their romantic relationship had strengthened since she moved in, but Nick was ever fearful of her pulling away, though he so often championed her departure and independence. Now in the face of it, he wanted to be by her side again, just as Quinn was now; a man who had been attracted to her, not knowing perhaps who she was. And to his credit, it seemed it was not a factor anymore, but Nick had developed a minor jealous streak in his time with Kate. Something he had never experienced before in past relationships, not even when Georgia slept with another man.

He reached for the bottle and gripped it as though it might slip through his fingers and despair would settle around him. He grabbed a glass and walked to the balcony, slipping out through the sliding door and into the cool breeze that drifted in from the bay. Would it get better when he truly accepted Kate deserved autonomy and deserved to grow and become whoever she was meant to become at the Bureau? That was the entire premise of their friendship. From the very beginning, that was what he had wanted for her. And no matter how different he thought he was from Marshall Avery, the true love of her life, and someone with whom he could never really compete, it was turning out that he might be more like him than he ever thought possible. This was something that was not in Kate's best interest.

Nick poured the whiskey into the old-fashioned glass until it was half-full. That was where things usually started. And by the end of it, there would be no glass, only the bottle until there was nothing left.

TURNED OUT, what they were looking for wasn't as hard to find as they'd expected, which drew even greater concern.

"He just left these emails here? Didn't try to delete them?" Kate looked at Dwight. "This doesn't seem right."

He peered over her shoulder at the screen and shook his head. "We can't pretend to understand what goes on in the mind of a killer and especially one who's driven by a twisted notion of love."

"Jameson's right," Quinn replied. "These emails between Sue

Copeland and Phillip Vega display a desperate man who would do anything to get the woman he loved, while not admitting it outright. And she used that to her advantage. She was playing him." He looked at Kate. "This is what we talked about the other night."

"It is. Someone was pulling the strings and it was her. Although nothing in these emails proves she asked him to do anything. She's playing the victim here. Look at her wording. Asking why her husband hadn't come home on a particular night. Or why Vega kept him at the office to work late. Often suggesting that Vega come over for dinner, that she could use the company."

"I think anyone reading these would come to the same conclusion," Dwight replied.

"She manipulated him, that is obvious." Quinn pointed toward the screen. "She was instilling in him the notion that whatever her husband was doing was taking its toll on her emotionally. Though not once does she outright say that he was cheating on her. She was convincing him that he was working for a dishonest and deceitful man through wordplay."

"It appears Sue Copeland had set out to destroy her husband. Maybe she finally got fed up with his philandering," Vasquez began. "And from what I see here, in these emails, she used every possible means at her disposal to get Vega to feel for her. And it worked. He developed affection for her. What do we want to do?"

"We need to move on this before much longer," Kate added. "Once the Copelands are released from the hospital, Sue Copeland is going to know what we found and I highly doubt the woman will still be around waiting to be hauled off to jail."

"We can bring her in for questioning." Dwight moved back to his seat. "The problem, again, as I see it, she didn't pull the trigger and there's nothing in these emails to suggest she asked Vega to do it."

"What about the 1am phone calls? Can we trace any of them back to Sue Copeland?" Quinn asked.

"You mean the calls we found on two of the victims' cell phones?" Vasquez asked.

"If any one of those numbers traces back to her, we would stand a much better chance at bringing charges of conspiracy." Dwight turned his attention to Kate. "You have the records handy?"

"I do. Most traced back to burner phones. How the hell are we supposed to know who purchased them?" Kate turned her sights upward, recalling the one person who just might be able to help. "I think I know someone."

"Who?" Vasquez replied.

"Agent Caison. I ran into him a few months back. He's been transferred to Headquarters, Counterterrorism." She looked at Dwight. "You remember him?'

"Aside from the fact that he was instrumental in uncovering the conspiracy regarding the mall bombing, yes, I remember him. You two were at Quantico together. What makes you think he can help?"

"Because he'll have contacts at NSA who will be able to trace those numbers and look up the registration information. Once he gets that, chances are very good he'll be able to track down the buyer."

Quinn noticed the time. "It's almost 4am. Maybe we should all try to get a couple hours' rest and then make contact with him."

"What happens if the Copelands are released?" Kate asked.

"Let me take care of that." Dwight began to leave. "I'll make sure they don't get released until later in the morning. But I can't guarantee more than a few extra hours. You and Caison will have to work fast."

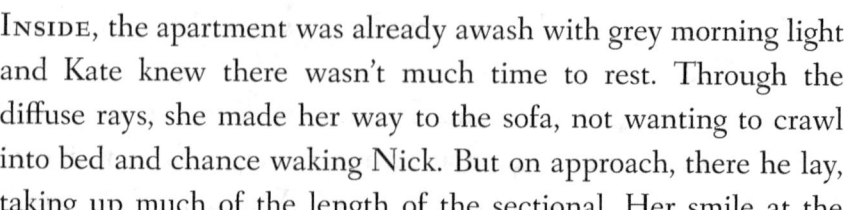

INSIDE, the apartment was already awash with grey morning light and Kate knew there wasn't much time to rest. Through the diffuse rays, she made her way to the sofa, not wanting to crawl into bed and chance waking Nick. But on approach, there he lay, taking up much of the length of the sectional. Her smile at the sight of him soon faded when she noticed the empty bottle of Jack sitting on the coffee table. Her heart dropped into her stomach.

So many times, she'd picked him up and dusted him off, and she thought all of that was behind them now. He'd gotten it under control again and her confidence in him had returned. Something had brought on this setback, but she could hardly think of anything that would send him reeling back so far. Things were going exactly as they had planned and they were happy.

Perhaps she was jumping to conclusions. Yes, of course. It was entirely possible he'd only had one or two and fell asleep awaiting her return. He deserved the benefit of the doubt.

"Nick?" She shook his arm. "Babe? Wake up."

He began to stir and his eyes flickered, attempting to focus on her in the minimal light. "Kate? You're home." A sleepy smile formed on his lips as he sat up and was noticeably unsteady.

"Are you okay?" Calling him out for drinking was a difficult thing for her to do. She'd watched her father drink to excess and often found herself rousing him from a drunken stupor as a teenager. Of course, she hadn't known the reason for his behavior until many years later. But it wasn't an easy thing for her to confront, even now with Nick.

"Me? Yeah, I'm fine. I guess I fell asleep waiting for you to come home." He caught her gaze only briefly before looking away.

She knew he had been drinking and while he appeared to be mostly sober, there was no mistaking the slight redness in his eyes and sway as he sat up on the couch. Kate glanced at the bottle and back to him. "I'm sorry it's so late. I only have a couple of hours before I have to get back. We think we've got the congressman's wife on a conspiracy charge, but I won't know yet until I can get some help from Will Caison."

"Caison? I thought he was in Kentucky."

"He was transferred to Headquarters earlier this year. I need his help to trace burner cell phone numbers. Geez, I'm sorry. I'm rattling on and you're still half-asleep."

"You should go put your head down while you can. Go on to bed. I'll leave you in peace."

She studied his demeanor but was much too exhausted to dig any deeper, though she should have. "Okay, yeah. I'll set my alarm." Kate leaned in to kiss his cheek. "Go back to sleep." This was not over, not by a long shot, but it would have to be put on the back burner. Why he turned to alcohol whenever things didn't go his way left her stunned. And what hadn't gone his way lately? He'd gotten everything he'd ever wanted. His dream job, her. Was it still not enough? Would anything ever be enough?

"Kate?" Nick sat on the edge of the bed. "Kate? You slept past your alarm. Hon, you got to wake up."

She opened her eyes to the bright morning light and Nick's haggard expression and overgrown five o'clock shadow. "Shit. What time is it?"

"It's 6:30."

Kate shot up out of bed. "Damn it. I'm supposed to be at the office in thirty minutes. I have to hop in the shower."

Nick moved out of her way. "I'll put on some coffee for you to take."

"Thanks," she shouted from the bathroom.

He walked gingerly toward the kitchen and upon waiting for the coffee to brew, he rubbed his throbbing temple.

Within minutes, Kate rushed out of the bedroom. "I have to get out of here."

He handed her a travel mug. "All ready for you."

"Thank you."

"Listen, about last night. I just needed..." It was clear he'd picked up on her disappointment and leaving the bottle on the table was a pretty clear sign as well.

"I have to go, Nick. I'm sorry." She held his gaze. "I'll call you later, when I know what's going on."

"Yeah. Okay." He kissed her cheek. "Be safe."

She left the apartment and walked along the corridor to the elevators. As the numbers lit up, she exhaled a heavy sigh. "I can't deal with this right now."

Her rubber-soled sneakers squeaked on the concrete floor of the parking garage, and once inside her car, Kate texted Vasquez that she was a few minutes late but was on her way.

The sun was fully awake and so were the thousands of people on the road impeding her progress. Will's cell number was still in her contacts list and she made the call, hoping he would answer; figuring he would.

"Caison here."

"Will, it's Kate Reid."

"Kate? Wow. Hello. How are you? I'm surprised to hear from you."

"I wish I could say this was a social call, but I need your help."

"Anything. Name it."

"I've got some phone numbers I'm pretty confident came from burner cells. What are the odds you can get a trace on those numbers for the registration information?"

"I don't have access to that. You'd have to get in touch with NSA."

"I know. I was hoping you would know someone there. I've never had to ask them for anything. And, to be honest, this is urgent. So chances are my request would be put on the back burner in any case."

"How urgent?"

"Oh, a couple of hours—at the most."

"I see."

"It's important. If I don't get this information, I have a sinking feeling my case will fall apart. Will, I really need your help here. Not that you owe me anything."

"You know I'd do anything for you, Kate." He paused. "Send me the numbers. I'll see what I can do."

"Thank you. This means a lot to me. You have no idea how much."

"Don't thank me yet."

"I'll text them to you now. I'm on my way to the WFO."

"Got it. Like I said. I'll do what I can and get back with you as soon as possible. Talk to you later, Kate."

SHE SOON ARRIVED, travel mug in hand, and stepped out into the buzzing bullpen. Catching Vasquez's eye, she approached. "What's going on?"

She pointed toward the monitor mounted on the wall. "You aren't going to believe this shit."

Kate watched as the congressman, with his wife by his side, stood in front of the hospital where several reporters pointed microphones in their faces. "I thought they weren't getting released until later this morning."

Dwight approached her. "I tried, but the Copelands still have powerful friends, for now at least. I think our time's up, Kate."

"Our rights have been grossly violated."

Kate watched the screen as Copeland spoke to the crowd, appearing frail.

"We have been treated as though we are the criminals in this, instead of the man who attempted to take my wife's life and my own while he sought to lay blame at our feet for the murders of innocent women with whom I had professional relationships. Our home was ransacked. Our lives turned upside down. This will not stand. The man responsible has been killed in self-defense. My wife, the brave, amazing woman you see standing next to me now, saved both our lives. While we are deeply saddened by the deaths of these young women, we cannot sit by while our good name is dragged through the mud in an attempt to cover up the gross negligence by local and federal authorities."

"What the hell is happening here?" Kate asked.

"He's trying to look like the hero. He and his wife," Vasquez replied. "Deflecting from the truth is all he has now. We know he didn't kill those women, but the truth as to why they were killed is more detrimental to him and his political career."

"What has Campbell said about this?"

"He's in his office, getting his ass handed to him by the assistant director for allowing us to get a warrant for the Copeland house."

"He should be talking to the judge then, not Campbell. And it was Quinn who put in the request anyway. I don't understand. How the hell did Grant Copeland pull this off so quickly?" She paused for a moment. "Phelps. He had to have played a part in this. He must have his hands in so many pockets in this town. He had to have called in favors because if it got out he was paid by

Copeland to sweep this under the rug, he would be in just as much hot water as Copeland."

"That's right." Vasquez folded her arms and peered at the television. "If we don't get something on Sue Copeland today, it's over for us." She turned to Kate. "And I don't just mean this investigation."

25

In the window of the café, Kate spotted him. "That's Agent Caison." She turned to Vasquez and Quinn, who'd gone along rather than face the music with Campbell.

"And you're confident he'll help?" Vasquez was generally a positive person, but after this morning's press conference, things had gone south and fast.

"He already has. I don't know how much he'll have for us, but it's better than nothing." Kate raised her hand as he entered to gain his attention.

"I didn't think I'd hear from you so soon."

Kate stood and greeted him with a warm embrace. "Neither did I. Thanks for coming down." She turned to Vasquez. "This is my partner, Agent Vasquez, and this is SSA Quinn, BAU Quantico."

"It's an honor to meet you both. Reid asked me to trace some burner phones for you all."

"Please, sit down." Kate took her seat and waited for Will to settle in. "I'm sure you're aware of the developing situation with Congressman Copeland?"

"It's pretty hard to miss."

"We were brought in to consult with Metro PD, but the detective there didn't have much faith in us and has been about as helpful as a dead head of lettuce. And so we took it upon ourselves, or rather, I took it upon us, to delve into a theory that would link the congressman's wife to the murders."

"I thought it was some congressional staff member who was responsible?" Will continued.

"Directly, yes." This time, Quinn stepped in. "However, we believe Sue Copeland was the principal influence and that's why Kate asked for your help."

"She sent me the numbers in question at around 7am. I reached out to my contact at NSA and asked him what he could do. However, I haven't heard back from him yet. And frankly, I don't know if what you're asking can be done in such a short time frame."

"We have to know if they trace back to the wife. And I'm afraid we have very little time to make our case against her," Kate continued.

"Agent Caison, if you can help, it'll mean putting behind bars the driving force behind the deaths of those women," Quinn said.

"I'll reiterate the urgency of the request, but it won't just be up to me. It's the NSA's call."

"Thank you. That's all I ask," Kate replied.

"What will you all do in the meantime?"

"Keep a low profile, stay away from the media," Quinn began. "Which won't be easy. And we'll continue to work the facts and see if we can come up with something more concrete."

"We have emails, but Mrs. Copeland was smart enough not to

implicate herself. Her words were vague, directions unclear, but we know what she wanted Phillip Vega to do," Vasquez said. "We just need your help to prove it."

Will stood ready to leave. "Of course. I'll keep plugging away. Reid, can I have a quick word?"

"Sure."

The two stepped outside as the hour approached noon.

"Thanks for coming down. I hope we're not wasting your time."

"Like I said in there, I'm not sure how much help I can be and I'll use whatever pull I've got to get my contact at NSA to provide me with the information quickly, but in the event I don't get it, or if it doesn't trace back to Sue Copeland, what's your strategy?"

"I'll be honest with you, I don't have one. I can try to use the emails we have to hold her on charges, but any lawyer worth his salt will see that all we have is speculation and no judge will keep her after that. I mean, she's still a congressman's wife."

"And the two were held hostage by the man who did kill those women."

"Right. So I just have to believe those numbers will point to her."

"I've always known you had a knack for hunches." He gently grasped her shoulders. "It is good seeing you again, Kate. I wasn't sure, after we passed in the night, so to speak, that you'd get in touch again."

"And you've become a national hero, so there's that."

Modesty revealed itself in his crooked smile. "I don't know about that. I had plenty of people to lean on and work with. And one very determined woman, not unlike you, who wouldn't stop until she got the truth."

"I'd better get back inside. You'll let me know as soon as you get anything?"

"Of course. Bye, Kate."

She watched him walk ahead and step into his car. After he drove away, Kate returned to the others. "I guess that's all we can do for now. You ready to head out?"

"I need to check in at Quantico. I don't want to leave you in a lurch, though."

"No, no, it's fine. This isn't your fight, but we really appreciate what you've done for us. I don't think we'd be this far without your insight."

"Don't sell yourself short. You two know what you're doing. But keep me posted and let me know if there's anything else I can do. You are on the right track."

"Just need to get something solid," Vasquez replied.

"Exactly."

As he began to leave, Kate turned to Vasquez. "We might as well go back to WFO and take our licks."

"I wouldn't count Campbell out yet. We'll tell him and Jameson what we're working on and hope they can stave off the worst of the pressure from the Copelands and their five-hundred-dollar-an-hour lawyers."

WITH A LINGERING HEADACHE, even after tossing back several tablets, Nick sat in his office, reviewing the testimony of his team in the Figueroa trial. He was concerned for Kate, especially after watching the news conference, but he maintained restraint and didn't reach out to offer help or guidance. It was the only way he would be able to distance himself from the events of this morning when she'd found him passed out on the sofa. It wasn't his intention and in fact was surprised by his own lack of self-control. It had been some time since that had happened. But it happened and he would have to make amends. The first step in that process was to not jump in and try to save the day for her. She could handle this. He knew that. Though he knew it could mean the end of her career if Campbell didn't back her, but Campbell had changed and he would have the team's back.

"Scarborough, you have a minute?" Quinn stood at the door.

"Yes. Come in. I didn't realize you were back."

"Just arrived. Not much more I can do for the WFO. It's out of my hands. I do, however, believe Agent Reid will find the answers she needs to bring the case to an end. She and her team are very capable."

"No question."

"It's clear your guidance and training paid off."

"Thank you, but I certainly can't take all the credit. Jameson, Reid, and Vasquez are bright, resourceful people. They'll be able to see this one through." He leaned back in his chair. "So, what can I do for you?"

"I'd like to talk to you about Agent Reid. I've seen her in action. I've seen the way she thinks and I am nothing if not impressed."

Nick displayed a proud smile.

"That being said, I have to say that she seems incredibly suited to the work she's currently doing. I'm not saying she wouldn't be an asset to me here, but I feel as though I'd be doing her a disservice, taking her away from what is clearly her calling. She's a little hot-headed, but that's probably a defense mechanism given the uphill battle she has faced throughout the course of her career."

The smile on Nick's face quickly faded. "Are you saying you intend to pass on her application?"

"You know her better than I, obviously, but I don't think I'm off-base here, do you?"

"Agent Reid can do whatever she puts her mind to. I've seen it first-hand on more than one occasion. Her determination alone is awe-inspiring. Having said that, I think the disservice would be in not asking what it is she wants to do, although I thought she'd made that clear when she requested the position in the first place."

"Are you saying this because it's what you want, or what she wants?"

"I guess I thought they were one and the same. Look, I know she's buried with this investigation and I also know she won't stop until she gets to the bottom of it. And I have every confidence she will. So, maybe the best thing to do in the interim is to put your decision on hold until you see what she accomplishes at the end of this investigation. I think that will be enough for you to make the case that she has the drive, the intelligence, and the desire to work as a profiler. I've seen her. I've seen her face when she realizes she got it right."

Quinn regarded his boss. "It seems like you're her biggest advocate. I hope your enthusiasm isn't misplaced." He inhaled a deep breath. "I need to think about this one. And you're right. She's got her hands full and that's going to take up a good portion of her time for the next several days, at least. I'll consider what you've said. And of course, when she's ready, she can come in and discuss what it is she wants to do." He began to leave.

"What about the others in contention?"

Quinn stopped and turned back. "They're all extremely well-qualified candidates. No question. And they've all got many years of service under their belts."

"But that doesn't make them more suited for the job."

"No. It doesn't."

THERE WASN'T much for Kate and Vasquez to do upon return to the WFO. After meeting with ASAC Campbell and Dwight, they were given a slight reprieve. But if something didn't turn up soon, they would have little in the way of protection and would have to face the music that they'd tried to implicate the wife of a congressman of colluding with a murderer. But Kate refused to believe anything to the contrary. She was right and now it was in Agent Caison's hands. A man she respected and trusted, even after their brief affair whose time and place was completely amiss. And now she was with Nick.

"Any word from your friend?" Vasquez appeared next to Kate with two mugs of coffee. "Here, you look like you could use a pick-me-up."

"Nothing yet. It's only been an hour."

"Yeah, well, it's not like we've got a lot of time to spare. The Copelands will be returning home soon and unless we come up with something, they'll get their belongings back. Then we're hosed."

Kate spun around in her desk chair to face her. "You didn't find anything that had been erased? Nothing deleted on Sue's laptop? What about the email Copeland sent to Karen Hildebrand?"

"That just shows us he was concerned for her and tried to warn her. Not that he knew his chief of staff was the killer. Although it sure seems the reason Vega went to the Copeland house that day was to find more victims. More women who'd slept with Grant. And Sue Copeland was extremely careful in her use of language toward Phillip Vega. Now, if they ever met in person and discussed anything, and by some miracle, we had evidence of collaboration from that, we'd be golden. If that exists, I don't know where the hell it would be or how we would track it down."

"And the bed sheets, we know, Vega took from the hotel."

"I can see your wheels spinning. What are you thinking?"

"Meredith Bowen didn't have anything to do with Grant Copeland apart from putting up with harassment."

"So why go after her in the first place? She didn't sleep with him, by all accounts. Why make her pay a price she didn't owe?" Vasquez asked.

"She had something on Vega, is the only thing I can gather. She could've gone to the press and spilled the beans about Copeland's unwanted advances."

"Yeah. But something's not right about that. The others, okay, I get it. They screwed around with her husband and according to her and Vega's twisted minds, they should be the ones to suffer. Never mind her husband, apparently. But the death of Meredith Bowen." Vasquez shook her head. "She doesn't fit the profile."

"Maybe we should go there—to her place—and check it out. Beats the hell out of sitting here and waiting for Caison to come through with something." Kate peered over her shoulder toward the corridor. "Let's talk Jameson into making a little trip with us. Maybe we'll find something. Maybe we won't. But at least we'll be doing something."

DWIGHT HELD the key in his hand. "Phelps pushed back on this until I told him it would be for his own protection, if we conducted our own search of the apartment. Right now, he's on edge and it's easy to figure out why." He pushed the key into the lock and opened the door, breaking the police tape seal.

The apartment had little trace anyone had actually lived in it. The furniture was still there, but it was spotless. No dishes, no personal effects, no trash.

"Looks like Metro PD cleaned the place out." Vasquez continued inside and switched on a light. "Power's still on."

"It's only been a few days. Bill was probably paid up through the month." Kate moved around the apartment and upon reaching the sofa, she began to upturn the cushions.

"Looking for loose change?" Dwight approached her.

"Might need it after this gig." She surveyed the immediate area until spotting something peeking out on the floor between the sofa and the side table. "Anyone got a glove?"

Vasquez approached. "Here. What'd you find?"

Kate slipped on the latex glove and reached for the device. Returning upright, they both began to examine it. "Looks like an audio recorder."

"Who still uses those?"

"Transcribing notes maybe?" Kate turned to her. "She attended policy meetings. It's possible she kept a record."

"What are the odds she was using this the night she was murdered?" Dwight asked.

"About as good as us finding something on Sue Copeland." Kate turned on the digital recorder. "There's something on here. It shows eleven minutes on the screen." Kate played the file that was cued up on the device.

What sounded like Meredith Bowen's voice broadcasted through the small speaker. Her tone was calm as she began reciting an agenda of some sort of meeting.

"Transcription," Kate said.

But as the recording continued, she was interrupted. A knock sounded on her door and crackling filtered through the speaker as it seemed she'd set it down on the table. Her feet padded softly, almost indiscernibly on the audio. Then the shift of a deadbolt and the turn of a handle broadcasted lightly.

"*What are you doing here? Do you have any idea what time it is?*"

"*We need to talk.*"

A man's voice, deep, filled with gravitas, sounded. Kate shot a look to her team and returned her attention to the recording.

"*I know he's been in contact with you again.*"

"*Hey, you need to take a step back. We talked about this at the office and I have nothing more to say about it.*" Meredith's tone shifted to near-panic.

"*You've been warned to stay away from him. You should've listened.*"

"*Are you crazy? I don't know what the hell you're talking about. I haven't done anything and you know it. Grant's insane if he thinks I'll fall into line like his other women. I'm not one of them. I never wanted anything to do with him. You'd better tell him to back the fuck off.*"

As they listened, the growing sense of what was to come fell upon their shoulders.

"*And you tell his goddam wife to stop calling me. I know she's the one who's been calling and hanging up, or uttering the occasional threat. I don't think you want me going to the police with this.*"

A scuffle began as Meredith was heard grunting, and a crash of perhaps a vase or something glass emerged as it hit the floor.

"Oh no." Kate knew, they all knew, what was about to happen and the idea that it had been caught on tape and they were about to listen to this woman be murdered sent chills down her spine.

More scuffling noises and then it sounded as though the device had been knocked from the table and had fallen to the floor. The gunshot rang out.

Kate gasped. "Oh God. It's the first shot, the graze on her

head." Her heart pounded and she wanted to drop the device. And then the other shot reverberated.

"Give me the recorder." Dwight extended his hand. "Kate, give it to me."

With trembling hands, she handed it to him. "It's all right here."

Vasquez placed her hand on Kate's shoulder. "We got her, Kate. We got Sue Copeland on conspiracy."

26

The silence in the room conveyed the deafening proof that they all needed. Kate looked to her colleagues before returning her attention to ASAC Campbell. "There it is. She mentions Sue Copeland. This is what we need to bring her in. But I need to know if you're on board with this."

"What do you think, Jameson? This is your team, your party."

"I think if we get more regarding the phone numbers found on the victims' cell phones, tying Sue Copeland to each of them, that, along with this audio, and the emails, then we have a case against her."

"Are you serious? I don't know how long that's going to take. We need to do this now." Kate looked at Vasquez. "Am I right? I don't see how we can wait."

"Calm down, Reid," Campbell replied. "Jameson's right. What you've got is damning, but not damning enough. The victim proclaimed Sue Copeland made harassing calls to her, with as of yet, no proof. That's not enough to assume she directed Bowen's death. We need more. We need the trace on the phone numbers.

Then we'll have something we can work with. Until then, keep looking. The Copelands aren't going anywhere. If they did, it would defeat the purpose of their claims that they'd been treated as criminals."

"Campbell's got a point," Dwight began. "The best we can do is make another attempt at reaching Agent Caison to find out how much longer he thinks this will take. Then we can develop a plan of action."

Kate shook her head. "It's never enough, is it?" She turned on her heel and left the room.

As she marched through the halls, Vasquez caught up to her. "I know you're pissed, but if we don't get this right—the first time— we won't get another chance. Phelps has worked hard to derail us and now we're on the verge of a huge find. You got to stay level-headed. I get it. It was hard as shit listening to that woman…"

"You can't even finish your sentence. And that's what I'm talking about. It was horrific and yet we wait."

"Yes. We wait."

They reached the bullpen and Vasquez stopped her again. "Call Caison. This could all be for naught."

"I guess we have nothing to lose. He did say he'd call when he had something."

"Press him anyway. He knows you. I'm sure he's used to it."

A half-cocked smile emerged. "I'll call him now." But before she'd had the chance to dial his number, she heard her name and upon turning to see who had called out to her, she spotted him. "Fraser? What's going on?" She set her phone down and rose to meet him.

"I found something I think you'll be interested in." He handed her a flash drive. "I didn't want to email it. Call me overly cautious. After what I've seen in the recent past, it's hard to trust again."

"You got that right." Kate placed the drive into her computer and waited for the files to load.

"Open that one there." He pointed to the screen.

She clicked on the icon, and within seconds, the information flashed before her.

Vasquez peered over her shoulder. "Oh my God. Where did you find this?"

"You asked me to do some digging on Phelps and I did. Frankly, it wasn't that hard to find. The guy didn't protect himself very well."

"Neither did Grant Copeland, by the look of it." Kate revealed her satisfaction. "I knew he was on the take."

"You've got good instincts. And Copeland wasn't his only benefactor. For the past few years, he's taking a fair sum of money from several politicians and even a few political consultants."

"You have to tell me, how on earth did you get access to this?" Kate continued, in awe of Fraser's work.

"I did some background on Phelps, and through a series of credit checks, I was able to ascertain which bank he primarily used. I then reached out to a contact at FinCEN and asked about any SARs that had been filed."

"Okay, you're going to have to stop right there," Vasquez began. "We're BAU. I don't know about you, Reid, but I have no idea what he's talking about."

"Of course, I'm sorry. FinCEN, or Financial Crimes Network is a bureau inside the Treasury Department. Basically, their job is to identify money laundering operations, among other things. And a SAR is a Suspicious Activity Report. The banks start getting suspicious when a person regularly deposits amounts just under the $10,000 marker. Because when that much is deposited, the banks have to file a CTR or Currency Transaction Report. This lets the government track down people who get paid in cash in order to ensure they pay taxes on that money."

"Of course they do," Vasquez replied.

"Yeah, but it's generally for a noble cause. Capturing money-launderers, drug lords, etc. Not really going after Joe Taxpayer. But anyway, several SARs had been filed for Phelps' account over the past two years. And, not only does it tell us who received the money, but who sent the money, for example, a wire transfer. And in the most recent cases, SARs were filed for two deposits under ten grand, which were cash, meaning we don't know who gave him that money."

"Or if he took it from say, I don't know, the evidence room?" Kate said.

"Possibly. However, the final deposit did arrive in the form of a wire transfer. It was for $9,950 and it came from an LLC that traces back to Grant Copeland."

"The same one that also owns his apartment in D.C?" Vasquez continued.

"Yes."

Kate nodded as her smile continued to widen at this most welcome news. "So now, we're on the verge of solidifying a case against Sue Copeland and her conspiracy to commit murder and now Grant Copeland for bribery. This is not going to be a good day for the Copeland family. And if it happens to backfire on Phelps too, well then..."

"What about the call to Caison?" Vasquez asked.

"Caison's involved? Since when?"

"Since this morning," Kate began. "We needed his NSA contacts, figuring because he works in CTD."

"Right. That makes sense. But what has NSA got to do with any of this?"

"We asked him to trace the registration of what we believe are burners. See if they trace back to Sue Copeland. We have several numbers that showed up on some of the victims' cell phones. We think they're tied to her. And, we just got audio indicating her direct involvement. We're getting close and this here? This will help seal the deal and bring down the others."

GRANT COPELAND FOUND himself back in familiar surroundings and again peered through his bedroom curtains, just enough to see the hordes of media that again occupied his driveway and spilled over into the lawn. Life as he knew it was decidedly over. And what would become of him? It mattered little that he didn't kill those women. They would only focus on the affairs, once they were discovered, and they would be soon. He knew they'd traced the notes left behind by Phil. Where they'd come from and probably had security footage to boot. There was blood in the water and the sharks were circling. Out the window flew his political career and what could have been a lucrative speaking career that followed. He was saddened by the deaths of the women with whom he'd shared intimacy, though Meredith's death seemed out of place in this horrid situation. But after all that has happened, he realized now he never loved any of them, not even Janine, which forced him to bear even more guilt for their deaths. The idea that his close friend could have done such a thing haunted him and watching him die would be forever burned in his memory. Sue had saved him. After he'd wronged her, she defended him.

He dropped the curtain when someone spotted him peering out and began snapping photos. Upon turning around, Sue stood before him.

"You should stay away from the window, honey."

"I know. This all just seems like a nightmare."

"Oh, make no mistake, this is a nightmare—for all of us."

"Of course it is." He took hold of her hands. "I'm so sorry. This is all because of me—my arrogance—my need for adulation. But I swear to you, I had no idea what Phil was capable of doing. I never would have believed it if I hadn't seen it for myself. And you saved us."

"To face this?" She peered over his shoulder toward the window. "We're prisoners in our own home. We'll never be free of the scandal."

Grant turned away, not wanting her to see his eyes redden. "I'm so very sorry. You deserved better. I've always known you deserved better."

"Why don't we go downstairs and I'll make us some dinner?"

Her smile could not hide her resentment. He could feel it piercing his very soul, assuming he had a soul left. Or had it been purchased by the highest bidder? "Sure. We should probably eat something."

The downstairs was quiet. Sue had persuaded the children to stay with her parents today and for the foreseeable future. The last thing Grant wanted was for the press to get hold of them. They were going to suffer enough humiliation in the coming weeks. Learning of their father's infidelities, which led his closest friend to commit such atrocities. That was how this was going to play out. Phil would be seen as a fiercely loyal man who would go to any lengths to protect his leader. However misguided, that was how his portrayal would be. They needed a villain in this story and Grant was the only one left who could fill that role.

"Sit down. I'll dish you a plate." Sue walked toward the oven and retrieved the casserole she'd defrosted on their return home and placed in the oven. The consummate housewife and caregiver.

With plates in hand, she set his on the table in front of him and placed hers opposite. Upon taking her seat, she carefully unfolded the napkin and laid it across her lap. "Should I say grace?"

He nodded.

Sue began the prayer as Grant bowed his head and closed his eyes. But all he could see was Phil holding the gun to his head, confessing to the murders.

"Amen." She returned her sights to him. "Eat. You should eat and keep up your strength. We're going to need it to see this through."

Grant picked up his fork and cut into the lasagna, taking a sizeable bite. "It's delicious, sweetheart. Thank you."

They continued to eat in silence as there was nothing left to say, only the assurance that they would each be greatly tested in the coming weeks and months ahead and Grant could not say if their marriage would survive this. Or if it did, how he would support Sue. She deserved the best in life, and for a while, he'd given that to her. But that was gone now.

"I'm quite full. It was a lovely meal, sweetheart." Grant placed his napkin on the table and pushed back his chair. "You don't mind if I lie down, do you? I'm feeling exhausted."

"I'm not surprised. Please, go on. I'll clean up."

He stood from his chair, feeling the slightest bit woozy.

Sue noticed his unsteady stance. "Are you all right?"

"Yes. I—I'm fine. I stood too quickly, that's all." Grant continued toward the staircase to climb to their bedroom, but as he reached the banister, his head grew even lighter. He gripped the post and lowered himself onto the first step.

Within a minute or so, Sue happened upon him. "Grant? What's wrong? Why are you sitting here?"

"I don't know. I don't feel well. I think I might need a doctor."

"Are you going to be sick?"

"No. I—I don't know. I'm dizzy. The room is hazy. Sue, I don't know what's wrong with me. Please, please call a doctor."

"I'm sure you're just coming to grips with what you've done."

"What?"

"The lives you've ruined because you wanted the warmth of a younger woman. I wasn't enough for you and I haven't been for some time."

"No. You're wrong. Of course you're enough for me." He pressed his fingers against his temple. "Sue, I need a doctor. Now."

"No, you don't. No one can help you now, Grant. The time has come to pay the price for your betrayal. This is the price you pay for the lives you cost."

"What? Sue, what have you done?"

"You've ingested a poison by the name of aconite. Some more well-known names for this are wolf's bane and monkshood. It's been around for centuries. What you're experiencing now are the initial signs of the poison entering your body. Dizziness, nausea. Soon, you'll have difficulty breathing, begin to experience cardiovascular arrhythmias. And eventually, your heart muscle will become paralyzed and you'll die. It's quite a miraculous poison and quite undetectable. In the end, it'll appear as though you died from cardiac arrest. It's incredibly elegant in design and function. And frankly, it wasn't that difficult to find, what with the internet and all."

"Why did you do this?"

"Why? Isn't it obvious?"

"Because I cheated on you? You decided to kill me rather than divorce me?"

"Well, that would be entirely too messy. A divorce. Grant, you earned this. For years, I've overlooked your indiscretions. Years I've been pandering to your fragile ego. Helping you win elections by playing the perfect wife and mother. I thought it would pay off in the end, but a woman can only take so much."

"They'll find out what you did."

"I'm willing to take that chance, but I don't think that'll happen. With all that's been going on, they'll assume your heart gave out. Simply couldn't take the stress of the murders that weighed on your shoulders. And the good news is that I'll still get your life insurance. And I'll be entitled to your life-long health care benefits as a congressman. There's no real downside for me. And best of all is that I won't ever have to smell another woman's perfume on you. I won't have to see you at all."

"Please, Sue. Don't do this. Call 911. They can help me. Please don't let me die like this. I know you love me."

"I used to love you, Grant. But I haven't for a very long time. And Phil knew that. He loved me, though. Too bad things didn't work out between us. But I couldn't let him live after what he'd done. You know, I did actually believe he might kill us. Probably just you, but still."

"You're fucking crazy." He clutched his chest and moaned in agony.

"You made me this way."

Grant tried to pull himself up, but his strength was leaving his body.

"Just relax. This will go much more smoothly if you just let it happen."

"No!" He pulled up again, this time taking to his feet. He only needed to make it to the door and the reporters would see him. They would help.

With unsteady steps, he moved forward, still clutching his chest.

Sue stepped aside and watched as he tried to make it to the door. "You won't make it, Grant."

"The hell I won't." He pushed on and was within a few feet before he collapsed.

Sue meandered toward him and stood over his limp body. "I told you."

27

When Agent Caison entered the bullpen with a buoyant air, Kate prayed this was the moment she'd been waiting for. The hour was growing late, evening had set in, and the clock was running out.

"I thought we should go over this in person," Will began. "You have a minute?"

"You bet. What'd you find? Vasquez, you want in on this?"

"Is the pope Catholic?" She moved toward her as Will approached. "Thanks for coming down, Caison. We could really use some good news right about now."

"I think I've got that for you." He handed Kate a printout. "This is from my NSA contact. There's no email trail. I met him and picked up the docs directly. It's better for him and for us that way."

Kate began to examine the documents, which listed phone numbers and registration information, along with activation dates. "This is excellent. My God, Sue Copeland used a credit card to purchase two separate phones. Guess she didn't think the registrations could be traced back to her."

"Right," Vasquez began. "But do any of those numbers correspond with what was found on the victims' cell phones?"

"Here." Will took hold of the report and sifted through it. "These are the call logs. I highlighted the numbers that show the date and time, as you mentioned the calls came in around 1am. I also verified if the numbers popped up at any other times and highlighted those for you as well. These should directly correspond with your phone records of the victims."

"Vasquez, you have those handy?" Kate asked.

"Yep. Right here."

As they cross-referenced the documents, it became clear that this was exactly what they needed. Proof that Sue Copeland had, at the very least, been intimidating the victims, harassing the victims, and had direct contact with them days before their deaths. While it didn't prove she was the murderer, since they already knew it was Phillip Vega, it did show a conspiracy to commit murder, especially when combined with the persuasive emails sent to Vega in the days and weeks prior to the killings.

Their attention, however, was soon diverted upon Dwight's approach. "What are you all working on? Agent Caison, pleasure to see you again."

"You too, sir. I brought the information Reid requested. They're cross-referencing the records now."

"Any luck?"

Kate turned to him. "Yes. This is exactly what I was hoping we would find. This gives us what we need to bring her in under conspiracy charges."

"I hate to be the bearer of bad news, or good news, depending on how you view it."

"What happened?" Kate's heart dropped into her stomach, fearing Phelps had done something to screw this up for them.

"A 911 call was made and Fairfax police were dispatched to the Copeland residence a short time ago. Grant Copeland is dead."

"What? How?"

"Heart attack. At least, that's the prevailing theory."

"Oh my God. Are you serious?"

"As a heart attack."

Kate's face drained of color and her earlier enthusiasm had just been doused.

"What does this mean for the investigation? What about Sue Copeland?" Vasquez appeared distressed as though all they had just worked for was about to vanish.

"We still have enough." Kate peered at her colleagues with an underlying uncertainty.

"We do have enough," Dwight began. "However, if it's deemed circumstantial by a Grand Jury, then we are in some serious hot water. They'll try to twist Copeland's death to undue stress we put on him. It'll be bad for all of us."

"It'd be a stretch to say all of this combined is circumstantial," Will added.

"Especially with the evidence we have on Phelps. He was taking money from Copeland in an attempt to impede the investigation," Kate added.

"Jesus. This is one convoluted mess you're dealing with."

"Tell me about it." Kate returned her attention to Dwight. "Are they going to do an autopsy?"

"Highly unlikely, unless we can show we have enough on Sue Copeland to suggest it could have been murder. In natural cause deaths, the family would have to request an autopsy. Criminal investigations require one."

"We should bring her in. This is entirely too coincidental and I think we all know that. Bring her in, talk to her. Then have a sidebar with the federal prosecutor. We'd have to convince him on the conspiracy charges and then tack on the murder of her husband."

"Let me talk to Campbell and let him know what you all have found. We'll need him to have our backs on this one. It's going to get very ugly." Dwight turned to Will. "Good to see you again, Caison. And thank you for your help." He turned toward the corridor and headed back to see Campbell.

"Where do we go from here?" Vasquez looked to Kate.

"We still have Phelps on bribery charges."

"Without any corroboration from Copeland, seeing how he's dead."

"I wouldn't have expected him to willingly turn over information anyway. We have the bank records and that should be enough. We throw this wrench into the cog and we stand a decent chance the federal prosecutor will take seriously our inquiry into Sue Copeland. This entire investigation reeks of a cover-up. And we all know how much our government wants to show transparency." She turned to Will. "Especially after what you and your colleagues unearthed."

"That will probably work in your favor," he replied.

"So we'll start there."

"Listen, I need to get back to Headquarters. Is there anything else I can do?"

"I don't think so. You've been incredibly helpful and we wouldn't have much of a leg to stand on without it; without you and Fraser. Thank you for that."

"Anytime, Reid. It was good working with you, even for just a minute."

"You too, Caison. Maybe we'll do it again some time."

"I hope so. Agent Vasquez. Pleasure."

"Same here."

He began to walk away. "You still owe me a beer, Reid. And I'll tack on an extra for this."

"Definitely." She watched him leave.

Vasquez eyed the two of them before returning her attention to Kate. "He's a good guy."

"He is."

"Why do I think there's more to this story?"

Kate regarded her with a knowing smile. "Come on. We've got work to do." As she returned to her desk and continued to cross-reference the calls and build their case, Dwight came back.

"Campbell wants to see you—both."

She looked at Vasquez and nodded. "We're up." As they walked with Dwight, Kate continued. "What's the temperature like?"

"Warm. He wants to hear from you, though. You'll have to convince him. I've done my part." Dwight pulled open the ASAC's door. "After you."

Campbell sat at his desk, fingers laced behind his head and leaning back in his chair. Kate had an amicable relationship with him, though she often sided with Nick when the two would disagree. Now it was her turn and she'd better make a good case or this entire thing would fall apart and the woman she was sure had orchestrated the murder of innocent people and possibly her husband would undoubtedly go unpunished for her crimes.

"Take a seat, you two. Jameson's filled me in, but I'd like to hear your position. We need something solid on this one, you understand?"

"Of course. And I believe we now have that." Kate held the phone records in her hands. "We just received information that proves Sue Copeland was in contact with the victims in the weeks before their deaths. And not only that, but we also have proof that Detective Phelps was taking bribes from Grant Copeland to hide pertinent information regarding our investigation."

"Agent Reid, this was never *our* investigation. This was Metro Police's investigation. We were simply asked to consult and provide details we believed they could attribute to the unsub."

"Yes, sir, that's how it started."

"But?"

"But things developed quickly and it seemed as though Phelps was attempting to withhold vital information on the case."

"And you took it upon yourself to dig into his background?"

"I did."

"We did," Vasquez interrupted.

"But we have the proof. We know what Phelps did. And we have evidence that points to Sue Copeland's involvement. Including, as we discussed before, emails she'd sent to Phillip Vega, the man who pulled the trigger." She watched as he seemed to process her words. "ASAC Campbell, we've got her. We've got Phelps. We just need your authorization to move forward."

He peered at the three of them. "You've all worked very hard on this investigation. Gone above and certainly beyond the scope of work. I believe you've been able to get to the bottom of these murders. Bring Sue Copeland in. I'll take the case to the federal prosecutor."

The collective sigh of relief was almost audible. "Sir, we'll need an autopsy on Grant Copeland."

"You don't think he died of a heart attack as has been suggested?"

"No, sir."

"Neither do I. Once we open an investigation into Sue Copeland, it'll warrant an autopsy. Let's do it."

Amid the reporters still parked on the front lawn and driveway of the Copeland residence, Kate, Vasquez, and Dwight emerged from their vehicle, followed by Fraser, whose attendance was mandatory in this instance.

"Just walk on through. Don't talk to any of them." Dwight held open their doors and as the three began their approach, heads turned and lights pointed in their direction. It was almost 10pm, about three hours after Grant Copeland had been hauled away by ambulance, dead on arrival. Sue Copeland was still holed up inside her fortress.

Dwight knocked on the door. "FBI."

Several seconds passed before the door opened a fraction of an inch.

"I have no comment. My husband just died. Can you please give me some peace."

"We're here to take you to our office for questioning," Dwight continued.

"Excuse me? Questioning for what?"

"Mrs. Copeland, please don't make this harder than it has to be. We have a warrant for your arrest." Agent Fraser had accompanied them because he was a designated Special Deputy US Marshal, and was thereby authorized to make the arrest. The Bureau and particularly the resident BAU Agent Jameson still had to follow protocol.

She peered at them through the sliver of an opening and spotted the cameras' flash in the distance. "On what charge?"

"Conspiracy to commit murder," he replied.

"What? Are you serious?"

"Mrs. Copeland, you need to come with us now. We don't wish to cause any more of a scene than what's already happening."

With hesitation, she responded. "Can I at least grab my purse?"

"Yes, ma'am. After you let us in."

She opened the door and the agents filed inside. Kate closed the door behind them.

"You cannot be serious. In the past 48 hours, I've been held hostage, killed my captor, and lost my husband to a heart attack. This must be some kind of sick joke." She reached for her purse.

"I assure you, ma'am, this is no joke." Kate stared her down.

"Let's go." Fraser took hold of the woman, and upon opening the door, lights flashed in their eyes with even greater vigor than on their arrival.

Microphones pointed at them and questions were hurled at them from every direction.

"I would advise you not to say anything, Mrs. Copeland," Fraser began. "You will be allowed to contact your lawyer on intake." He continued to shield her as best as he could until they reached the car. "Please, watch your head."

Sue Copeland now sat in the back seat next to Kate and Fraser while Dwight pulled away from the curb. "I hope you all know what you're doing. The press will have a field day with this."

"Not in the way you believe it will," Kate replied.

Spread out on the table were crime scene photos on display for maximum effect. Sue Copeland continued to stare at the wall behind Kate and Dwight.

"We understand how difficult this must be for you, Sue," Dwight began. "But given the evidence discovered on Phil Vega's laptop, along with the phone numbers registered under your credit card, you can see that this is damning evidence, highly suggestive of your involvement."

She looked at Dwight with dead eyes. "I was in contact with Phil. I won't deny that. He was fond of me and forgive me for admitting that it felt good to be wanted. My husband certainly didn't want me."

"But it was more than that," Kate began. "You used Phil. You used his affection to get what you wanted and that was revenge against your husband and the women who enjoyed his company." She watched as Sue continued to avoid eye contact with either of them or the images laid out before her. "He was doing what you asked, even if you didn't ask directly."

"So I'm responsible because he took it upon himself to kill those women to defend my honor? I cannot possibly be held accountable for his crimes."

"Maybe not. But a conspiracy to commit murder charge is extremely likely, Mrs. Copeland," Dwight added. "And your husband's death will be looked into, given this impending charge. Are you sure there's nothing more you'd like to say on the matter of Grant Copeland's death?"

"You don't need to say anything more, Sue." Her lawyer peered at Dwight. "Agent Jameson, do you intend to charge my client with a crime?"

"Yes. The federal prosecutor will charge Mrs. Copeland with conspiracy to commit murder and she will be held until a bond hearing tomorrow morning."

"You're keeping me here overnight?" She turned to her lawyer. "I can't stay here."

"Given the circumstances, it's unlikely she'll be allowed bail. But that's not up to me."

"No it isn't, Agent Jameson." The lawyer turned to Sue. "It's just one night. We'll get you in front of the judge tomorrow and he'll set bail. You'll be home by the afternoon."

"I can't believe this. You are making a mistake. I'm the victim here. Those women destroyed my marriage. Destroyed my husband."

"Don't say anything more, Sue," the lawyer began. "I will accompany her to processing."

As they left the holding room and continued to processing in the federal complex, Kate turned to Dwight. "The US District Attorney's office has already filed for a Grand Jury. When do you expect an indictment? We can't hold her for long."

"I'm aware. However, I suspect they're going to want the autopsy results before proceeding."

"We won't have it before the 72-hour deadline."

"We have to or she could get bail and then we've lost."

"I'll take Vasquez and we'll go to the ME's. We'll sit there until he's finished if we have to." Kate stood ready to leave. "I'll call you when I have something."

Upon arrival at the Office of the Chief Medical Examiner, Kate and Vasquez waited for authorization to enter.

The man behind the desk ended the call. "He says you can go back."

"Thank you." Kate took the lead and headed beyond the double doors. She pressed the buzzer and the door clicked. Entering the autopsy room, she immediately spotted the examiner. "Thank you for agreeing to see us, Dr. Carr. And for taking this on yourself. I know how late it is."

"Frankly, I'm not sure why you're here. The body was only just admitted. As you can see, I haven't begun my examination.

Not to mention the time it takes to get lab results. You know this, Agent Reid."

"I do. And I'm sorry to put undue pressure on you. But we have someone in custody and the only way we can continue is to get to the bottom of Grant Copeland's death. A member of congress is dead and we are eager for answers."

"And mounting pressure from the media probably has something to do with this as well, I imagine."

"You imagine correctly," Vasquez replied. "Please, do you have any preliminary thoughts on cause of death?"

The doctor approached the body and pulled down the sheet to the waist. "The call came in as a suspected heart attack."

"That's right," Kate replied.

"So, given that assumption, I wouldn't expect to see any outward signs of stress on the body. No contusions, lacerations, or anything of that nature, unless the victim had fallen, which I don't believe was the case in this situation."

"Not from our understanding." Kate peered over the body. Something she'd done many times in the past, only this time, she felt detached. Like Grant Copeland simply didn't matter to her. It was a startling revelation to feel nothing for someone and was a far cry from the previous times she had been in this very position.

The doctor continued to view the body as he placed latex gloves on his hands. "What I'm seeing here gives me pause."

The agents glanced at one another with anticipation.

"You see this?" He pointed to the mouth and gently pulled it open. "Lips are slightly purple. Much too soon to be considered a result of rigor. No." He shook his head. "The tongue is purplish in color too."

"Meaning?" Kate asked.

"It's too early to surmise, but my initial reaction is asphyxiation." He looked at Kate.

"But this man died of a heart attack?"

"That's what's been said." He continued to view the body and remained silent, leaving them to wonder what he was thinking.

Finally, he spoke again. "As I said, it's too early to be sure, but given what I'm seeing right now, I'm inclined to rush a toxicology."

"Why is that?"

"Well, because there are no outward signs of asphyxiation. No finger marks around the neck, nothing, from what I can see right now, lodged in the victim's throat. So I would want to look for something in the bloodstream that could cause such a reaction."

"Such as?" Kate was growing more anxious by the minute.

"One possible cause could be poison." He looked at them. "This is where I would begin because with no outward signs, I must look inward. And poison is a logical place to start. Especially poisons that would lead to cardiac arrest."

"How long will it take for you to run the tests and receive results?" Vasquez asked.

"Anywhere from several days to a week. Maybe more."

"Dr. Carr, this man is a United States congressman. We are in urgent need of answers."

"Agent Reid, I will do my best to get you those answers. However, if it helps at all, I can with confidence offer a preliminary report suggesting what we just discussed."

"That might be enough to present to the DA's office."

"It's all we've got for now." Vasquez looked to the doctor. "Then that is the route we'll have to take."

28

Almost every agent residing on the 5th floor of the WFO now stood in the bullpen watching the televisions mounted on the wall. A press conference was about to begin and the Metro Police Department Chief of Police stood at the podium.

Kate, along with Dwight and Alicia, the team that had already grown closer since Nick's departure, stood in anticipation with the rest.

The morning sun shone in the chief's eyes as he began. "First of all, it is with great sadness that I convey to the people of this district along with the people of the United States the loss of one of our public servants. A member of the U.S. House of Representatives, Grant Copeland, was murdered last week. And with the help of the men and women at the FBI and our own tireless officers, the perpetrator of this horrific act is in custody.

"In addition, this has allowed us to solve the multiple murders who this very same perpetrator orchestrated. Innocent lives were lost, but justice has been won. The efforts of our department, the

FBI, and our friends at the Baltimore Police Department were rewarded for the capture of this individual. It proves that once again, our communities can come together, can work together, for the good of the people."

"Sounds like he's about to announce his run for office." Kate cast a sideways glance to Vasquez.

"Wonder if he'll say anything about his Detective Phelps?" she added.

"Doubt it," Dwight replied.

One of the staff from the front office approached. "Agent Reid?" She held out an envelope. "This was left for you."

"Thanks." Kate opened the manila envelope and pulled out the papers.

"What's that?" Vasquez asked.

Kate read the title. "It's the toxicology report on Copeland." She began flipping through to the summary page. "Oh my God. Well, here it is in black and white."

"Can I see?" Vasquez leaned in and began to read. "Aconite, otherwise known as wolf's bane, this poison is virtually unde-tectable and mimics symptoms of cardiac arrest. The only tell-tale sign is asphyxiation." She looked at Kate. "Guess she thought it would be untraceable. Jameson, you see this?"

He took the papers from her and upon reading the page, shook his head. "Sue Copeland was smart but must've missed this. You two did good work on this. I know it wasn't easy. And especially given the pushback from the detective."

"I notice the chief isn't mentioning Phelps. You hear anything about what's going to happen to him?" Kate asked.

"He'll go to prison on bribery. And in this instance, it'll be a federal charge because Copeland was a congressman."

"Yeah, I bet that doesn't get mentioned in the same breath as all this amazing cooperation between jurisdictions and us," Vasquez said.

"I think I've heard enough," Kate began. "Time to get back to work. What's on the agenda for today?"

~

Nick sat across from Kate and watched her push food around on her plate, hardly taking a nibble. "I thought you'd be famished."

"More exhausted than hungry. And I guess I still can't help but feel as though I should've picked up on the possibility that Sue Copeland had been behind the murders. I was wrong, Nick. And it could've cost the investigation."

"But it didn't. And believe it or not, sometimes even the best of us get it wrong. Quinn helped point you in the right direction. You two worked together to figure it out."

"It was a lot more than just the two of us. If I hadn't had the help of Agents Caison and Fraser, I think Mrs. Copeland might still be sitting in her home, free as a bird."

"You think I haven't called on help from other departments? We don't work inside a vacuum. Look, I know you shoulder the burden for what you perceive as failures, but this was not a failure. And from what Jameson told me, you took the lead on a good portion of this case."

"I stepped on toes, that's for sure."

"Maybe. But Jameson knows what you're capable of and knows when to let you take the lead. He's not like me and that's probably a good thing."

"I'm supposed to meet with Quinn tomorrow." She regarded him with trepidation. "I think he's made his decision. Has he mentioned anything to you?"

"Even if he had, it's best if I let him do his job. This is his call."

"You're going to let me hang out to dry on this?"

"Look, if the possibility exists that you and I are going to be on the same team again, then I can't offer you information that isn't mine to offer. You know Quinn's already expressed reservations for that very thing."

"I know. I'm just nervous."

"But this is still something you want to pursue? You haven't changed your mind? Even after getting a taste of a greater leadership role?"

"Quinn's shown me that I still have a lot to learn and I want to learn. This has become more important to me than I expected."

"So long as it's what makes you happy. Don't do it for me."

Kate smiled. "I have no intentions of making you happy, Scarborough."

"Well, that's good to know."

The laughter broke the rising tension between them about the still-unresolved issue of his slip into the bottle. Kate wanted to address it, knew it needed to be addressed, but after what she'd just been through, she was exhausted and it would no doubt result in an argument, or worse, a fight. She'd reverted back to a time when it was easier just to let things lie, but in doing so, decisions about their future would be made based upon an issue that couldn't be ignored.

Nick held her gaze. "You look like you want to say something."

Maybe she wasn't the only one who was thinking of the problem, yet was unsure of how to tackle it. "You want to deal with this now?"

"You're meeting with Quinn tomorrow and it could change the trajectory of your career. I'm the last one who should want to discuss this, but for you, I think we should." He waited for her to say something, but when several moments passed, he continued. "I screwed up—again. And for that, I'm sorry."

Kate set down her fork and folded her hands in her lap. "Why? I didn't think it was something to be concerned about any more."

"That's the secret of an alcoholic. Making everyone think there isn't a problem."

"That's the first time you've admitted that. You're saying there is a problem?"

"I'm saying I'm not sure, but I want to be upfront because this has reared its ugly head in the past and I can't sit here and pretend it won't happen again."

"What set you off? What made you reach for the bottle?"

"The only thing I can figure is that I knew I couldn't step in and help you."

"I didn't need help."

"I know. You rarely do and yet I find myself wanting to anyway."

"So what do we do about that? Especially if I'm to work in your department?"

"I've worked too hard to get here, Kate. To be with you. We both know that was years in the making. I won't destroy that. Most of the time, I'm okay. It's not a problem. Then I let my feelings get in the way of what's right and I do my best to drown them out. It's not an excuse."

"No, it's not, but you didn't answer my question. If we are to get past this—once and for all—what do we do?"

He was now the one pushing food around on his plate. "I'll talk to someone. I've made some positive changes in my life. The job, which I've strived for for much of my career, and you. And now the possibility you and I can work together again. I'm thrilled at the prospect." At this final point, he looked her in the eyes. "So I'll talk to someone. I'll—get help—before it gets out of hand."

Kate nodded. "Okay."

"Agent Quinn?" Kate stepped into the doorway.

"Reid? Come in. Thanks for meeting with me." He stood and waited to greet her. With a solid handshake, he continued, "Sit down, please." When he returned to his chair, he wasted no time in cutting to the chase. "I'm sure you've already figured out why you're here."

"I assume you've made your decision regarding the position."

"I have. But before we get into that, I'd just like to offer my congratulations on solving a very complex investigation."

"I certainly can't take all the credit. If it weren't for your help..."

"There you go again, underestimating yourself. You really should work on that. Yes, I was able to offer insight, but this was your collar. Yours and your team. I was impressed by what I saw out of the WFO. Jameson runs a tight ship."

"He does. He's a remarkable boss who allows me to take the lead when he believes I'm on the right track. And if I'm not, he won't hesitate to let me know that too."

"I have no doubt about that. He'll do well assuming Scarborough's role there. That being said, I would like to discuss your future placement. But there is something I would be remiss in not mentioning. I would just like to clarify your intentions."

"My intentions? I thought I'd made them clear."

"Reid, I watched you for several days. I watched as you pushed through road blocks. Pushed past the difficulties you experienced with what turned out to be a crooked cop. Now, apart from some hot-headed moments, you did what you believed was best for the investigation."

"I did. Why do I detect a note of concern?"

"I'm concerned about your true intentions. What you really want from your career at the Bureau."

"I want to learn criminal profiling. That's why I'm here. To learn from you."

"See, I'm not so sure about that. Don't get me wrong, I think you are inclined to that type of research, no doubt. But what I saw over the course of this last investigation were the qualities of a leader. One who could one day be the Senior Supervisory Agent in the WFO when Jameson moves on, because he will likely move on. He's talented in his own right and that will be recognized, just as Scarborough's talents were. But the question is, do you have the constitution to wait that long? Is this venture into profiling merely a stepping stone to a leadership role?"

"Doesn't everyone want that? I mean, to grow within their organization?"

"My goal isn't to become Section Chief or Unit Chief. My goal is to continue to help field offices and other law enforcement by giving them information about who they are looking for and get inside the mind of the criminal to anticipate his or her next move. But I don't see that in you. I see a person who will continue to ascend the ranks. Perhaps even one day rivaling Scarborough. Though I wouldn't want to be around when that day comes."

"I don't get why you're saying these things. I want to learn profiling. I'm good at seeing inside just like you. I mean, not exactly like you, but hopefully one day, like you. I want to find them and bring them to justice as any agent would."

"What I'm saying is this. Without question, you are qualified and perhaps even more so than your counterparts, due to your unique background. However, my concern is that this position will not be enough for you and my training will have been—not wasted, but maybe not put to as good of use as it could've been were someone else sitting in that chair. Neither of us wants to waste our time here, Reid."

A part of her knew he was right, but she grew irritated none-theless, feeling as though it had all been a waste of time. The past six months of additional training courses at Quantico just to be able to apply for this position. Overcoming the implications that she would only get the position because Nick was the new Senior Unit Agent. It was as though she was stepping into the WFO for the first time again. The initial days when other agents looked at her as though she didn't deserve to be there. Wearing that chip on her shoulder had become tiresome. And now here was Noah Quinn, telling her exactly what she had been afraid to hear. That the chip would be the reason she would not do what she wanted in her career at the Bureau.

"No. I don't want to waste my time, even though I've spent the better part of six months preparing for this. Working my ass off to take the required additional training, keeping up with my position at the WFO. However, in the end, it seems as though you're the one who is wasting my time. Not the other way around. I've put in the work. This is your hang up, not mine." She pushed up from the chair and started to leave.

"Wait."

Kate turned on her heel. "Yes?"

"You might not think I'm looking out for your best interest, but I am. Now despite that, I simply wanted you to consider your choices and out of fairness to the other applicants, be completely sure this is where you want to be. And frankly, to be sure that your relationship with Scarborough will not get in the way. I won't have that become an issue, no matter what happens between the two of you."

"Are you saying you're offering me the position?" Her firm

stance did not waver. "Because it sounds as though you're not sure yourself."

"I am hesitant, Agent Reid, and for good reasons, as I've just stated. But you have put in the time and I've overlooked that. I'm sorry. I will offer you the slot. You will train with me. You will take orders from me. We will work long hours and will rarely be recognized. This is not a position that will bring you glory, not in the way you've received in the past. I guess I can't insist you swear some sort of oath of loyalty, but I do ask for it." He paused. "And there is one last thing. I don't want you to answer now. I want you to sleep on it. Because I do believe some of the things I've mentioned matter to you. And I want your absolute certainty before you accept the offer. Come back to me in the morning with your answer."

"Okay. I will."

THIS WAS NOT something anyone else could answer for her. Kate had to decide what she really wanted and Quinn had laid it on the line. No one had ever seen through her the way he had and it frightened her. And he wasn't doing it for her—not really. He was doing it for himself. To preserve his values. He wanted a partner in the truest sense of the word.

"I didn't expect you back so soon." Vasquez returned from the break room. "Why do I get the feeling Quinn bailed on you? Oh man, I'm so sorry, Kate."

"No. No, he didn't bail. He just—well, he was just upfront, that's all. I was offered the job."

"What'd you say?"

"He said he wanted me to sleep on it and tell him in the morning."

"Oh. Are you having second thoughts or something? Did he pick up any hesitation? I don't get it. I thought this was sort of a done deal."

"I'm sorry, Alicia. I can't talk about this right now. I'm trying to figure everything out."

"Oh, sure. I understand. It's a big decision. You just let me know if you want to talk. I'm here for you, and I always will be."

"I know." Kate grabbed her things. "Tell Dwight I headed out for the day, would you?"

"Of course."

Standing inside the elevator, watching the numbers descend, Kate didn't know where to go. Nick was at Quantico and she'd avoided him. He would call soon and she had no answers.

She got into her car and drove. Just drove, no particular destination in mind and until arriving at a place entirely unexpected, she hadn't even realized she'd been driving in that direction.

Kate pulled alongside the curb of the home that was the first place she could really call her own. The little yellow house that reminded her of Sam's place. The house she rented after leaving behind her life in San Diego. Working so hard to put the pain of losing Marshall, of losing Sam; putting all of that behind her and becoming something she never believed was possible. An FBI agent.

She chuckled at how her life had done a complete 180. No one back in San Diego would recognize her now. In fact, her own parents would be hard-pressed to realize the depths at which she'd evolved.

Her phone rang. "No. Not yet." Kate silenced the call and continued to stare at the little house that still had a For Sale sign hanging in the yard. "Well, who wouldn't want this house?"

Paralyzed. That was what she felt in this moment. So much of what Quinn said rang true. About wanting to be a leader. About enjoying the accolades when they got the bad guy. It was all true. But did that really mean more to her than getting into the mind of someone like Hendrickson. The man who altered the very fabric of her being. The man who hurt so many people and destroyed so many lives. Watching him die was the single most vindicating moment in her life. And that meant *everything*.

"I know what I have to do." Kate reached for her phone. She didn't need to sleep on it. She just needed to see clearly her reason for doing this. And now she had. There would be more Joseph Hendricksons. There already were more. And she would be the one to catch them.

"Hey, it's me. Are you busy?" She waited for Nick to answer. "Okay. I won't keep you. I just wanted to let you know that Quinn offered me the job." She smiled as he sounded overjoyed at the news. "He actually asked that I sleep on it, but well, I've already made my decision. And of course, would want you to be the first to know. Nick, I'm going to take it. I'm going to work at Quantico." This time, Kate flung her head back with laughter. "I thought you'd be happy about that. Just don't say anything to Quinn. I'll respect his request and really give it more thought." She shook her head. "No, of course I won't change my mind. This is what I want. I know that now and I won't let anyone sow seeds of doubt in my mind again. I know what we'll be up against and I don't care. I'll take what they dish out and ask for more." Kate stared at the house again. "I love you. And I'll see you tonight. Bye."

It was done. "Now let's see what happens next." Kate started the engine and drove away.

THE END

ABOUT THE AUTHOR

Robin Mahle has published more than 30 novels in the mystery/thriller genre. She also writes historical fiction as <u>Christine Chase.</u>

It is Robin's fast-paced style of storytelling combined with tense action and thrilling twists that bring her readers back for more. So be sure sure to subscribe to her newsletter to keep up on all the latest releases, sales, and giveaways. Go to robinmahle.com and sign up today!

Robin lives in Coastal Virginia with her husband and two children.

If you enjoyed Ms. Mahle's work, please share your experience by leaving a review on <u>Amazon.</u>

For more information, visit Robin's website.
www.robinmahle.com

ALSO BY ROBIN MAHLE

The Kate Reid FBI Thriller Series (17 books)

The Chef (stand-alone psych thriller)

The Man in My Attic (stand-alone psych thriller)

The Compound (standalone psych thriller)

The Remy Fontaine Fugitive Hunter Thrillers (4 books)

The Det. Rebecca Ellis Thrillers (5 books)

The Allison Hart PI Thrillers (5 Books)

The Lacy Merrick Thrillers (4 books)

**Sign up to receive <u>Robin's Newsletter</u> so you can stay up to date on her new releases, events, contests and even exclusive new material!